LORD OF THE KNIGHT

Gentlemen of Knights
Book Seven

Elizabeth Johns

ARE YOU SIGNED UP FOR DRAGONBLADE'S BLOG?

You'll get the latest news and information on exclusive giveaways, exclusive excerpts, coming releases, sales, free books, cover reveals and more.

Check out our complete list of authors, too!

No spam, no junk. That's a promise!

Sign Up Here

www.dragonbladepublishing.com

Dearest Reader;

Thank you for your support of a small press. At Dragonblade Publishing, we strive to bring you the highest quality Historical Romance from some of the best authors in the business. Without your support, there is no 'us', so we sincerely hope you adore these stories and find some new favorite authors along the way.

Happy Reading!

CEO, Dragonblade Publishing

Additional Dragonblade books by Author Elizabeth Johns

Gentlemen of Knights Series
Duke of Knight (Book 1)
Black Knight (Book 2)
Knight and Day (Book 3)
Dark of Knight (Book 4)
Shining Knight (Book 5)
Dangerous Knight (Book 6)
Holiday Knights (Boxed Set)
Lord of the Knight (Book 7)

PROLOGUE

MARIA LLOYD SIGHED and set down her book and stared through the parlor window of her parents' country house. She gazed in abstraction, seeing nothing of the view beyond the glass. The romantic tone of Lord Byron's verse had brought on a wistful mood.

Love. It was such a simple term for such a wide array of emotions and feelings, she thought... which rather begged the question, how do you know when you are in love?

One loves one's parents, grandparents and siblings from birth. It is scarcely questioned, although exceptions are made for the latter, of course, yet most people would lay down their life for their siblings, no matter how much they may vex them.

Then there are things. Maria loved her bed. As a girl, she loved her books and her dolls and her house.

The animals, she mused, ticking each item off on a finger. Often, she thought she liked them more than any of the humans she had met, though most of them she liked quite well. Truer devotion Maria had yet to find than that of her pets.

Places. Maria had not been to as many as she would like, but she loved beautiful buildings and pretty views in equal measure. The country was lovely, but London was its equal in different ways.

Food. Now, there was something one could not live without.

Porridge one did not love. On the other hand, there were certain delicacies to send one into raptures and pure ecstasy.

But love of another, to last a lifetime? Maria's friends had spoken of love striking them like a bolt of lightning or an arrow to the heart, but that had not happened to Maria.

Philip had always been a part of her life and she felt as though she had always loved him. From the first time they had met as children, when he had greeted her as she sat in her favorite swing in the meadow, then pushed her high until she laughed. He had never asked to be pushed in return—her delight had been enough. That was true love.

CHAPTER ONE

OUTWARDLY, THE BEAUTIFULLY appointed stone town home on Brook Street portrayed all that was good *ton*. Inside, Maria's mother ran, screaming in hysterics, from the drawing room, calling for her maid and her smelling salts. This had happened countless times since the incident earlier, but this was the first time they had all been in a room together. Earlier, her brother had been suspected and publicly accused of being a traitor in the middle of Hyde Park, even though he had been trying to prevent the truth of a scandal involving her father coming out. Maria was left in the middle of the room, looking at her father with disgust, while her brother lurked in the corner, his arms crossed over his chest.

"How dare you look at me in judgment? You are the one who made the public spectacle!" her father yelled at Gabriel.

She knew her brother would not defend himself. "Gabriel was trying to protect our family!" she answered hotly.

Her father snorted. "Both of you have been brought up to a life of comfort, with every luxury, due to your name. But do you know how that came to pass?" He began to pace the room, growing more agitated with every step. His face was red and beads of perspiration dotted his brow. He turned sharply back to face them. "It came to pass because I did what was expected of me. Sometimes that meant silence."

"When a man and his wife were murdered for being honorable?" Maria could not hide her disgust.

"That is easy for you to say, miss, when you have no notion of how the military works, and years ago whilst in India, no less. It is not civilized like England! And yes, I had to save my own neck. He would not have thought twice about murdering me!"

Maria shook her head. It was not worth the effort to argue the point that India was every bit as civilized as their native shores, just different. What was done was done, but what would become of her?

As if her father could read her thoughts, he turned on her next. "You stupid girl! If you had only married any of your suitors during the last three Seasons, your future would have been assured, but now you will rot in shame as a spinster."

"I see. This is now my fault." She stood up to leave. There was no point in trying to reason with him, just as always.

Maria walked calmly until she passed the threshold, but instead of going to her chambers, she went out to the garden. The family would have to leave for the country before dawn in disgrace; the servants were already bustling about in preparation. Her father had been right about one thing. She should have been married long ago and this would then have no longer been her problem. Perhaps this would come to nothing—her father had not been the criminal, after all – but no one wanted any hint of scandal attached to their bride or their name. She had seen it many times before. If they removed to the country quickly, then a wealthy, landed gentleman might be willing to have her.

Maria wanted to cry, but the tears would not fall. She was not a watering-pot, but often thought it would be nice if she were.

She sat in her childhood swing and mindlessly rocked back and forth. It was difficult to assimilate all that had happened—all that had changed in her life overnight. The scandal would doubtless die down eventually but nothing would ever truly be the same. Besides, now she had lost respect for her father. She did not wish to return to the country and pretend nothing had ever happened.

"May I?"

Maria jumped.

"Gabriel! You are far too good at sneaking up on people."

"I have had a great deal of practice," he remarked, sitting next to her on the bench swing that barely fit the two of them. Gabriel was a man of few words, so if he had sought her out, then she would listen. Still, he remained silent for a few minutes before speaking. "I am sorry you are caught in the middle. I had hoped to prevent you and Mother being hurt."

"I know you tried, Gabriel, and the real traitor was caught in the end. What do you mean to do now?"

Maria looked up at her brother, whose face was now hardened. Gabriel had always been more serious than most, but gone were the vestiges of boyhood. He was looking off into the distance, somewhere beyond the gardens and brick fence that surrounded it. "Disappear."

"You are leaving, then. Will I ever see you again?"

"I do not know. Perhaps when Father is dead."

Maria tried to choke back the emotion she felt. "I cannot blame you. I wish I could leave so easily. Things will not be pleasant for some time."

Gabriel nodded. "I know."

At least he did not reiterate the fact that her chances of marrying a gentleman of her choice were virtually gone.

He pulled a letter from his pocket. "This came for you."

Maria could not imagine why anyone would have written to her. She would not be appearing in public for some time. She flipped the letter over. "It is from Kate," she said as she broke the seal. Kate was one friend who would stand by her, she was sure of it. She scanned the words quickly. "She has invited me to go to Paris with her."

"You should go," he said without hesitation.

"Society is small. People there will know."

"Perhaps, but you will find it matters less. And I will be nearby should you have need of something."

"Are you still intending to work for Wellington?" she asked quietly.

He nodded quickly. "Yes, but it will not be widely known. However, there will always be someone who can reach me."

Maria had wanted to go to Paris for many a long year, but she doubted all of her woes would suddenly disappear once she was across the Channel.

"You doubt me, but following the drum is different. There are still some of these Society games to be endured, but they matter much less to those who must deal with war."

"I know you have found it difficult at times, to go back and forth between military and civilian life."

"I have no patience for Society, that is true. They have little appreciation for what it takes for them to have their freedoms."

Maria knew she was guilty of that herself. She was grateful for those in the military and had seen veterans missing limbs before, but it was still difficult to imagine what it was like. "Will I be near any battles?"

"Lord willing, Bonaparte's reign is over, but you will be with the army so one can never be certain. I expect, being with Owens and his wife, you will be quite protected as part of Wellington's entourage."

Maria had little choice, really. If she chose to hide in shame, the country would be her lot forever. At least this provided her with an opportunity to see some of the world. She could always retire to the country later to live out her life as a spinster, if that was to be her fate.

She reached over and took her brother's hand and squeezed it in a rare display of affection between them. He was several years older and they had had little opportunity to be close.

"I will go. It will be a change of scenery, if nothing else."

"And you will be among friends. Everleigh will also look after you."

Philip. She closed her eyes and tried not to think about it.

Friendship was better than nothing and he would stand by her.

"Just remember that sometimes Wellington's officers are called on to play a role. Try to remember that."

Maria thought it very odd advice, but refrained from remarking upon it. "Do you travel with us?" she asked instead.

He shook his head. "I am leaving now, but I will make certain you know how to reach me when you arrive in Paris." He kissed her on the cheek, then rose and disappeared into the darkness.

Maria did not like hasty decisions, but at least she had a choice to make, which she decidedly had not had half an hour before. She returned to the house and penned a reply to Kate, accepting her invitation and informing her she would call in the morning. There would be no sleep that night for anyone in the household, Maria reflected, although sleep would be a welcome escape from reality. She climbed the stairs to her mother's apartments, where maids were packing trunks and footmen were then carrying them down to the waiting carriages.

"Mama," Maria called to her mother, who was lying on the chaise with a damp cloth over her eyes. She did not know how Lady Mottram would react to the news.

"Is it time to go?" her mother asked, holding her hands out.

"Not yet, Mama. I wanted to tell you Kate has invited me to accompany her family to Paris and I have accepted."

Her mother sighed deeply. "I do think that is for the best, although I will miss you dreadfully. It is very kind of Kate."

HOW HAD EVERYTHING changed in a few short weeks? Philip had returned to Paris rather disillusioned. When he had left with Jack Owens, his best friend, they had been bachelors—enjoying a fast life on Wellington's staff without any other responsibilities. Now Jack was married, and the knowledge smarted despite the fact that he was very happy for Jack. Kate, his friend's wife, was a most excellent female and if someone had to follow the drum with them, he would as soon have Kate as anyone.

Also weighing on Philip's heart, though, was what had happened in London. He could not stop thinking about his friend, Lady Maria. Her family had unfortunately been involved in a nasty scandal immediately before the three of them had left Town and he had not had a chance to speak with her. Before leaving with Wellington, he had stopped at their home and the house had already been boarded up. It was a travesty of Society that a scandal automatically tainted everyone in the family. Maria had always been a good friend and in all likelihood would now lose her chance of making a good marriage. Philip resolved to write to her and see if she needed anything. If only he had been able to speak with her!

That ship had sailed, so to speak, and he had asked his brother to ensure Maria was well.

It would not be long until everyone arrived. Jack and Kate would be there soon. They had just returned to London from their wedding trip when he left.

He looked out of his window over the beautiful city that was Paris. At least there would be distractions from his morose thoughts here.

A knock on the door disturbed his thoughts. "Enter."

It was Wellington. "I have a late invitation to a dinner at the Austrian minister's house. Somerset is a little out of sorts. Can you accompany me?"

"Of course." Philip could hardly say no when he had nothing else to do.

"Excellent. I should hate to disappoint the ladies by presenting only myself for them to dance with. Why is it that most of the gentlemen at these assemblies are fat old men?" He did not expect an answer. "I will see you downstairs in half an hour."

Philip inclined his head as his commander left and then began to dress. He had been intending to find something with which to occupy his time, anyway—although he probably would have chosen another avenue than a tedious dinner party.

In less than an hour, they were at the hôtel of the Austrian minister, a mansion similar to the one Wellington had purchased for his post there as ambassador. It was of a white baroque style that stood six stories high. Flaming torches guarded either side of the doors, along with soldiers in uniform.

Wellington never cared to be early or on time. He had quite perfected the fashionably late arrival. An orchestra could be heard playing from the ballroom, with the familiar sound of feet tapping in a rhythmic dance. No doubt the waltz would be in full swing, as it were, being in Paris and at an Austrian's house.

All eyes turned upon them when they entered. Wellington commanded that respect wherever he went. He had great presence; ladies wanted to be with him and men wanted to be him.

They were quickly greeted by their host, Duke Klemens von Metternich.

"Your Grace." A man in full dress uniform bowed before him. "I am pleased you were able to return in time for our little party. May I present my wife and daughter? His Grace, the Duke of Wellington, this is Duchess Eleanor and her niece, the Archduchess Pauline Klementine."

Wellington and Philip both bowed with a deference fit for a princess.

Wellington introduced him as Lord Philip, of course, but he barely heard. He was so taken with the beauty standing before him that he doubtless embarrassed himself with such awkwardness.

He had heard the rumor of a beauty in the Austrian court and this creature must surely be the proof. Rumor also held that she'd left a string of broken hearts and ruined men behind, but it seemed irrelevant at the moment.

When he stood back up from his bow, she met his gaze and there was no pretense in it. He knew that look. "Would you care to dance, Archduchess?"

She smiled knowingly – there was no coyness – she knew she was beautiful.

"I would be delighted, my lord." She dipped into a curtsy, then took his arm. Apparently they were to dance in that moment.

One day, Philip might reflect on what had made him so careless with his feelings, but for now he allowed himself to be swept away in infatuation. He needed something to fill the void he felt at the loss of his best friend and the disillusionment from the accused betrayal of one of their own.

It was as if the Austrian beauty cast a spell over him. From the deep chestnut color of her hair to the mahogany of her eyes, the curve of her nose and perfection of her figure that fit perfectly in his arms, he could find no fault in her person. The glittering tiara and necklace of diamonds she wore were nothing in comparison to her. He was smitten.

As the strains of the waltz began, he bowed before her. "I am yours to command, Archduchess."

"Please tell me you will not be a bore," she remarked as she placed one hand on his shoulder, and he put his own on her waist. He immediately felt a quickening of his pulse. He must not allow his enchantment of her to show. He knew well, from playing the game, that she would lose interest quickly. She must have thousands of men at her feet. Philip supposed he'd had equal attention from the fairer sex, but none had captured his interest thus immediately.

"I have never been accused of being a bore," he remarked smoothly.

"Somehow I knew you would not be. I suspect women do not hold your interest long."

He inclined his head. It was the truth. "And yourself? Let me guess: men make fools of themselves."

"How did you know?" She laughed. "You would never do such a thing. Ironic, is it not, that people do the opposite of what they should."

"Indeed."

"Tell me about yourself, Lord Philip. I suspect, beneath your finally chiseled demeanor, that you keep some very dark secrets."

"Oh, but I will never tell," he bent over and whispered in her ear.

She looked up at him with a seductive smile. "We will see about that."

A challenge. It was exactly the right thing for her to say to secure his interest. "At least I know Paris will not be tedious," he said, answering her indirect query.

The tempo of the dance increased and there was little place for words as he spun her about in the glittering candlelight amongst the sea of other dancers caught up in the rhythm. It was a heady feeling to have the most beautiful woman he had ever seen in his arms and he allowed himself to be drunk on her charms.

When the dance ended, he knew that keeping her wanting more was a matter of how he handled this moment. "Shall I return you to your aunt?"

"Oh, my allotted time with Lord Philip has ended," she said, looking wholly amused, her eyes twinkling. She looked about and her gaze landed on Wellington. "I think I should like to dance with this infamous duke of yours. I hear he is very charming, but will he measure up to you?"

Philip gave her his arm and led her slowly from the dance floor, trying to prolong each moment. "I can hardly disparage my commander, can I? He undoubtedly has a list of conquests miles long."

"A diplomatic answer. I believe I prefer one whose conquests are not so well known."

Philip kept his face impassive as they reached Wellington. "Your Grace, Her Highness has requested the pleasure of your company next."

She gave Wellington her hand.

"I will not take offense that you chose Everleigh first, or shall

I?" Wellington teased.

"Most definitely not," she answered, casting a look at Philip. "How else would I know with what to compare you?"

Philip tried not to bristle as he heard Wellington laugh while he led the archduchess to the dance floor.

CHAPTER TWO

PARIS WAS BEAUTIFUL. In some ways, it was very like London, but there was a certain magic in the air of the French capital that Maria could not quite describe. They had arrived in darkness last night and she'd had only a hint of what the city looked like. By morning, with the sun peeping over the Mansard-styled, grayish roofs peppered with chimneys, she had the first taste of its unique charm. While it was not enough to make her forget about her troubles, not everyone she saw there would know who she was and whisper behind her back, so that was something.

Kate and Jack did their best not to pity her and for that she was grateful. It would have been too much to be borne whilst watching them be so in love, which they could not hide, nor would she want them to. It did not make it any easier, but she would learn to bear it.

They were to stay at Wellington's town house—hôtel in French, which Maria had not anticipated. At least most of the people there knew the truth of the story, though that would not stop the looks of pity.

She had yet to see Philip, which she was looking forward to. He always had a way to lift her spirits and knew just what to say.

A knock on the door announced Maria's maid, Bisset, who then helped her to dress. Captain Owens had insisted she and Kate bring a wardrobe befitting the London Season, for the whirl of social events was always active in Paris. Maria could not imagine what that would entail but perhaps they would call on other officers' wives, and she would again feel the sting of awkwardness of being single and wondering if they were judging her.

Maria had no intention of going anywhere alone, so she waited for Kate to come and fetch her for breakfast.

When Kate at last appeared, she looked incredibly beautiful in a lime-colored sprigged muslin, alongside which Maria felt her jonquil one looked dull in comparison. Maria had never been jealous of her friend before, but she could not deny being envious of the happiness she had found with her husband.

"Bonjour!" Kate said with a giggle. "I never before thought to find Miss Bell's lessons of use!"

"You must know I was never very good at languages," Maria reminded her. Maria understood the languages quite well, but speaking them was altogether another matter.

"Pooh. You are too modest. I know you at least speak German, French and Italian quite competently."

"Competent does not mean fluent—or well."

"Let us break our fast," Kate said with a hurrying motion of her hand. "I cannot wait to explore the city."

"Will the gentlemen be working?"

"Yes, meetings and such, Jack says. We are to avail ourselves of any mounts or carriages we need, as per His Grace's orders."

"What would you like to do first?" Maria asked as they made their way through the maze of passages in the direction of the breakfast room.

"Oh, I have no specific plans. Perhaps take a ride around the town, stop at shops, and eat a lot of pastries?"

"Kate wanting to shop…. will wonders never cease?" Maria forced herself to smile despite feeling weary.

They descended one side of the curved, dual staircase to the checkered marble floor of the entrance hall.

The gray-haired butler greeted them jovially. "Good morning, ladies. Breakfast has been laid on the terrace this morning. His Grace enjoys eating outside when the weather is so fine."

"What a lovely notion," Kate agreed.

He directed them to the doors leading outside, but none of the other guests were present. Maria tried not to feel disappointed. She would see Philip later.

"Perhaps we do not need to go anywhere to eat," Maria commented, seeing the display of delicacies before them. Pastries unlike any she had seen before were displayed like an artistic masterpiece. There were other such items as caviar and *l'escargot* with the typical English breakfast of bacon, eggs, and toast.

"Perhaps we should walk to view the city so our figures do not suffer," Kate remarked as she piled her plate with the delicacies.

Maria agreed, a moment before biting into a flaky croissant.

When they had finished their repast, they gathered their cloaks and bonnets and set out for an adventure. They began by walking south along the Rue du Faubourg Saint-Honoré. "Jack says, if we stay alongside this pretty avenue and the river, we should not become lost," Kate said.

"I think there will be quite enough to see on the nearby streets for several days," Maria said as they looked down the wide thoroughfare at the numerous boutiques and eateries.

"Yes, there are also many wonderful museums and parks, do not forget."

One of the first shops they entered was a modiste's establishment, to make an appointment for a future date. Anything from Paris couture was coveted in London.

"Perhaps it is silly to want a dress from here, but I have always coveted the Parisian fashions worn by ladies of the *haut ton*," Kate confessed.

"Perhaps it would be nice to have one," Maria agreed. She still did not feel in the least excited by the prospect of attending numerous social engagements. There was little to smile about.

Nevertheless, they did make appointments for a week hence,

and then they set about exploring the various milliners' emporiums. Maria watched impassively as her friend tried on at least fifty bonnets. Everything looked good on Kate's fair beauty, no matter how ridiculous it appeared on the shelf.

Lifting from a cabinet a beautiful creation of blue with silver netting and three jaunty feathers, Kate turned towards her friend and set it atop her head.

"I do not need any hats," Maria protested and began to take it off.

"I insist. I have always thought this color suited you very well. And the hat is perfection itself. Take a look."

Reluctantly, Maria turned to the mirror. She did not recognize the person in front of her. The hat was smart, of course, but the liveliness of the person usually reflected back at her was not.

By the time Maria had removed the bonnet and turned around again, Kate had already arranged for the purchase of it. Maria did not have the heart to argue and they were soon back in the streets, walking towards their next shop.

"Oh, look!" Kate exclaimed. "Is that not Lord Philip over there?"

Maria perked up immediately. Although she disliked to be so influenced by one person, she could not seem to help herself. She scanned the bustling street, full of pedestrians in the main, but it was difficult to distinguish who was who amongst the ladies' parasols and gentlemen's hats. And then she saw him.

Kate was already waving and calling to him, but he did not see them. His eyes were for one person alone and she was one of the most beautiful ladies Maria had ever seen. She felt physically sick as she watched them flirt with one another, but forced herself to smile as they drew closer.

When Philip finally noticed them, some strange emotion crossed his face and he brought his companion forward.

"Maria!" he called. "Are you well? I am so relieved to see you here. I called at your parents' house before I left London, but the house was closed up."

Maria's spirits lifted at his words and then fell again when she looked at the lady on his arm. Despite knowing she was dressed in the latest London fashion, Maria could not but feel frumpy and plain next to this model of beauty and mode. There was something about her –perhaps her confidence—that even made her cast Kate into the shade. But Philip would not be blinded by beauty alone, would he? Maria struggled not to hate the woman instantly and forced herself to answer. "Yes, Mama and Papa went to the country, and I went to stay with Kate."

"I am very pleased to see you. Forgive my manners! May I introduce my companion, the Archduchess Pauline Klementine? Archduchess, allow me to present Lady Maria Lloyd and Mrs. Owens, wife of my friend, Captain Owens."

The ladies curtsied to each other, but Maria could not help but assess the woman on Phillip's arm. She had her arm intertwined possessively through his, and there was little doubt she wanted Philip. Who would not? She could not compete with such beauty. Maria's heart sank even further. She knew she could not win Philip's hand, but something inside her had never lost hope. If she were being honest, it was why she had not accepted those offers made to her. She was indeed the stupid girl her father thought her.

"Will you be at the hôtel later?" Philip was asking and Maria forced another smile. She had become very good at doing that over the years, but now it was much harder. Now, of all times, when she could not afford to have any aspersions cast on her character.

"Yes, of course." Kate answered for her and sent her friend a worried look.

"I will see you later, then. Enjoy your shopping," Philip said with a bow before leading the duchess away.

The woman looked back and smiled knowingly as Kate and Maria watched the pair walk towards la Place de la Concorde. How could she compete with such a woman? Not only was she beautiful, but she was sophisticated in ways that Maria could only imagine. Maria felt every bit the naïve innocent.

"I do not like her," Kate said in a supportive way, patting her on the arm.

"You are a great friend, Kate," Maria said, attempting to be strong though her chin quivered. She inhaled a deep breath and willed herself to feel nothing. "He was never going to have me, I know. But why must it hurt so?" she whispered.

Kate said nothing. Maria knew her friend could not answer that question, because she herself had been trying to do so for years. She shook her head and looked away, but a warm tear still escaped down her cheek. They walked back to Wellington's residence in silence, Kate not attempting—thankfully—to divert her with more shopping.

PHILIP WAS IN the throes of infatuation and yet he could not seem to care. Perhaps it was—dare he say—love? In the back of his mind he knew it was reckless for someone in his position. However, the archduchess was Austrian, one of their allies, and did he not deserve to have some amusement? Reality was likely to crash down upon him soon enough, but she was like an addictive drug and he could not seem to stop, even though he knew it was bad for him. If only to prove his point, for some reason he had been embarrassed when caught in public with the archduchess by Mrs. Owens and Lady Maria. It was almost as if he had a secret he did not wish to share. Reluctantly, he returned Her Highness to the Minister's house and walked back to the British hôtel.

At least Maria was there. Since they were both children he had always enjoyed Maria's company. He was very glad that Jack and Kate Owens had brought her to Paris. Nothing good would have come from her being hidden away in the country.

He walked up the steps of Wellington's new residence, the

Palais Borghese, and the butler opened the door for him.

"Good evening, my lord."

"Jenkins," Philip returned. "Have you any knowledge of Lady Maria's whereabouts?"

"I believe she is taking a walk in the gardens, sir."

"Very good, thank you." He found her sitting on a bench, surrounded by a backdrop of trees and roses, looking lost in contemplation.

"Penny for them?" he asked as he stopped beside her.

She noticed him and a flicker of pain crossed her face before she masked it with a smile. "Philip, good afternoon."

"May I join you?"

"Yes, of course." She made room for him on the bench.

"I am happy to see you here."

"You are?" She sounded surprised.

"Of course I am. I am always happy to see you, but I am pleased you were able to leave England."

"Because of the scandal, I collect. Yes, I had little choice but to leave or hide."

He was surprised by the vehemence in her voice. He had never before seen Maria ruffled, truth be told. She looked down at her hands and fidgeted with the ribbons on her gown. She must be more upset than she appeared.

"The scandal will go away. Your brother is not a traitor." He attempted to reassure her.

"No," she whispered.

"Cheer up, pet." He tried to raise a smile by using her nickname from when they were children. "I cannot stand to see you sad."

"Self-pity is not becoming, is it? I beg your pardon. I will come about. The emotion is just still very raw."

"Indeed."

"The soldier's life is different from how I expected," Maria remarked, changing the subject.

"How so?" he asked, his curiosity piqued.

"It seems a great deal like being in London."

"I take it you had envisioned we were engaged in fierce battle all the time?" he asked, amused.

"Something like that," she agreed.

"Most of the battles happen behind the scenes, as beautifully veiled diplomacy or acts of spying. I hate to be the one to disillusion you."

"Is the archduchess a part of the latter?"

He paused, uncertain how to answer that. Along with most gentlemen of his acquaintance, he was uncomfortable when speaking of his feelings, but this was Maria, after all. "I do not know yet what she is. Flirting is a very deep game in these circles."

"Because it has hidden meaning?"

"It can have." How could one explain such things to an innocent?

He heard her swallow. "But do you like her?"

"I do," he confessed, "although doubtless she is only toying with me, since she is far above my station…"

Maria protested with adorable indignation. "I beg to differ! She is royalty?"

"She is part of the court." He realized then he did not actually know where she was ranked.

"And do people use courting as a disguise for obtaining information in these circles?"

"I would not call it courting, precisely."

"But you are interested in her, are you not?" she persisted.

He shrugged. There was no point in lying to Maria, but he was not certain he was ready to bear his soul either. "She intrigues and fascinates me."

Maria sighed and he did not know quite how to interpret it. Disappointment? Something else?

"Will you be joining us for dinner?" he asked instead. Maria was like a sister to him, and if she disapproved, he did not wish to hear it.

"Yes, is it time to dress already?"

He pulled out his pocket watch to see. "Soon enough, I believe, considering the hours you ladies like to spend on your toilettes." When she did not rise to the bait, he continued, "You will meet several new faces, I presume. If there is anyone in particular to whom you would like an introduction, just give me a sign."

"Philip, I may be desperate, but I am not here to martyr myself."

"Is that not the very definition of marriage?"

"Not you, too!" She was angry.

"What did I say? Is that not the desire of most young ladies? To find a match?"

"As Father was quick to point out, had I done my duty these past three seasons, I would not now be a dried-up old spinster and a burden to him!" She rose and walked a few paces away.

He stood up and followed slowly. "Maria, I did not intend to be presumptuous or harm your feelings, but it would remove you from Lord Mottram's jurisdiction. I am aware of your feelings on that subject."

She turned back to face him and closed her eyes. "Yes," she said on a sigh. "My feelings with respect to my father are no better than they were. Forgive me. I am unsuitable company."

"No, never. If you cannot unburden yourself to one of your oldest friends, then I am not a true friend indeed."

Her face softened at his words. "Thank you, Philip. Is there anyone in particular I should consider? Someone with an intelligent mind, who would not care about the slur upon my family's name?"

Philip tried to think. He mentally ran through the list of eligible officers of his acquaintance, but could not find one without some fault. Some were penniless younger sons, some had gambling habits, some were overly fond of women and drink, and the others were simply boring. Many of them intended not to marry because of their profession at arms. "I will need to think upon that," he said. The thought of Maria with anyone dismayed him. No one seemed to be good enough for her.

She waved her hand in a dismissive way. "Please do not trouble yourself. Truly, I am happy enough to see Paris for the nonce. Perhaps, when my fascination with the city has ended, I will ask you again."

"I should not expect that to happen very soon, then." Despite England having long been at war with France, he had a deep love for the city.

Maria's mouth formed into a smile, but she still looked sad.

"What can I do to make you happy again, dearest?" he asked, looking down into her face. If he were to describe her, it would be in a similar way to the archduchess. She had beautiful chestnut hair, though she styled it very simply in a tight chignon. Her eyes were a light brown color –the color of tea with a splash of milk– and were perhaps one of her best features, while her skin was as soft as dew on rose petals. He had heard her described as plain by her parents, but Philip did not think so, especially when she smiled. Yet she did not inspire him to madness like Pauline Klementine did.

More than once it had occurred to him to offer for Maria. To do so would at least provide her with the relief of being a married woman and the support of having his family name behind her. In fact, it was what he had gone to her home to do when he had found her gone. It was still probably what he should do, but since then he had met the archduchess, and the words would not form on his tongue.

"Philip?" She was looking up at him in concern, with her big doe eyes. "For a moment it seemed as if you went somewhere else entirely."

"Forgive me. I was lost in contemplation. I believe I was asking what I could do to make you happy again?" He forced himself to smile. A number of emotions crossed her face in rapid succession. What he would not have given for her to share them with him, he thought. She was not being open with him.

"Being my friend is all you can do for now, Philip. Time will surely heal some of the wounds."

Clearly she did not believe the words she spoke, but she was striving to remain calm.

"You know you may always tell me anything. Anything at all."

"I wish that were so," she whispered.

He pulled her into a hug and held her against his chest. Her family was not very affectionate, but if anyone had ever needed a hug, it was she. They had been friends a long time, after all. "Everything will be well, pet."

CHAPTER THREE

MARIA CLOSED HER eyes and relived the warmth of Philip's arms around her, his telltale signs of woods and pine and wished things were different, that he would see her in the same way he saw the Austrian woman and want her in return. But loving someone meant you wanted what was best for them, and she wanted him to be happy. She would cherish the tender moment in his arms forever.

She rang the bell to summon her maid in order to dress for dinner, and suddenly she wanted to be noticed. She wanted to inspire men to be irrational. After a few minutes, Bisset came into the bedchamber, and Maria decided to be bold.

"Bisset…" Maria began, wondering if her maid of many years would agree. "Would you help me style my hair in a different fashion—dress a little more maturely?" Maria knew Bisset was capable of much more. In the beginning, she had tried to make Maria more stylish, but because of her father's comments on her plainness and her mother's strict sense of propriety, Maria had never been comfortable being on display. Now, it seemed, she needed at least to try.

"Yes, my lady," the maid said, instantly brightening and waving her into the seat before the dressing table. "What did you have in mind? We must hurry if we are to achieve an acceptable result before dinner."

Maria shook her head. "I do not know. I have always relied on my mother to advise me."

Bisset made a little face before quickly disguising it. "Then what do you wish for? Have you seen a style you like?"

Maria laughed nervously. "I confess I find Caro Lamb's short curls delightful. I wish I had the courage to do something so drastic."

The maid stood back and tilted her hair behind Maria while considering her reflection in the mirror. "I do think shorter hair would be becoming and without all of the weight, I think you would have a pretty wave."

"If you can, then do so," Maria said, seized by a brief moment of bravery…or lunacy.

The maid smiled and left to fetch a pair of scissors and other items she needed. While she was gone, Maria went to look over her gowns. They were also very demure and subtle in color, as was expected of a young lady in England. Not all her gowns were yet pressed, but there was a dark green velvet with a low bodice that was nowhere near so crushed as the muslins and jaconets. She had never been brave enough to wear it despite the accompanying fichu. Although she had dreamed of wearing it to the theatre one evening, she had never done so. It had been one of the few dresses she had selected without her mother's approval. She took it and laid it on the bed, scrutinizing it critically.

Bisset returned and came to stand beside her.

"What do you think, Bisset? Would this go with shorter hair?"

The maid slanted her head. "Perhaps without the fichu at the neck. You do have a beautiful neck, if you will pardon my saying so."

Maria blushed a little at the praise, yet felt bolstered enough to take the momentous step. She gave a swift nod, and the maid removed the finely embroidered cloth from the neck of the gown. Having directed her mistress to sit at the dressing table, she then brushed out her waist-long hair. By the time the maid picked up the scissors to cut, Maria was shaking with fear and gripping the edge of her seat.

"Have you changed your mind, miss?"

"No," she choked out. "Do it, please."

"Very good, my lady." The sound of the steel scraped as the scissors opened, then the cutting of the hair was a strange sound which made her cringe. The stakes were so very high that her nerves were on edge. What if she looked a fool? She had not the personality of Caro Lamb to pull off such a feat if she looked a fright. There was only so much hiding beneath a bonnet of such a mistake that a girl could do. Wrapping her head in a turban would definitely make the statement that she had placed herself on the shelf.

But something drastic had to be done. If Philip could not love her romantically, then she had to make someone else take notice of her.

The loss of weight was noticeable each time the scissors passed around her head. Long lengths of hair fell to the floor and Maria could scarce credit her locks had been so long.

"All done, my lady," Bisset finally pronounced.

Maria was afraid to look. "Is it an improvement?"

"Well, it is difficult to say with you looking down, but there is a nice, natural curl to it that is pleasing."

Maria dared to look and shook her head back and forth, studying the new person staring at her as the curls bounced this way and that. She smiled.

"Oh, miss!" the abigail exclaimed. "It becomes you to perfection!"

"I think so, too. Splendid, Bisset. Splendid."

"We had better get you dressed so you aren't too late."

"Indeed. It is essential I arrive before His Grace."

Maria had never wanted to be the center of attention before and now, suddenly, when all eyes were upon her, she disliked the sensation very much. But she had made her bed, so to speak, and must now deal with the consequences.

Soldiers she was not yet acquainted with cast appreciative

glances her way, but there was as yet no sign of Philip.

"Maria?" Kate asked, her voice startled as though she did not recognize her friend.

"Forgive me if I am late."

"Forgive you? I hardly recognized you!" Kate declared, pulling her away from the crowd of officers her husband, Jack Owens, was speaking to. "What have you done?"

"I gather you do not care for my hair?" Maria tried to sound unaffected, but if Kate thought her ridiculous, then all hope was lost.

"That is not it at all!" Kate surveyed her critically. "It is actually quite fetching, but very out of character for the Maria I know!" she whispered with some urgency. "Did you do this because of that woman?"

"No," Maria said emphatically, then thought better of it. "Well, perhaps a little. It made me realize I must do something to be noticed."

"You were beautiful the way you were. You do not need, nor ever had a need, to change."

Maria refrained from retorting that the way she had been was not achieving her greatest wish. "Is it really so terrible?"

"No, I rather like it, but I cannot like the idea of you doing such a thing so suddenly for the wrong reasons."

"I do not have the luxury of time, Kate. I will never have Philip, but I need someone. I cannot afford to be over-nice in my choice, and I cannot return to England unmarried."

"You are in earnest," Kate said, searching Maria's face. "Very well. I will ask Jack if he can recommend anyone."

"If so, that would be more than Philip could do. He could think of no one."

Kate looked thoughtful, but said nothing to the fact. She looked Maria up and down, then took her arm. "I have never seen you in anything so daring. You must know I always suspected your figure was excellent."

"I decided enough was enough. I bought the gown at the

beginning of the Season, without Mama's knowledge, and have never been brave enough to wear it."

"Should I surmise from this that you are secretly harboring a bold side?" Kate teased.

"I suppose I am." Maria laughed. "With Mama such a thing was not to be borne."

They walked over to Captain Owen's side, whereupon he broke off his conversation and looked at them with a smile. "Why, Lady Maria, may I say you look very fetching tonight? Did you change something?" He frowned, as though he ought to be able to realize what it was. Sometimes, she thought, for the intelligence work the gentlemen did, they were exceeding blind to the ladies in front of them.

"Jack," Kate scolded, "she has cut her hair."

"Ah, yes, that's the ticket."

"We need to introduce her to some worthy gentleman."

"No one wants to be referred to as *worthy*," Jack retorted. "Such a fellow would be a dead bore, my dear."

"Kate, you are putting me to the blush! Must we be so *outré* about it?" Maria's voice held a hint of panic even she could not miss.

"Trust me, my lady, there will be plenty of gentlemen clamoring for an introduction," he replied with a wry smile.

Taking Kate's arm, Captain Owens then presented his other one to Maria. "I am the envy of every man here," he said with a teasing smile as he led them over to a group of officers by the window.

Maria pasted a smile upon her face, determined to try being more coy and flirtatious, when she spied Philip enter the room with the archduchess. Her Highness was attired in a bold red gown which left few of her charms to the imagination.

"Well, not every gentleman," Maria muttered, trying not to feel jealous and hurt, feelings which were threatening to cause her to run from the room. Watching the archduchess clinging to Philip's arm as they made a slow progress through the assembled, she felt horribly self-conscious when, to her chagrin, she met the other woman's eye. Maria instantly felt transparent. It was as though the woman knew Maria was trying to compete with her, and was not even a worthy foe.

Maria turned away, determined to find someone else. Surely Philip was not the only gentleman on earth she could love?

PHILIP LOOKED TWICE when he entered the room and saw Maria. He almost tripped over his own feet. Pauline gripped his arm.

"Your mousy friend has improved herself a little."

Philip looked again. Was that cropped-haired creature Maria? "I do not think her mousy at all," he replied shortly. In fact, she looked very attractive in a green fitted velvet gown which showed her figure to advantage. It was not a word he had thought about Maria before, not in the physical sense. Not that he had thought her ugly, he corrected himself hastily, but he had always considered her more in line with a sister. And one did not think one's sister attractive. Handsome, perhaps, but decidedly not attractive. But he had never noticed her curves in the unattractive sacks dripping with ruffles and lace her mother had prescribed.

"Then I will have to make certain your attention is on me so you may not be distracted," Pauline said.

Philip turned to the beauty on his arm. "There is little doubt of that."

Despite his prompt response, Philip could not but notice the number of officers begging for an introduction to Maria. "I must make certain she stays away from Weston. He is a definite fortune hunter. And Patten—he defines the word libertine."

"Lady Maria is a grown woman."

"Yes, but she is my friend and friends have a care for one another."

"If you say so, then it must be so. However, I do not wish to talk about Lady Maria all evening. There can be no mischief in harmless flirtation." She waved her hand dismissively.

Philip turned his attention to the beauty on his arm. She was correct. Maria was of an age to know how to go on and it would perhaps benefit her to have some male attention. But he would keep an eye on her, as he knew Jack would.

"What would you like to speak about?"

"I would like to engage in some harmless flirtation myself," she said, looking up at him from beneath lowered lids as though he were the only man in the world.

"Is it harmless? Somehow I do not think I will leave your company unharmed."

"Who says I will let you go?" She looked at him knowingly and he laughed. The last thing he was going to do was fall into her clutches so soon. Of a certainty, he would not let her know if he did. But he loved how she made him feel. His pulse quickened at the mere thought of her. The sight of her caused goose pimples on his flesh. Pauline was a heady addiction, that he would do well to remember.

"I will fetch some refreshment. What do you prefer to drink on such occasions?"

"Surprise me, my gallant *Philippe*. But no ratafia, if you please."

Philip found a waiter and took two glasses of champagne.

He heard Maria's laughter and turned sharply. Maria would never have allowed herself to laugh in such a manner in London. He narrowed his gaze to see what she was reacting to.

Colonel Strickland, the handsome heir to one of the oldest titles in England, even if it were only a barony, was whispering in her ear. He had several brothers and had purchased a commission because he wanted to serve his country, not because he had to.

Philip searched his mind for anything that would recommend Strickland or otherwise, and no fault came immediately to mind. He was perhaps a little old for Maria, but she had never been drawn to the younger set. She had always been mature and thoughtful, so perhaps an older man was just the thing.

He caught Jack's gaze and gave him a thoughtful look which he knew his best friend would understand. Jack inclined his head, indicating that, yes, he was keeping a watchful eye on Maria.

Satisfied, Philip made his way back to the archduchess, who was already surrounded by a court of admirers.

"You leave for five minutes and someone takes your place," a pompous Prussian soldier remarked.

"That is assuming I am replaceable," Philip riposted dryly, moving straight to Pauline's side, and handing her the glass of wine.

Pauline smirked as she held his gaze and took a sip of the gold liquid.

All eyes turned as Wellington chose that moment to enter the room. He strode directly toward Pauline. He always did have an eye for beauty, but Philip was not concerned. Wellington was very much enchanted with Lady Georgiana Lennox at the moment.

Philip tried to pay attention as his commander charmed Pauline, but he could not keep from looking towards Maria. He had been with her only a few short hours before and he had had no sense of her contemplating anything so drastic. What had made her do it?

He could not decide how he felt about the change. Part of him reasoned, why should she not? And the other part of him stubbornly preferred Maria the way she had been: witty, warm...comfortable. Perhaps she would not like to think of herself in those terms, but he could not think of her as a flirt. Would men not gain the wrong impression of her, and thus not value her finer qualities?

Was this merely a product of her family's scandal and her supposed desperation to find a husband? Or was this the true Maria emerging from her mother's vastly over-protective shell? Did he really know her at all? Somehow, the last question smarted the worst. Maria had always been one of his closest friends and confidants, however unlikely that might seem to others. They had been thrown together constantly at their family's gatherings, their brothers being several years their senior and often away at school. Philip's sister had still been in the nursery. He had never quite thought of Maria as anything other than a dear friend. She had not been a silly girl and had enjoyed tagging along on his adventures. This was only over-protectiveness. It had to be.

"Who is that distracting all my officers?" Wellington's voice boomed, causing Philip to start and remember where he was.

Philip looked where Wellington indicated, although he knew quite well to whom he was referring.

"That is Lady Maria Lloyd, sir."

"By Jove, it is, is it not? I am not accustomed to seeing anyone else steal your thunder, Pauline. I should pay my addresses. She is an old friend."

Wellington kissed Pauline's hand and then excused himself, striding straight toward Maria.

"You should not scowl, *mein liebster*. People will get the wrong idea."

"I am not scowling. This is my contemplative face when I am trying to solve a mystery."

Pauline burst out laughing and several heads turned to stare. "If you say so, it must be true."

Then Philip did scowl. She had said that phrase more than once.

"Come, walk with me through the gardens and I will take your mind off your mystery for a while." Her voice was low and seductive.

Philip hesitated, but he was saved from rejecting her by dinner being announced.

"Later, perhaps. Wellington's chef will have to cure your mood for the nonce," she said, as though amused, while he led her into the dining room.

Before, when there had been beautiful women at Wellington's dinners and dances, Philip had been greatly diverted, but now he was questioning the wisdom of so much female distraction. There was the archduchess, who could be called one of the great beauties of Europe, holding court at one end of the table, and then there was Lady Maria at the other. Despite her transformation, she could never compete with the archduchess in looks. However, she could rival anyone with her quick wit and keen mind if she chose to. Philip bit into his *Canard à l'Orange* but scarcely tasted it as he listened to Maria's laughter and saw her cheeks flush becomingly in response to something Strickland had said to her.

He knew he should be glad Maria was receiving so much attention. Why, therefore, did it disconcert him so?

CHAPTER FOUR

THAT EVENING, MARIA returned to her room exhausted. She had spent the last three Seasons doing the social whirl of routs, balls and parties, dancing and being convivial until dawn, but she had never before been on display. To be sure, it was a smaller audience, but how could cropping her hair and wearing a more daring gown change everything so completely? Or was it simply her attitude which had changed?

Most certainly she preferred not to draw attention to herself, but Kate had been correct in that Maria was desperate. Whatever it was, it had succeeded in attracting male attention.

You had offers before, her conscience reminded her.

But not the one I wanted, she snapped back.

At first, she had believed Philip not to have noticed her, but realized her mistake when she caught his scowl from across the room.

Deliberately, she had avoided his gaze, pretending she had not seen him. She had laughed a little too loudly, against her mother's strict upbringing, as though her partner were the most riveting gentleman in the world. Colonel Strickland was handsome, his dark hair was silvering around his ears and his pale blue eyes were framed by dark brows and lashes, the whole presenting a pleasing picture, if a little stern and older than her preference, but she knew he would not play games. In fact, he had asked her to go for a morning ride before he began his duties for the day. Recklessly, she had accepted, grasping at any chance she had. Desperate she might be, but not enough to make a wretched marriage where there was no reciprocal respect or friendship.

A few other, younger officers had shown interest but clearly would not step on their superior's toes. She knew something of Lieutenants Patten and Weston from repute and suspected they were more likely game for flirtation than marriage, although she did have a very respectable dowry which would make her a fair catch even when her looks did not.

She sat before the dressing table and critically surveyed her reflection. It was rather startling to see her hair short, but it was flattering. If truth be told, she had attempted to play the coquette with a confidence she had not felt. In fact, if it had not been for the archduchess entering on the arm of Philip, she might even have believed in her own charms. Instead, she now felt as though she were second-rate and the men she had attracted had either no hope of the great Austrian beauty, or the fish in the sea were so thin they had paid her attention out of courtesy.

The look the archduchess had given her had spoken volumes. Full of pity, it had said, *I know what you are attempting to do and it will not prevail.*

Thankfully, during dinner they had been seated at opposite ends of the table, but Maria had been conscious of her opponent's presence nevertheless.

It was not until after the meal had concluded that Philip had spoken a word to her, and then not until the archduchess had taken a moment to visit the retiring room.

He had walked over to Maria and with one look, the other men had scattered. Part of her wanted to reprimand him, but her treacherous heart leaped at his attention.

"Good evening, Maria."

"Good evening, Philip. I was uncertain if you had noticed I was here." Even Wellington had taken the trouble to greet her.

He looked at her thoughtfully—critically—before speaking. It was difficult to stand where she was in a room full of people, and let him look, without cringing. She could feel her neck and cheeks warm. Her tendency to blush annoyed her.

"I noticed. Why did you do it?" His hand reached up as though he would touch her hair but then stopped midway as though he realized it would be inappropriate.

"Why should I not? It is time for a change, Philip."

"You look lovely," he said, almost as if he had only now realized she was female.

"Thank you," she barely whispered, her throat constricting with emotion. How feeble she was to be so starved for praise from him!

"Would you care to ride with me in the mornings while we are here? Although most of the day is taken up with duties, riding is allowed for exercise."

"Perhaps I might accompany you the day after next? I have already promised to ride with someone tomorrow."

"May I ask whom?"

She looked up with surprise, feeling her brow furrow. Why she hesitated, she had no notion, but she did.

"Be careful, Maria. Some of the gentlemen dangling after you tonight are not suitable for marriage."

"Surely, you can have nothing to say against Colonel Strickland? I have been acquainted with his family since birth."

"No, there is nothing to say against him. Is he the one you are to ride with?"

"Yes," she answered softly.

Why the conversation had been so painful, she mused now, she could not say. It had turned to mundane matters about Paris and as soon as the archduchess had re-entered the room, he had returned to her side. It was time to cast aside dreams of Philip.

Maria brushed her shorter hair a hundred times and then shook it back and forth, relishing the freedom from the heavy weight she had carried for as long as she could remember. Then she laughed, and decided she did look rather well. Perhaps, she reflected hopefully, if Pauline Klementine, or even Kate, were not in the room, then Maria might be considered pretty.

What she had done, she had done for her own satisfaction and she would not allow herself to regret it. Desperate times called for desperate measures and perhaps Colonel Strickland would be just the thing. She was certainly willing to consider him, although he must be more than ten years her senior. She wished she had a Debrett's *Peerage* to consult, but if she recalled correctly, one of his brothers was of an age with her and he was the next youngest.

Marrying an older gentleman was not unusual and Maria could find no fault in doing so, for she had little in common with the boys her age. For they were boys; that was undeniable—and mayhap why a gentleman older than oneself made a superior husband. Such gentlemen were more seasoned and cultured, and had a calm confidence about them which set them apart from those who were still sowing their wild oats.

Colonel Strickland was also a large man – broad and tall – and she could imagine opponents seeing him on his horse across the battlefield and wondering if he represented all that the British army had to offer. It would not be a comforting sight.

He was quieter and more stern than Maria would prefer, but perhaps she could draw him out. She suspected a smile from him would be worth the effort, for it was not recklessly bestowed.

Having decided that being courted by Colonel Strickland would be a good thing indeed, Maria rang for Bisset to help her from her gown.

When Bisset duly stepped into the room, she gave Maria a hopeful smile. "How did you go on, my lady? I have been most anxious while waiting to hear."

"Mrs. Owens was shocked," Maria confessed with a smile.

"And the gentlemen?"

"They seemed pleased. It becomes me not to boast but I spent the whole evening surrounded by dashing army officers, and have promised to ride with one of them in the morning."

"Is he handsome?" That was clearly the most important bit of news to Bisset.

"He is Colonel Strickland, eldest son of Baron Ingram… and yes, he is handsome."

"I will spy on him," Bisset announced without shame as she helped Maria step out of her gown.

"Discreetly, if you please," Maria added. There was no point in telling the maid not to discover what she could; the girl might be an inveterate busybody, but she guarded her mistress' confidences as her own. Besides, Maria wanted to know. If a person was not well thought of below stairs, then they were generally not pleasant behind closed doors.

"Which habit shall I press for the morning, my lady?"

"The dark green one." It was new and had neat black frog fastenings in the military style and braided trim, topped by a simple beaver hat.

Bisset nodded her approval. "It will look well with his uniform."

"Were there any noteworthy adventures in the servants' quarters?" Maria and Bisset had always gossiped about the goings-on to be witnessed after parties.

"There was a handsome groom. He was Austrian."

Maria tried not to show a reaction. There had been more than one Austrian present that night. "Was he interested?"

"Of course." Bisset waved her hand as though it were nothing. Her beauty had caused many a disturbance in servants' halls and stables across England.

"All he could talk of was his mistress and how she was a great beauty." Bisset scoffed. "He said I would make a lovely addition to her household. As if I would leave you for her."

Maria smiled at her maid's loyalty.

"Her maid thinks she is above the rest of us."

"Her maid was here tonight?"

Bisset smiled knowingly. "Oh, yes, in case a hair falls out of place. She always attends with her."

"She is beautiful," Maria said, forcing a neutral tone. Nonetheless, it was painful to admit, as though not being so was her own failing. "Lord Philip is much taken with her."

"Oh, my lady, how can you say so? Lord Philip cannot be smitten by such a one! She treats gentlemen like puppets and has no heart."

"Why do you say that?" Now Maria was concerned for Philip. She had never known him to form any real attachments and very likely he could hold his own against the archduchess, yet she still could not but be concerned.

"Because her marriage has been arranged from birth, yet she allows gentlemen to think they have a chance to win her. At least, that is what is said amongst the servants."

Maria wondered if Philip knew the archduchess was promised to someone else.

PHILIP HAD INVITED Pauline to ride with him the next morning since Maria was otherwise engaged. As he rode along the Avenue de Maringy to her residence, he contemplated Maria's situation, not realizing he was spending more time reflecting upon her person than his own.

He could not decide how he felt about his friend riding out with Strickland. Maria had never refused him before. Had he taken her for granted? Had he assumed she would always be there for him? Of course, everything would change if she married – if he married. Yet it was one thing to know that in your mind but another to acknowledge the same in your heart.

Perhaps Maria had attracted as much attention in London, and he had been unaware of the fact. He had been away with the army for most of the time since her come out. If that was the case, and she had had a court of admirers, then there was no reason for her to have changed her hair or the way she dressed.

"Why are you frowning? I think I should be duly appreciated for rising so early to ride with you," Pauline said with a hint of petulance. She looked up at him, one hand on her hip and a riding crop in the other. Defiance only made her eyes sparkle with tantalizing allure.

Philip had intended to dismount and go to the door to call for the archduchess, but he had been so lost in contemplation he had not even noticed he had arrived.

He dismounted and bowed over her hand. "Forgive me, your Grace," he said and brought her fingers to his lips.

"I think you are the first gentleman ever to have kept me waiting."

"Then I am fortunate you did not rebuff me." He assisted her into the saddle of a white-socked gray which a groom was holding ready for her.

"Unfortunately, I am not wearied by you," she said, as if she were mystified. "'Twould be so much the better if I were."

"So you tolerate me until you tire of me?" Philip knew the game well.

She looked at him in a knowing fashion before urging her horse forward. "Where shall we ride? Along the riverbank?"

"Anywhere we may gallop is acceptable to me." They cantered along to the Pont des Invalides and down to the promenade beside the Seine, where they could give the horses their heads.

No sooner had they reached the wide thoroughfare than the archduchess called for a race to the next pont, and urged her gray to a gallop. Philip allowed her to lead until the bridge came into view, then relaxed his grip on the reins and squeezed his own hunter's sides with his legs. He won easily, by several lengths.

"What is my forfeit?" Pauline asked. "I am not used to losing, you know."

"Neither am I." He had never seen the value in letting someone else win. "I will settle for a kiss and a cup of chocolate at the Café le Procope."

"Done."

They dismounted, loosely holding on to the horses' reins as he swept her beneath the edge of the bridge and pulled her close for a kiss. Instead of ravishing her mouth, his lips grazed hers, teasing and promising more. Her hands gripped his shoulders and tried to bring him closer, for a deeper caress, but Philip resisted. The desire in her eyes was tempting, but he would not succumb.

He aided her to regain her saddle and they cantered back the way they had come, passing other soldiers who looked at her appreciatively. Some even called out, professing their dying love and some offered for her hand.

They continued to canter along the Quai de Tuileries, a pretty avenue lined with trees in full leaf, with a gentle breeze from the Seine in their faces.

It was a heady sensation to be singled out by Europe's greatest beauty, and Philip felt more alive than he had done in years. Many of Europe's greatest gentlemen had lost their heads over her and the sensations their infatuation created. He was infatuated enough that he determined not to do so.

They pulled to a halt at the bridge next to the river before returning to the streets above.

"Do you intend to marry soon, Lord Philip?" she shocked him by asking once they had reached the wide expanse of the palace gardens.

"Marriage is not something I have seriously considered, ma'am." Except he had been willing to propose to Maria, he silently reminded himself.

"Would you, sir? Consider it, that is?"

"Why, Archduchess, are you asking for my hand?"

She looked at him without any of her usual coyness or pretense and he realized she was serious. Was this not merely a game of flirtation? It would seem not, yet was he ready for marriage—and to someone like her?

"Possibly," she replied slowly. "My father insists I marry this year."

"And I imagine he has someone in mind," Philip stated. It had not occurred to him before, but doubtless her family intended her to make a great dynastic match. Philip was from one of the finest families in England, but he was hardly descended from royalty, as she was.

"Yes," she said, looking out over the water. A mother duck swam by with her ducklings trailing behind, then disappeared under the bridge.

"Is he so abhorrent, your intended?"

"He is arrogant, corpulent, and tedious."

"So your father has given you an ultimatum?"

"Yes, of sorts. If I find someone else before the vows are spoken, what can he do?"

Philip thought there was a great deal that could be done but did not speak the words. Certainly, he was not about to throw himself into the fire before finding out a great deal more about Her Highness and her situation. Therefore, he did not proffer an answer and was saved by Maria and Colonel Strickland riding into view. He waved, forcing the pair to rein in and greet them.

"Colonel Strickland, you are acquainted with the Archduchess Pauline Klementine?"

"I have had the pleasure of an introduction," he said, tipping his cocked hat to her.

"How do you do? Your horse and mine look as though they are twins."

The colonel's stallion did, in fact, have almost identical markings, down to the white socks on all four legs.

"Is, by any chance, your horse an Andalusian from Babieca's line?"

"Indeed he is, your Grace. I purchased him while on campaign in Spain. I have never owned such a splendid horse. I hope to breed him one day, in my retirement." He looked pointedly at Maria, who flushed prettily at the insinuation.

"Do you plan on selling out soon, sir?" Philip found himself asking, as though it were his place to know.

"Perhaps in the next year or so, when Wellington finds a suitable replacement or it is time to set up my nursery. My father is no longer in the first pink of youth, and I should like to have time with him before he is called to his maker. Now Napoleon is exiled, it seems the right time."

The colonel was serious, then, and that would appeal to Maria. Strickland was a good catch. He would try to be happy for her.

CHAPTER FIVE

MARIA HAD BEEN courted before, but she had never taken any of her suitors seriously. With Colonel Strickland, things were different. She could no longer afford to hold out hope for Philip. It was ridiculous girlish sentiment anyway. Yet, still she could not make it go away no matter how hard she tried.

As she finished changing from her habit to her day gown of lavender muslin with a dainty floral print, there was a knock on her door. She had planned to have luncheon with Kate at the Café de Foix before exploring one of the museums there, but she thought she had some time before they were to leave.

Bisset left her and she went over to the window, gathering a book to settle in while she passed the time. But there was a light knock on the door before she even had a chance to settle her skirts.

She opened the door to see her maid staying there. "What is it, Bisset?"

"Mrs. Owens asked me to inform you that she is not feeling up to an outing today."

"Oh dear, is she all right?" Maria asked. Come to think of it, she had not seen Kate at breakfast that morning.

Bisset leaned in and whispered. "Between you and me, I think she might be increasing."

"So soon?" Maria asked, slightly appalled. She knew these

things happened, of course, but selfishly she had hoped she'd have more time with Kate.

The maid flashed a knowing look. Maria closed the door behind her, disappointed. She wanted to go somewhere anyway. It was a beautiful day and should not be wasted inside reading a book. There were enough rainy days at home for that. Perhaps one of the other ladies might wish to visit a museum or do a little shopping. Maria penned a note to Mrs. Johnson, gathered her bonnet and went downstairs to ask the butler to send the note to their lodgings.

However, there was a group of officers there and Maria quickly turned to go back upstairs until they left.

"Lady Maria?"

Maria stopped and turned back around. She could hardly pretend she had not heard. It was Colonel Strickland's deep voice and there was no reason at all to avoid him.

"Do not leave on our account."

She smiled. "I was only going to wait for you to finish your business. I did not wish to interrupt."

"We are finished." He inclined his head to the group in a silent command and they began to leave. "Are you going out?"

"Mrs. Owens and I were, but she is indisposed." She held up her note. "I was going to see if Mrs. Johnson was available to accompany me to the Louvre Palace instead." It had been called *Musée Napoléon* during his reign, but that ended, praise be.

"If you can bear my company twice in one day, I would be happy to go there myself. Would you believe I have not been there once since we arrived in Paris?"

"Some would call that criminal, sir!" she teased. "I think it is your duty to come at once. Let me summon my maid."

"I will call for a vehicle while you do that."

A few minutes later they were all ensconced in an open landau taking in the beautiful city on their way to the museum.

The carriage drove slowly through the traffic along the Tuileries Garden where it seemed the equivalent venue of the fashionable Parisians to Hyde Park's Rotten Row. Hundreds of pedestrians meandered along the avenue, ladies twirling their parasols, while gentlemen in their top hats strolled alongside.

Maria was not uncomfortable with the colonel, but neither was she relaxed. Deliberately she resolved to make an effort to become better acquainted. If she had not known Philip so well, then likely she would not be comfortable with him.

"You mentioned you might be retiring soon. Will you be content do you think?"

He smiled. "I was always told I would know when it was time. Would you believe I have been a soldier for nearly twenty years?"

"You must have commissioned when you were a babe."

He smiled and crinkles formed at the edges of his eyes. He looked more handsome smiling, to be sure. "A very diplomatic answer, my lady."

WHEN THEY ARRIVED in front of the palais, they were surrounded by a Renaissance masterpiece of cut stone and carvings. To someone who adored symmetry, it could not have been more pleasing. The palace itself, as well as all of the buildings around were of uniform height and color, walls of windows and beautiful sculpture adorned each roof. The buildings looked upon the garden and the stone courtyard.

He handed both Maria and Bisset down. A kind gesture that many gentlemen would have overlooked.

The building itself was a stunning piece of art. She stood in the courtyard and looked up, circling slowly, to take it all in. It was even more magnificent when standing there.

"The continent does grandiose architecture and squares well."

"I have not seen its equal in England," Maria admitted.

He extended his arm and he took it, feeling her heart race a bit at the contact. That was a good sign, was it not? She had not been so close to him before that she could recall and it was pleasant.

They climbed the steps and a carved wooden door opened for them. They entered the large entrance hall, then they were shown to the grand gallery. The room was hundreds of feet long, the walls were lined by large paintings and portraits set off by red marble columns topped with sculpture, the ceilings of windows, alternating with arches.

"It is magnificent," she remarked. "I have been in Burlington House, but this is so much to take in."

"This is only the grand gallery. There are many more, though many are statues and sculptures." He looked amused.

"How can the works to be properly appreciated in such a manner?"

"Would it be better to have to travel to many separate places to see each one?" he countered.

Maria had to think about it. "Personally, I could stare at one picture for an hour. But I see your point. This offers more people an opportunity they might not otherwise have. But, I will have to spend days and days in here to see everything!"

"Then it is a good thing we will be in Paris for a while," he said with a warm smile as they stopped to look at a Botticelli.

They stood in companionable silence as they studied the life-sized *Venus and the Three Graces*. Maria had always enjoyed art and never ceased to be amazed by the depth of feeling a picture could evoke in her.

"Do you paint?" he asked.

"What I do could not be compared in the same breath as this. Of course I was taught watercolors, but never oils."

"Do you like this artist?"

"I do not know if like is the precise word, but I certainly feel him in the work. I sense a strong sense of passion."

Her cheeks flushed when she realized what she had said, but Colonel Strickland did not seem to think her inappropriate.

"I agree. Certainly these are not the staid landscapes that line the walls of Ingram Park."

"I do not mind some staid landscapes myself," Maria chuckled. "Nor do I mind paintings of horses and hounds."

"Then perhaps you would not be disappointed with our collection."

They moved on to DaVinci, whose portraits were something to behold.

"Now this this is very pleasing to me. The color palette is my not favorite, as they are very dark, but create this perfection as a whole that makes you feel as if you are in the room with these people." She waved her arms in front of the large display. "It is quite fascinating!" She turned to see if the colonel understood, but he was not looking at the painting; he was watching her.

"Yes. Fascinating," he agreed quietly with a warm look.

Maria could feel her cheeks heat and lowered her eyes, not quite certain how she felt about his open admiration.

"Would you care to go for some refreshment now? There is a *chocolaterie* nearby where they spread it in a crepe and top it with finely ground sugar. It melts in your mouth."

"That sounds divine. I do not think there is an artist to surpass this one and the rest would be a sad disappointment anyway."

He laughed. "We will save the rest for another day and give Titian his proper due. But I do recommend you return and see the rest. Rumor has it that many of the collections Napoleon's Army confiscated will be returned to their rightful owners now that he has abdicated."

"As they should be."

Maria left the Louvre on the arm of the colonel feeling quite in charity with him and the world, thinking perhaps happiness was within her grasp after all.

PHILIP MADE HIS way to the offices in the hôtel with a spring in his step. His ride with the archduchess that morning had ended with a pleasant interlude of passionate kisses—something she had previously withheld—and he was quite in charity with everyone and everything at the moment.

Jack, Captain Owens, was postured irreverently leaning back in his chair with his boots crossed at the ankles atop his desk.

"Oh, come to pretend to write some reports, have you?"

"I thought his duty was to look pretty on the arm of a certain Austrian princess," Johnson teased.

Philip smiled as he went to pour himself a cup of coffee, then slid into one of the armchairs near an open window. "Work is work, gentlemen." He took a sip, then leaned his head back and allowed the sun's rays to hit his face.

"Can someone please tell His Grace to assign me the most beautiful woman on earth for once? I have the Prussian countess, for goodness' sake." Schunk's was arguably the sharpest mind on the staff, but he was lazy and his boyish face and figure did not lend themselves to always being taken seriously, nor did his nickname, Chunk.

All of them groaned uniformly. The countess was an ugly shrew and if it were not for her dress, it would be difficult to tell she was a female.

"She could best me in the ring. Don't want a woman like that," Schunk remarked glibly with an unfeigned shudder.

"You have your German heritage and fluency to thank for that pairing," Johnson pointed out.

"The things we do for king and country," Owens agreed. "If you married, the task would fall to someone else," Owens added with a blissful smile.

"Perhaps I will marry," Philip said, surprising himself that he said it aloud.

"Pardon me, but could you repeat last?" Owens said sitting up straight with a thunk of his boots on the wood floor.

"Your ears do not deceive you. I am considering the matrimonial state."

Even Chunk looked up at that.

"His Grace will not be pleased. You are his secret weapon. As a matter of fact, I am not sure I am pleased. Who will I live vicariously through? You have been the Holy Grail of bachelorhood for the entire army – the entire kingdom. But of course for someone like the archduchess, I suppose a more beautiful male could not be found than Everleigh," Johnson reflected.

Philip watched this exchange with amusement.

"I think she will lead you a merry dance," Owens said.

"You do not think Everleigh man enough to maintain her loyalty?" Johnson asked.

"Of his honor, I have no doubt. Of hers, I pray my impressions are wrong, but I heard rumor she is already betrothed."

If Philip did not understand that Jack said these things from Phillip's genuine concern, he would probably call him out. But still, he remained silent.

"Well, I think you are the luckiest dog alive," Chunk said. "Even if she leads you a merry dance, may it be merry all the way."

Philip raised his mug in acknowledgment.

"It may be time for Wellington to recruit some new blood. I hear Strickland has made known his intentions to retire and take a wife. That would only leave Chunk here with Weston and Patten."

"Heaven help the kingdom!" Owens exclaimed.

"Excuse me, but you said Old Stick is retiring?" Philip asked with nothing short of alarm.

"Oh yes, he was just closeted with Wellington and told us the news on the way out."

"You can imagine Wellington's thoughts on the matter," Owens remarked.

"Yes, Everleigh, do have mercy on the rest of us and wait to make any pronouncements till this one blows over," Johnson agreed.

Philip barely heard what Johnson said. Had Strickland already made Maria an offer? "Did Old Stick give a reason?"

"Something about ready to settle down and take over family responsibilities," Chunk said with a dismissive wave. He was likely two decades Strickland's junior and had no notion of matrimony anytime soon. But even Philip, with his strong affinity for bachelorhood, felt some pull towards life beyond the army.

But not yet. There certainly was no rush to become leg-shackled and be a gentleman farmer. What else was there for him? Politics, he supposed. Then he began to wonder what Pauline would want or expect. Would she be willing to follow the drum? She was used to glamour and glitz. Would she be satisfied with the British beau monde?

He hoped she was not in a rush. He was quite willing to martyr himself for the right cause, but was this it? He heard Lady Maria's name and he snapped back to attention.

"Lloyd's sister?" Chunk asked.

"Yes, you should've seen her. I had not seen her in years and never remembered how pretty she was," Johnson reflected.

Philip could have told them that. Maria often tried to hide her light under a bushel or behind her mother's fashion choices.

"I always liked Lady Maria. Pluck to the backbone, she was. Could ride like the devil himself," Johnson added.

"We could use some more cavalry officers," Owens teased.

"She would make you look bad," Philip remarked, not even completely jesting.

"What is she doing here, though? She can hardly follow her brother. He is…"

Owens coughed loudly, interrupting Johnson. "We are not to speak of it."

"Oh, that's right," Johnson tapped his head as though it needed a hit to make it work properly.

"Lady Maria is here as a friend to my wife," Owens answered. "We thought she would enjoy companionship."

"Not enough for her, are you?" Chunk teased and promptly received a wad of paper tossed at his head, which he ducked.

"I certainly do not mind having her here. There are never enough pretty females about. We need them to offset the likes of the countess." Chunk shuddered dramatically.

There was a round of laughter in the room causing Wellington to poke his head out from behind his door.

They all stood to attention and quieted.

He frowned at their formality. "I was only trying to hear what the fuss was about."

"The Countess von Schleiben's ankles," Chunk answered, which brought on another round of laughter the way he pronounced it with an exaggerated nasal intonation.

Wellington shook his head. "Who is desperate enough to have looked at her ankles? I will have him drawn and quartered." He turned and shut the door behind him without waiting for an answer.

"I bet the archduchess has trim ankles," Chunk said longingly.

All heads swung towards Philip. He lifted a shoulder. "But of course."

CHAPTER SIX

WELLINGTON HAD DECIDED to host one his grand fetes and Maria's new gown had come just in time. It was a colorful and daring neckline –for her—and she felt somewhat conspicuous. It would be nothing to the archduchess, she knew, but when she looked at herself in the cheval mirror, she thought she would do very well.

Colonel Strickland had already reserved two dances, speedily requesting them when he had seen her with Kate that afternoon, on the terrace having tea. Patton and Weston had also reserved sets.

She stopped to look at the ballroom on her way to the drawing room, where Wellington was receiving his guests. She always liked to view the empty room before it was filled with too many people.

The ballroom was as luxurious as one might expect from Napoleon's sister's former home. Chandeliers twinkled, casting a bright glow, shadows of the flames doing their own dance on the parquet floor. One wall was covered in framed mirrors, the other a wall of doors leading outside to the gardens.

The fragrance of fresh roses wafted strongly through the room, while their leaves of green and petals of peach and pinks brought the garden into the ballroom.

Once it was filled with people, such subtleties would be difficult to appreciate.

"I did not expect to find you here," Philip said from behind her, causing her to start.

"I could say likewise," she said, turning around with a smile.

"You look beautiful, pet," he said, studying her up and down appreciatively. She tried not to blush. He had never quite looked at her like that before.

"I find that a great improvement on the scolding you gave me last time."

"I will never hear the end of that, will I? May I blame sur-prise—and humbly beg your forgiveness?"

"You may, but it does not mean I will forget it," Maria teased.

He held out his arm. "Shall we go to the drawing room?"

She took it and tried not to compare the feel of him with the colonel. She was quite determined to be pleased with her new beau, if that is what he was.

"And will your lady interest be present?"

"Of course." They walked a few steps before he paused and gazed down at her. "Is Colonel Strickland being a little hasty in his suit?"

Maria did not mask her surprise. "Not at all. Why do you ask?"

"It is nothing." He frowned, walking on again.

"You should know me better than to think you can succeed with such evasiveness. I will wring it out of you one way or another, you know."

He smiled and she was pleased to see her playful Philip. "Yes, I imagine you will."

Nonetheless, he walked on and did not elaborate. They were still alone in the hall but could hear voices and music as they approached the drawing room.

"Do not force me to cause a scene," she warned.

They stopped a few feet short of the doors and he turned to face her, their arms still linked. It was delicious torture.

"If you must know, he had an audience with Wellington this

morning, asking to be replaced. He indicated he was ready to take a wife and settle down in England." He spoke with an air of superiority, as one did towards one's little sister.

"And therefore you assume he has chosen me and proposed?"

"I could not be certain, of course. It seemed out of character for him and he has shown great interest in you—as have several other officers."

"What?"

"Precisely. And on such a short acquaintance."

"Is the pot calling the kettle black? Could not one argue your acquaintance with the archduchess is shorter than that of mine with the Strickland family?"

"No… and yes, indeed. However, I have not proposed," he argued.

"And neither has he."

He patted her on the arm in a rather brotherly and condescending fashion. "You know I only wish for your happiness, Maria. I do not want you to rush into anything for which you are not ready."

"And may I wish the same for you?" She did not mask the exasperation in her voice.

He looked at her strangely, but before she could interpret its meaning, they were interrupted.

"There you are!"

Maria closed her eyes and wished the archduchess to the devil.

Philip released Maria and holding out his hand to the beauty, bowed deeply, kissing her extended hand. "We were just about to enter."

He turned to give Maria his other arm. At least he had not forgotten her completely, she thought, her irritation hardly appeased. She shook her head, not trusting herself to speak, and followed them into the drawing room. Quickly spotting Kate and Captain Owens, she walked as properly as she could to their side.

These were the times she was grateful for the training to be a lady she had endured in the schoolroom, because she was quite unsure how she managed to smile at that moment. She wanted nothing but Philip's happiness, and she was quite certain the archduchess was as heartless as she was pretty. It was women's intuition, she mused, that allowed them to see another's true character when men were blinded by beauty. Hopefully, this was just a passing fancy, but she had never seen Philip so besotted before. While ladies had always thrown themselves at him, such behavior had only amused him. Now there was a different look in his eye.

"I trust you are feeling more the thing?" Maria asked Kate.

She waved her hand in the air as though it was an insignificant trifle. "You look lovely, Maria," she responded instead.

"She says this with so much calm when she was about to come searching for you," Captain Owens teased.

"I was talking with Philip in the hall," Maria explained.

"Move along, husband. Maria is here now, and come to entertain me." Kate gave him a gentle nudge.

"But I want to hear the gossip too..." He made a pout. "...especially so since it is about Everleigh."

"I am afraid I do not have any delicious tidbits to impart," Maria said apologetically.

"Did you not go to the museum with Colonel Strickland?" Captain Owens asked, clearly not believing her.

"I did. Kate was not feeling well and he happened to be available to accompany me."

Captain Owens looked at her thoughtfully. "That is quite a skill you have, you know, to make that sound as though you were simply breakfasting with your mother."

"Would you please leave? Maria will not confess the whole if you are here," Kate scolded, yet with a twinkle of affection in her eye.

He put a hand to his heart. "I thought we had grown close, Lady Maria."

She could not but laugh. "Truly, there was nothing to the

outing, I assure you. It was a lovely afternoon. We drove to the Louvre Palace but had occasion only to tour the grand gallery because I spent so long viewing each picture. Colonel Strickland was very tolerant. Then he took me to a café for some lovely crepes with a delicious mixture of cream and chocolate spread upon them." She closed her eyes in remembrance of the best thing she had ever tasted in her life. When she opened her eyes again, Kate and her husband were staring at her.

"Oh, good heavens." Kate turned to her husband. "It must all be true."

"What is true?" Maria groaned.

"Jack and the other staff officers are convinced Strickland means to offer for you. Would it be welcome?"

"I am not opposed to getting to know him better. I do not think he will make an offer so soon, though." She knew it was an evasive answer, but needed more time to consider. While it seemed wrong to accept another when her feelings for Philip were still so strong, she had to find a way, she told herself, even though time was not completely on her side.

A waiter then came forward with a tray of drinks, and each of them took a glass from the silver salver. Gracious, Maria thought, but at that moment she very much wished she could behave like a gentleman and pour the contents of the glass—several glasses, in fact—down her throat and cease the ability to think. She wished time might slow down, but she had prayed for God to find her husband quickly and a man she could be happy with. Who could better answer the purpose than the colonel? He was handsome, came from an excellent family, and she liked him. Theirs would never be a match of strong passions, and from all accounts, strong passions led to heartache later. Her marriage would be comfortable and respectful. She could imagine reading by the fire with Colonel Strickland when they were older.

"I think he is an excellent choice for a husband, for what it's worth," Captain Owens remarked, looking over to where the tall subject of conversation was standing.

"Thank you. I also think him a very good choice. But he has not spoken to me and time will tell."

Kate took her hand and gave it a squeeze. She knew most of the struggles Maria had, yet understood her need to find someone else to marry.

Just then, a strikingly handsome man entered the room with the Austrian minister. He wore a full beard, his hair was dark and curling, and his eyes piercing—searching for someone, it seemed. Maria had not seen him before. "Who is that?" she whispered.

"He is new to me," Captain Owens confirmed, "but with the amount of shiny gewgaws on his chest, he must be either a duke or a prince."

Maria could not suppress a smile at Captain Owens' phrasing. He had kept her laughing constantly on their trip to Paris.

Maria followed the man's gaze to the archduchess, who looked up and saw him. Her face grew pale and immediately her eyes shifted away, as if defiantly.

"How interesting," Kate said. as if noticing the same thing. "It appears our archduchess is not pleased with the new arrival, whomever he may be."

"Or perhaps the fact of being caught on our Lord Philip Everleigh's arm is something which would displease him," Captain Owens observed pointedly.

⇻⇻⇻✳⇺⇺⇺

"Do you know him?" Philip asked.

"We are acquainted," Pauline answered vaguely.

"You do not appear pleased with his presence," he added as he noticed her ill-concealed glare.

She looked sharply up at him and smiled brilliantly. "I am unaffected either way. Are we to dance? Because I would like to dance."

And avoid talking, he thought but did not say. "As long as I need not be concerned I will find a dagger in my back."

She smiled radiantly up at him, trying to distract him, he knew, but he played the game nonetheless.

He had trained for too long not to read people's emotions and hidden meanings. It was a blessing but also a curse. At the moment it definitely felt like a curse.

He took Pauline into his arms for a waltz and she was far more rigid and formal than she had been previously... except when he looked into her eyes, they were full of fire. This gentleman meant something to her, Philip was sure of it. Was he a brother come to discipline her, or was he a former love who had scorned and scorched her heart?

Philip could do nothing for now, but observe.

They did not speak for two full circles of the floor.

From the corner of his eye he watched as Maria received a great deal of attention. She was dancing with Colonel Strickland, which should please Philip more than it did, but he was resigning himself to the match. Their friendship would have to change once she married, of course, but it would be preferable to Philip if she chose someone with whom he was better friends. There was nothing at all wrong with Strickland, but his nickname, "Old Stick," was for a very appropriate reason.

They could still dance from time to time in cordial acquaintance, of course. She would bear many children and devote her life to them. Philip had always known she would be a good mother.

Normally, Pauline would have remarked upon his wayward thoughts by now, but she was obviously distracted herself. When the dance ended, she took Philips's arm possessively, even before he had had a chance to offer it.

"I need a drink," she said.

Pausing, Philip signalled to a waiter and took two glasses of champagne before cupping Pauline's elbow with the other hand and guiding her outside. Directing her to one of the seats thoughtfully provided by their host, he handed her one of the glasses.

She emptied the contents in one, long drink.

He raised his brows at her, waiting for an explanation.

Philip knew how to play the silent game as well as any expert in diplomacy. He deliberately calmed himself by breathing deeply and taking in his surroundings – the lush green gardens on a warm summer night, and the sounds of carriages in the distance mixed with the humming of crickets in the grass nearby. Thrusting his hands in his pockets, he looked up at the stars, searching for constellations while waiting for her to compose herself enough to talk—or grow nervous enough to fill the silence.

She was better at the game than he would have suspected, an accomplishment he didn't know whether to be suspicious of or to admire.

All the while, he was mentally searching the list of Austrian court enquiry agents for who the man could be. Somehow, Philip knew he was no mere courtling.

"Are you jealous?"

"Should I be?"

She laughed. She was a bit fuddled. That was his first indication she was nervous. Philip had not seen her drink too much before and it was one of the strict rules of diplomacy, never to become inebriated.

"He is here at the behest of my father, of course—and no doubt to chide me and order my good behavior."

"Are you afraid?"

She did not look up at him. "Only of a miserable marriage. There is naught that Friedrich can do to me here and now."

"Is he your betrothed?" Philip asked pointedly, not caring if he sounded rude.

"He is my cousin and my father's most trusted pawn."

"Would it be wise for us to stay apart whilst he is here?"

She looked up sharply. "Absolutely not! I will not be ordered around by him. My father may come here himself if he thinks I am so outrageous."

Light steps alerted Philip to another's presence.

"Pauline?" A deep voice spoke firmly in the dark. "I believe the next dance is mine."

Philip stood still in the shadows, assessing his competition, as it were, even though he was far from certain that was the case.

"Go away, Friedrich."

"You cannot avoid me forever and it is hardly proper for you to be out here alone so long." He spoke in rapid German, but Philip understood the words quite well.

"I am not alone."

"Come."

For a moment, Philip thought there would be a confrontation – for the man had to know who she had gone outside with and yet he had not acknowledged his presence whatsoever. Philip debated intervening, but decided to remain still and await a signal from her.

He expected her to argue or be more defiant, but instead she rose and took the stranger's hand.

After they had left, Philip waited a few more minutes in the shadows. He breathed deeply of the beautiful evening, waiting for his emotions to compart, but they would not cooperate.

It took a great deal of strength to quell his anger at himself for feeling such a base emotion as jealousy. Perhaps it was just protectiveness?

When he felt he would no longer plant the man a facer, he walked slowly back up the terrace steps, remaining in the shadows. He found a place by the doors to watch, where he might be unobserved from inside, to see if he could determine exactly what this Friedrich was to her.

First, however, he spotted Maria waltzing with Chunk and smiled. Philip tried to look at her from a stranger's perspective and realized she was quite lovely. As one of his dearest friends, he knew the sensation he felt towards her was protectiveness.

Pauline passed in front of Maria, in the arms of this Friedrich. They were a striking couple, and Philip knew it was no mere protectiveness he felt for her. This man was somehow a threat and Philip wanted to eradicate him.

He watched for any sign of affection or otherwise from the couple, but they hardly said a word. They stared into each other's eyes as though ice locked them in place, while a fire burned within Philip's chest like a volcano about to explode.

In his mind he knew he needed to distance himself, but he doubted his ability to do so.

When the dance ended, Philip moved toward where Maria and Colonel Strickland had stopped. The colonel had left her alone, perhaps to fetch some refreshments, and Philip took the opportunity to speak with her again.

"What do you think of our newcomer?" she asked without preamble.

"I wish I knew what to think. He has certainly raised Pauline's hackles."

"She did not explain why?" Maria asked.

"No. She assures me he means nothing to her, but she is definitely affected. I have not witnessed her composure to slip before."

"I do not know her well, but I noticed the same thing."

Philip inclined his head a little. Maria was very perceptive and he trusted her judgment. "She said something about him being her father's pawn, but I sense it is more than that."

"They are coming this way."

"Lady Maria, my cousin would like an introduction. Archduke Friedrich Klement, may I present Lady Maria Lloyd and my dear friend, Captain Lord Philip Everleigh?"

"Delighted." He bowed, acknowledging both of them.

"Lady Maria, would you be so kind as to partner me for the next dance?" he asked in a charming accent.

Philip could not help but glance at Maria with surprise. Giving no sign of a similar shock, she of course accepted gracefully, and he watched the man take away another of his women within the space of two dances.

CHAPTER SEVEN

MARIA HAD DANCED with English royalty, yet she was not prepared for this.

The archduke was a large, imposing man and gave the impression of a wild beast barely enclosed by this trim package of formal attire. She had sensed the virility amongst the soldiers since arriving in Paris and living beneath the same roof as many of the officers, but it was very strong with this Austrian.

If she could not be comfortable with Colonel Strickland, then she was several more degrees less so with this gentleman. There was a sense about him that he only acted with purpose, so why, from amongst all the other ladies, would he have chosen her to dance with after the archduchess? Clearly there was some relationship between those two which was thick with tension.

She took his hand and followed him to the floor, grateful the dance was not a waltz. If one were not destined to enjoy a dance, then at least it would not be sacrificed to one's favorite.

"Are you newly arrived in Paris, sir?"

"I am. And yourself?"

"Yes. We have been here only about a week."

"I, myself, do not know how long I will stay. It all depends."

Dare she ask on what, she wondered, although she was quite certain she knew.

"Do you travel often in your position?"

"Sometimes. I have been in your country frequently. I went to school there for a couple of years as a boy."

"Perhaps that is where I went wrong with my languages. Your English is excellent."

"Do you speak German?" he asked.

"Very little, I am afraid. No matter how hard my governess tried, I never had an ear for it."

He smiled a little but it did not reach his eyes. Maria liked to think she generally had a good sense of a person's character, but she could not read this man. She did have to give him credit, however: his attention was completely on her when they spoke, even though she had a feeling he was not in the least bit interested in her, but rather the archduchess.

They were separated by the dance and coming to the middle of the floor, she joined Lieutenant Patten for the next figure.

He smiled at her and flirted shamelessly. The same type of characters were to be met with here as in London, but on a different scale. The British community in Paris was smaller and tighter knit than would be found in London. Here, people who might not otherwise have been friends were drawn together by circumstances.

She returned to the archduke and he was surprisingly lithe and light on his feet for so large a gentleman. Philip, too, was quite graceful in his movements, yet more like a cat – part beauty, part predator.

Both are dangerous in every sense of the word, her inner voice warned.

"You are most fortunate, Lady Maria," he remarked.

"Oh?" She raised her brows as she extended her hand to him for their *en passant*.

"You have many people here with an eye for your well-being."

"Indeed, sir, and how come you to know this on such a short acquaintance?"

"I have but to look around me. See that colonel over there?"

He indicated Colonel Strickland. "He looks at you with approval."

She stared up at the archduke in fascination at his boldness.

"And that young Lieutenant who was flirting with you? He is curious about you."

"Really? And what about that one?" She looked towards Chunk.

"He is interested but he thinks you are above his touch."

Maria laughed. She dared not ask what he thought about Philip. She did not know if his assessments were accurate or not. More than likely, he was merely making conversation.

"But your Lord Philip, he watches you with a protective, almost possessive, eye."

Maria almost missed a step. "We are very old friends, practically from the cradle, you should know."

"Ah, I see."

What was he about? Could he be trying to pry information from her about Philip? Perhaps turnabout was fair play.

"Are you the same with the archduchess?"

"Pauline? Yes, I daresay you could say that. We have known each other from the cradle. She is a cousin of mine."

That was not perhaps as informative as Maria would have liked it to be. People married their cousins. "I think you flatter me, sir. If anything, they have interest in you."

"Me? No." He chuckled halfheartedly. "I am but another face to them."

"Or competition," she said with a smile before the intricacies of the dance paired her with Major Johnson.

"You are looking very pretty tonight, Lady Maria," he said.

"Thank you, sir," she answered, still unused to hearing herself called pretty.

"I am happy to hear the news about you and the colonel. Devilish fine fellow."

Maria tried to maintain a smile without answering. Why did everyone assume it was already a match?

She needed to accustom herself to the idea, because if he offered, she could hardly say no. She glanced over to where the object of her thoughts stood speaking with the Duke of Wellington. Colonel Strickland deserved better than that from her. He looked up and smiled at her. Inclining her head in polite response, she took the archduke's hand again for the last figure of the dance.

"Do you have any siblings, Lady Maria?"

"I do, sir. In fact, my brother is a soldier."

"I was wondering what brought you to Paris. Most of the beautiful ladies are already married."

Maria could feel her cheeks warm. Perhaps he did not realize what he was insinuating.

"Your brother, he is here?"

"Not tonight. His work often takes him away."

"A spy, then," he remarked. "Someone must do the dirty work."

"I do not know what his position entails, sir," She did not like the insinuations he was making, as if they were fact.

He smiled down at her as the dance ended and he looked sinfully handsome—enough that she thought he might indeed be competition for Philip with the archduchess. He also looked as dangerous as the devil himself.

PHILIP FORCED HIMSELF to dance attendance on other ladies besides Pauline, and the other gentlemen were more than happy to take his place. He ignored the looks of reprimand she cast him from time to time, but he needed to observe and assess, and he could not think clearly when close to her. It was as if she cast a spell on him whenever he was near.

He was surprised by the attention the archduke had paid Maria. At first, he had thought the man was simply being courteous by dancing with whichever lady was presented to him, but he had not danced again since the first with Pauline and the second with Maria, and that was singular.

When the last of the guests were finally leaving, Philip went to the smoking room, where most of the officers went to relax after an evening of "doing the pretty." There were sure to be one or two of his friends present, though Jack could no longer be relied upon, being newly married.

"Well, this is a surprise," he said involuntarily as he entered the masculine domain. Jack was sitting on one of the burgundy-coloured leather armchairs, swirling a glass of what appeared to be cognac.

"Trouble in heaven?" Jack asked.

"I could ask the same of you," Philip said as he poured himself a glass of the amber liquid and sat opposite Jack. He eased off his dancing slippers and with a loud sigh of relief propped up his feet on the table next to his friend's.

"Kate was tired and has already fallen asleep," Jack explained, "and I thought you might want to talk."

Philip raised his glass in appreciation. Something inside him warmed to know his friend had not completely set him aside. Not that he would blame him; Kate was a most excellent woman.

"Shall we have our conversation silently or shall we actually speak?" Jack asked.

"I am afraid I will only talk in circles, but I will not solve this quietly, I know that," Philip replied.

"Mm." Jack made a sound of understanding. "What do you make of him?"

Philip appreciated that his best friend did not have to be told what was on his mind. "So far, all I can say is that his taste in women is excellent."

"Hear, hear," Jack agreed. "Did she not explain who he was?"

Philip shook his head. "Only that he was a cousin, doing her father's bidding."

Jack half-grunted, half-scoffed.

"Precisely."

"I do not believe that is the whole story. I have a sixth sense about him."

"Do you sense something nefarious about him?"

"I do not know what I sense." Jack shrugged. "But I feel something."

"Very helpful."

"You are welcome," Jack responded, a half-grin twisting his mouth.

"It is good to have validation, I suppose. Yet I will admit I am finding it hard to determine whether he is a rival for Pauline's affections or a rival in the professional sense."

"Allies are supposed to be trusted," Jack objected in a mock stern voice.

"Keep your enemies close but your friends closer? In the generic sense of the word, of course, although we are speaking only in terms of countries and not actual people."

"I think it is the other way around, but I understand." Jack lifted his glass to Philip's and they both took a drink.

They sat for a moment in silent camaraderie before Philip spoke again. "But why Maria?"

"Ah," Jack said with understanding. "Why Maria or why Maria and no one else after her?"

"The latter, of course. Maria is one of the best, most kind and caring people I know. That much is obvious."

"Mm." Jack murmured his agreement.

"I do not want her to be hurt or used as a pawn." Philip took another sip of his drink.

"Do you think Strickland would let that happen?"

Philip nearly choked. He opened his mouth to object, then closed it and frowned instead.

"What?" Jack asked.

"I suddenly realized you are correct, and I do not know how I feel about it."

Jack slapped him on the back. "It was bound to happen sooner or later, old fellow."

"Being mortal must be insufferable," Philip quipped in return, casting a sly grin at his old friend. Jack simply shook his head, offering an ironic look at the ceiling for good measure, and tossed back the rest of his drink.

Meanwhile, Philip stared at the remainder of the liquid in his glass, still not quite ready to set aside ideas of Maria with Strickland. "Do you think Old Stick is a good match for Maria?" he questioned slowly.

"I can think of no one else here who would be better."

"I must object," Philip said.

Jack looked at him with condescension. "If you do not wish to marry her yourself, then you must allow that someone else should be allowed to."

"What I object to is that she evidently feels under pressure to marry now, and to make a selection from the limited stores of available candidates here."

"Very well, I will allow that objection, but you must admit there is nothing wrong with Old Stick other than he is older than she, and a bit dry. If Lady Maria does not object, then why should you or I?"

Philip sighed heavily. "I suppose you are right. Besides, I can think of no one else I would choose for her in London."

"On paper, he is a most excellent match. One could argue better than you or I, since he will actually inherit a title."

Philip scowled at his friend, knowing it was a fruitless gesture.

"Now, might we discuss the elephant in the room?"

"I must be blind, what is this elephant?"

Jack closed his eyes in annoyance. "Your mention of marriage to the aforementioned Archduchess before the subject was changed to Lady Maria?"

"Ah, yes… and the potentially nefarious Archduke."

"Does he change your opinion on the matter?"

"An excellent question, of which I am not yet sure of the answer. I do believe I need to find out his connection to Pauline, other than the fact of their being cousins, of course."

"He will, naturally, try to sway her, whether he is doing her father's bidding or his own."

"Assuredly," Philip agreed. Standing up, he took Jack's glass over to the cabinet to refill it along with his own. "How do you think she will react, is my first question?" he asked thoughtfully as he handed Jack his glass again and resumed his seat.

"What do you expect?"

"She brought up the question of a marriage herself, and one could also say she proposed to me."

"That is more than a little unexpected," Jack remarked, "although women have always thrown themselves at you."

"No one of her caliber, however," Philip added.

"Just so. But the fact that you are considering it, and are so clearly smitten, is what has my nerves all aflutter."

Philip could feel himself smile. "I wish neither to involve myself in a family feud nor a lover's quarrel. I would hardly ingratiate myself with the Austrian court or her father, either, if she actually went through with it."

"Do you think you are a pawn?"

"Well, it has been barely more than a fortnight since I first met Pauline and someone is already here to bring her back into line."

"It could be a coincidence," Jack argued.

"It could, but you do not believe that any more than I."

"No, I do not," he agreed with aplomb. "So what shall you do?"

"I think I shall continue to court her and see what happens."

"It will be such a hardship," Jack muttered dryly.

"The hardship will be in trying to remain detached and observe objectively," Philip admitted.

"How the mighty have fallen!" Jack laughed.

"I daresay. Had not this archduke arrived tonight, I would perhaps have already agreed to her scheme of marriage—if it is a scheme. How I hate that I must question her motives!"

"That is the way of things in our line of work," Jack reasoned. "I did it myself with Kate. It is hard to suppress years of training and habit."

"In the end, what won?"

"Instinct. I listen to that sixth sense that also tells me the archduke has illicit intent."

Philip exhaled a frustrated sigh. "I cannot deny that I feel it as well, but I can hardly cut the connection, against my every wish, at this point—for diplomacy, if nothing else."

"Then perhaps she is the one for you, but I feel you will regret making that decision in haste."

Philip leaned his head back over the chair. "Whoever would have thought Jack would provide me an ounce of sanity in advice to do with matters of the heart?"

"I have always told you I am a fount of wisdom," Jack retorted.

"And I have always said you should not have to tell someone how great you are."

"Ah, but that is one benefit of having a wife. She can do it for me."

Philip rose to his feet. "I can take no more. I am for my bed."

CHAPTER EIGHT

THE NEXT MORNING, Maria completed her toilette and then went downstairs to the garden to see if Kate was there since she'd not been in her rooms.

She found Kate sitting at a small iron table with a cup of tea and a croissant looking the very picture of a happy bride.

"Good morning," Maria greeted. Kate was looking out over the garden.

"Maria, I didn't see you there. Join me. I hope you do not mind I came down without you. Jack just left to see to his duties and I did not wish to disturb your sleep."

"Not at all. You retired early. Are you feeling well?"

"Yes, of course. I have just been more tired of late. I am sure it is just some adjustment to a new place."

Maria filled her plate with a roll and asked for a cup of chocolate before joining Kate at the table. It was a beautiful summer morning surrounded by the fresh scent of roses and birds chirping happy little songs of busyness.

"I want all the details," Kate said as soon as Maria had filled her mouth with a bite of pastry.

"About what?" Maria asked as soon as she could politely do so.

"The new duke or archduke or royal highness or whoever he is." Kate waved her hand in the air. "Jack said he only danced with the archduchess and yourself and so I want to know what he was like. You know that would set the *ton* abuzz back home."

"I cannot disagree. However, I do not think I was sought out for any particular reason. Who can know what society is like in Austria? Perhaps by dancing with one other person he thought his duty was done. If he even gave it that much thought."

"Was he pleasant? Or charming? He is very striking."

"Pleasant is not the descriptor I would choose," Maria said thoughtfully. "I certainly was not at ease with him. He is handsome and polite, but I do wonder if he chose me because he saw me talking with Philip."

"A little tit for tat? Do you think he is trying to make her jealous?" Kate asked.

"I hardly think I am one to inspire grand passions or jealousy, but perhaps he thought to extract some information from me." Maria pursed her lips. "Is that what he had been doing? He was more inquisitive than most new acquaintances are upon a first dance, but at the time I attributed it to his foreignness. Sometimes directness can be refreshing."

"Interesting notion," Kate said as she refilled her tea and added some milk. "Do you have the feeling that there is more going on than meets the eye?"

"It has crossed my mind," Maria confessed. "Although I dismissed myself as fanciful since we are living amongst diplomats and spies."

"Hush," Kate said, leaning in and whispering. "They aren't supposed to know that we know."

Maria laughed. "You are married to one and I am sister to one."

"I do think it would be prudent to pay attention. You never know what we might discover."

"They are one of our allies. It does not make sense," Maria said.

"Even England has traitors, Maria." Kate realized what she said and then blushed. She reached across the table and took

Kate's hand. "Forgive me. I do not think of you or your brother as traitors."

"I know. Thank you for that, but most people are suspicious. My father did not act honorably, in fact. I am still furious with him myself."

"But you are not he."

"What shall we do today?" Maria asked, deliberately changing the subject.

"There is a garden party at one of the embassies. The Dutch one, I think. Jack wanted us to attend."

"Did he say why?" Maria asked.

"Not particularly. I think it makes Wellington happy for the wives to socialize."

"Curious," Maria said. "But I suppose there is no harm in being friendly to the wives of our friendly nations."

"She will probably be there," Kate mentioned off-handedly.

"Probably," Maria agreed. "Although she seems to do what she wishes."

"Has Captain Everleigh said so?"

Maria tilted her head. "I am not certain if he said it, or it is my impression. She seems a bit wild and fast to me."

"Well, yes," Kate agreed. "Certainly her dress and mannerisms would label her such in England."

"But if Philip is determined to marry her, then there must be something good about her. I am determined to find it," Maria stated with a resolution she wished she felt more strongly.

"You are too good, Maria. I am perfectly willing to allow you to despise her and will think nonetheless of you."

"You are the best of friends, Kate. Shall we go?"

"Yes. Thankfully these gowns will suit. I always did favor you in peach."

"It is one of the few pastels that does not make me look like a ghost."

Kate laughed, looking up to the mode herself in a white dress with dark blue stripes.

Bisset joined them with their bonnets and parasols, and they were soon deposited on the steps at the home of the Belgian minister to France.

Maria had been attending these sorts of parties since before her come out. Her mother would allow her to attend ladies only functions if they were at their home. However, she was most definitely a foreigner and of no particular consequence in the hierarchy of European politics or diplomacy here, and she was not particularly looking forward to small talk with strangers.

They were shown to the back garden which was much more manicured and elaborate than that of Wellington's despite it having been home to Napoleon's sister.

There were stone pathways, fountains and trellises covered in bright blooms of pink roses and purple wisteria with cloth covered tables under tents erected for shade.

Ladies in the latest Parisian fashions stood about talking in groups, but Maria immediately honed in on the archduchess. There was something about her that drew one's gaze to her and others around her seemed to fade into the background.

She was certainly beautiful, but Maria suspected it was something more. Her boldness and her confidence perhaps. The characteristics that were discouraged and condemned in English society. Yet, if men were so attracted to it, why was it so wrong?

"I see you spotted the forbidden fruit," Kate said in a soft yet derogatory term.

"What makes you say that?" Maria asked. "I was thinking the same thing, but why?"

"I suppose because she tempts men to sin and tempts women to murder."

Maria could not but laugh. "You are not helping my resolution to befriend her."

"You are right. I am sorry. I shall do better."

"Let us go and greet her first. She is the only one whose name I remember anyway."

They first greeted their host who was very kind and introduced them to some other ladies.

When they were free, they took offered glasses of champagne from a waiter and then proceeded towards Philip's inamorata.

When she saw them she stopped speaking and turned to greet them.

"Good afternoon, Lady Maria and Mrs. Owens." She curtsied. "An unexpected surprise. Has Philip sent you to spy on me?"

"Of course not," Maria objected quickly. "Whyever would you think that?"

The archduchess scoffed. "I would not think you would approve. It is clear you want him for yourself."

Kate gasped at the woman's boldness and clamped her hand on Maria's elbow.

"Do you deny you are in love with him? I do not think I misread the situation," the woman proceeded to turn the knife in further.

"You do not mince words, do you?" Maria snapped.

"What is the point of doing so? Besides there is no one else to hear." She held her hand out and made a half-circle.

"Loving someone means wanting what is best for them. I came in an attempt to befriend you, but I do not think a friendship between us is likely."

She laughed a little, unseemingly affected by the words. "I suppose I am so unused to such a gesture from other women that I did not recognize friendship when it bit me in the face."

"I feel sorry for you if that is the case. Good day, Your Grace."

"Bravo," Kate whispered.

Maria bobbed a curtsy and then pulled Kate away with her. She did not bother to stop and take her leave of the hostess because she did not think herself capable of forming any more civil words.

As Philip dressed the next morning to meet Pauline for a ride, he hurried through his ablutions with anticipation. Being in new—attraction—was like a drug that you wanted more of. He knew with his mind what it was doing to him, but the feeling it gave him made him want it nonetheless. He paused as he tied his neck cloth and looked at himself critically. Nothing about him had changed outwardly, and for once he wanted to be reckless. Knowing someone else might want her and she wanted him made it more thrilling. It was juvenile, to be sure.

"I will be careful," he reassured his reflection and tied the final simple knot before taking his gloves, hat, and crop and leaving his apartment. After mounting his horse and trotting alongside the river to their appointed meeting place, he whistled a tune and doffed his hat to everyone he passed. He felt glorious and did not care if the world knew about it. In fact, he hoped his good cheer was contagious.

When he spotted Pauline standing by the bridge holding the reins to her mount, he almost called out to her, but she looked so beautiful, so serene, that he enjoyed the image it portrayed. He decided to take a different path and approach her from behind thinking to surprise her.

He veered right around a copse of trees and bushes and turned back towards where she waited. A large smile broke out on his face and it was all he could do to keep from urging his mount to a faster pace.

The diversion cost him. He pulled up to dismount himself and stopped short. Pauline was no longer alone but stood staring up at the Archduke.

They greeted each other with the more familiar kisses of Europeans but Philip could detect nothing particularly romantic in the gesture. Pauline began to speak with animation, and Philip strained to hear without revealing himself.

If the gestures Pauline were making were anything to go by, then she held strong opinions while the archduke was exasperated. Likely they were speaking of her father just as she claimed he was here for.

Surely Pauline had to know Philip would be arriving any moment. Was this some sort of performance for his benefit?

It was not a good feeling to be so cynical, but did he care? He did not like to be forced, and had not this man arrived, would he have felt differently?

He studied their interactions closely, but he could not accuse them of anything beyond close acquaintance. Certainly, they were not behaving as lovers. Unfortunately, he could hear few details without moving closer and losing his cover.

Straining to lean a bit more, he closed his eyes to home in on the words.

"I did not have the chance," it sounded like Pauline was saying. Chance to what?

"You must not fail," the archduke replied.

"I do not fail," she answered, then turned away.

Philip wanted to hear more, but he could not lest he step forward and reveal himself, which would be suspicious. Perhaps he should remount and approach from the expected way.

He hesitated a moment longer and then decided to stop overthinking it. He remounted his horse and walked around to rejoin the path that would lead him back to Pauline.

This time she saw him coming and raised a gloved hand in greeting, with no obvious shame for being found with her cousin. That was promising at least. He smiled and tipped his hat and rode up to them and slid off the side of his horse. He bowed to them both.

"Good morning." He greeted them.

The archduke returned his greeting with an inclination of his head.

"Will you be joining us on our ride? He would prefer Pauline all to himself, but there was benefit to observing the pair together.

"No thank you. I was unaware of her assignation. I would prefer not to be de trop as I believe the phrase goes."

"Come let us be away before he changes his mind," she said with a slight tug on Philips's arm.

"I will expect to speak with you later," the archduke said to Pauline which caused a mischievous look in response.

The archduke turned on his heel and left without another word.

"Is everything all right?" Philip asked.

She waved her hand dismissively. "Spying on me, of course. He wanted to know everything about you."

"There is little to tell," Philip replied.

She stopped and looked at him as though searching, memorizing, determining the accuracy of his remark. "I do not believe you," she said looking up to meet his gaze.

"Shall we ride?" he asked, instead of allowing her to pry further. He did not know why he was reluctant to share himself with her when he was considering marriage. Instead of exploring that thought further, he helped her to mount, enjoying having a moment to touch her and inhaling her scent of jasmine and something else a bit more exotic he could not put a finger on.

They rode a while at a canter enjoying the fresh morning air save the occasional stench of dead fish from the river which assailed his senses. It was easy to forget why he was there when he was with her.

Pauline pulled up at the next bridge and smiled at him, looking more beautiful than ever with rosy cheeks from the exertion of the ride.

He stopped beside her. "Would you tell me if he was harassing you, Pauline? Is he the one you are afraid of? Though he is hardly an old fusty man, is he?"

She laughed. "You do not think so? He has you fooled, then. He is my father's puppet. Sometimes I wonder if he has his own original thoughts at all."

"You are still in earnest though I caught you? I do not approve of anything hasty especially if it brings about division in your family."

She narrowed her gaze disapprovingly. "My father would welcome you for appearances if nothing else. It is hardly a disastrous match to be united with one of the best families in England."

"It depends on how you look upon it," Philip argued. "When you could easily secure an alliance with any of the royal houses in Europe."

"What serious talk. I do not wish to be serious. I want to have fun. Race you back to the bridge," she called as she urged her horse forward before he could object.

He kept pace with her, but did not try to overtake her. It would have been too easy and his mind was still warring with his heart and for the first time in his amorous career, he felt uncertain.

"What is it?" she asked when they stopped again, disappointment evident that he had not really raced her.

"Forgive me, I am distracted by work."

"The romantic words every lady longs to hear," she said, not masking her sarcasm. "Should I offer you kisses to remind you of the business at hand?"

He smiled. He was only so much of a fool.

They both slid down from their horses, he just in time to catch her in his arms. She placed hers about his neck and brought his head down to hers and did a very successful job of distracting him with her passion. He allowed himself the luxury and shut out thoughts of doubt. She might be a very successful actress, but he knew women and desire could not be completely feigned. She was enjoying it at least a little.

At some point he became conscious again of the fact that while hidden a little behind the bridge and their horses, they were still in public. He pulled away.

"Do you see what we have together?" she asked, breathless.

"Of course I do, but you know in our positions there is much more to be considered."

She laughed. "As if I could forget, but neither do I mean to settle for a cruel, loveless marriage. Will you at least be willing to become betrothed?"

"Did the archduke threaten you, Pauline? Why the haste?"

She hesitated as if unwilling to answer.

"I would never let him harm you. You know I would help you, surely?"

"Unless you are my husband, you would have no right."

"True enough. But neither is he your husband."

"No, but he acts on my father's authority."

Philip looked out over the water, jaw clenched, scarcely noting boats row by. He wanted nothing more than to be with this woman, but even to him it felt rushed. However, chivalry was as deeply ingrained as a gentleman's code of honor. "You speak of romance, Pauline, but I hardly call this betrothal such."

She looked away herself. "I will not force you if it is against your wishes. I certainly never thought I would have to beg for a proposal."

"It is not that, but the precipitous nature of it. However, it will ease the pressure from your father, by all means we shall become betrothed."

CHAPTER NINE

MARIA WAS HAPPY. She had enjoyed a lovely morning riding with Colonel Strickland, and an afternoon shopping with Kate. Simply being outdoors in Paris was a girlhood dream come true at last, and as long as she did not think too much about Philip, she could at least be content with her situation. She parted ways with Kate, who wished to rest before the evening, but not being tired herself, Maria headed towards the gardens. She was grateful to have a space in which to roam freely, since Kate was still occupied with her new husband for a great deal of the time. Maria also suspected, as Bisset did, that Kate was increasing but had not realized it yet. On the thought she smiled ruefully at a sprawling juniper. What did Maria know about increasing? The notion gave her pause. More than anything else she wanted to be a mother and at once felt reassured that she was making the right decision. With a little sigh, she took a few more steps and then stopped to smell a clematis vine which was growing up the side of a trellis.

She was so lost in her thoughts she did not hear Philip approach.

"Well, Maria," he said. "Will you wish me happy?"

"I beg your pardon?" Maria asked, turning around quickly. Her heart realized what he was saying.

"I am betrothed. I have asked Pauline for her hand and she

has accepted."

Maria did not know what to say.

"Are you not pleased?"

"Philip, all I have ever wanted for you was your happiness. If this is your wish, then of course I am pleased."

"Thank you. I could not bear it if you could not be friends with her."

"I am unlikely to move in your circles, Philip, but of course I will be pleased to become better acquainted with her."

So much for trying to convince herself she was content, her inner voice intoned bitterly. She wanted to run away and cry into her pillow.

"Do you not also expect to find yourself betrothed soon?"

"Perhaps," she answered distantly. "I suspect he is waiting to speak first with my brother."

He frowned, but she was not sure why. "Of course, that must be the case. I did not speak with Pauline's father, but she assures me it is not necessary. I cannot be certain why. It goes against every instinct and my upbringing as a gentleman."

"Perhaps they do things differently in Austria?" Maria suggested, trying to help.

"Well, if rumors are correct, we might be removing to Vienna for the Congress. I should have time to become acquainted with her family if that is the case."

"I had not heard of such a move to Vienna."

"Nothing definitive has been said. Wellington mentioned in passing that he had been recommended to go."

Maria did not know how she felt about the news. "Will all his staff be required to go?"

"I could not say. I imagine some will stay here for the nonce." He looked over at her from where he was standing before a pretty red clematis. "Why are you so sad, pet?"

"It will be difficult to remain friends, will it not? I do not fancy you will be living at the neighboring estate in England and becoming a country squire."

He smiled a little. "Very likely not. I imagine I will continue in diplomatic circles and remain on the Continent most of the time."

"I did not think so," she said, unable to hide her feelings. "Most ladies do not care for their husbands being friends with another lady, no matter how harmless the lady may be."

Philip took her chin in his hand and brought her face up to look into his. "We will always be friends, Maria, no matter what."

"It cannot be the same and you well know it." She could feel tears pooling in her eyes and wanted to curse her stupid sensibilities. But then he surprised her by bending down and kissing a tear away as it spilled onto her cheek. He put his arm around her and held her against his shoulder until she had composed herself.

She had never been one to cry, but this felt as shattering as the scandal she had left behind in England—perhaps more so, in fact, because deep down she knew that things would never be the same. How could they be?

She took a deep breath and moved back, although she would stay in his arms forever if she could. To prolong the inevitable would only make it all the more painful.

"Are you going inside?" he asked.

"I think I shall stay out here a while longer. With my new coiffure, it hardly takes any time for me to ready myself," she teased, managing a half-hearted smile.

"Very well," he said, though she could tell he was hesitant to leave her. That, in and of itself, was enduring and much of why she had always loved him. "I must write to my family of the news." he continued. "Will you at least save a dance for me tonight?"

"Is there dancing tonight?" She looked up at his beloved, handsome face.

"At any party Wellington hosts, my dear girl, there is always dancing." He made a quick bow and she watched his fine figure walk away until it disappeared.

Turning, Maria went away from the house, through the wide

expanse of lawn and back along the outer perimeter of the grounds for privacy. There were no large, manicured pathways as were common in England. She was not yet ready to face another person and was debating the advisability of pleading a headache that evening when she saw a movement out of the corner of her eye. She stopped and turned to see what was there, but everything was still. Telling herself it must have been a bird or a squirrel, she took a few more steps and then saw movement again. No, she was not imagining things. Heart thumping, she walked to the farthest point of the garden, where vines covered a wrought-iron fence. In hindsight, it was probably not the wisest thing to do, but Maria had always followed her instincts.

"I thought you were not going to see me," a familiar voice said. "I did not wish to call out."

"Gabriel!" she exclaimed with happiness. "Why are you sneaking about?"

"Hush. Because it is necessary for me to do so, at least during the day. I will be staying here tonight."

"For good?" she asked hopefully, wanting to be able to be with him during this trying time.

"No, I cannot remain above a night."

She did not trouble to mask her disappointment and allowed her face to fall.

"I like what you have done to your hair," he remarked. "You look very pretty, sister."

"Thank you, Gabriel." She could not remember the last time her brother had paid her a compliment, if he ever had.

"Mother always did try to dress you in the manner of some silly confection."

She could hardly disagree with that statement.

"Is it true that you might be betrothed soon?"

"You have been keeping well informed, I see. I could only wish I knew more of you."

"I met with Wellington earlier today. He told me about Strickland."

"Do you approve?"

"I suppose I have naught ill to say of him."

"High praise, indeed!" she mocked.

"Is any man ever truly good enough for one's sister?"

She smiled at him and wished she could see him properly—touch him—hug him.

"If he will make you happy, Maria, then I have no objections. He is a good man, although I will admit I always thought you cherished notions of Everleigh, so I am happy to see you settled."

Maria swallowed hard. Had she been so obvious to everyone? That was a lowering thought. She had seen other ladies wearing their hearts on their sleeves, in the words of Shakespeare, and had pitied them. She thought she had at least masked her feelings.

"No, I do not think the whole world knows, but remember I live and die not by the sword but by my powers of observation," he reminded her gently.

"Thank you for that comfort, brother. Have you heard any news from England?"

She could almost feel him tense his body. "As far as I know, Mother and Father are well. They are still in the country, I believe."

She nodded. It was what she had expected. "I thought to have heard from Mother by now. I have written to her every day."

"Do not fret. The post can be very unreliable across the Channel. If anything amiss had happened, I would have heard."

"When can I see you again?"

"I do not know. I have already been out here too long. People might become suspicious if they see you talking to the wall."

She laughed. "I had not considered that. Oh, but it is so good to see you. I have missed you." She had always desired a closer relationship with her brother than he had been prepared to give. The giving of affection was simply not in his nature. Nevertheless she still craved it, especially now with her family thus separated.

"Do not worry, I am here. I will know if you need me."

Without another word, just like that, he vanished.

"Brother I need you now," she whispered.

Maria remained standing there, staring at the vines for some time, not even worrying if someone could see her. Why was it that those she wanted to be close to were always out of reach? She had been pleased with life before, but now it was as though a big chasm had opened before her, one she could not cross. Reluctantly, she walked back to the house to dress for yet another night of dinner and dancing, far less cheerful than she had been before.

PHILIP'S HEART SQUEEZED at Maria's pain. She was not one to display her emotions openly so she must be wretched indeed. He wished he could help her. He would make a point of trying to observe her more closely when she was with Strickland. If he thought she was merely settling for the man without her affections being engaged, then he would try to discourage the match—although the thought of interfering was abhorrent to him. Was it his concern? Perhaps he did not have the right, yet her brother and father were not present to guide her and he believed he must act on their behalf should it prove necessary.

He could recall the other matches Maria's parents had tried to force upon her and it occurred to him that perhaps they did not, after all, have her best interest at heart.

It was quite obvious Maria did not care for his betrothal with Pauline, but he was certain that once they became better acquainted the issue would resolve itself.

Glad to have settled matters to his satisfaction, he dressed for the evening and made his way downstairs to aid Wellington in greeting his guests as they arrived. When Pauline finally made her appearance, she was on the arm of her cousin and Philip felt a fierce stab of jealousy. It was a base emotion he was unaccustomed to and it caught him off his guard.

However, she smiled with delight when she saw Philip and immediately released herself from the archduke's arm and came over to Philip. She looked ravishing in a shimmering gown of deep orange. The color would have overpowered anyone else, yet on her it only accentuated her unworldly beauty.

The jealous rage turned to pride and he soon forgot about it as he fell under her spell. *How does she do it?* he thought carelessly, kissing her hand before possessively tucking it under his arm.

"What has you looking like a kettle about to boil?" Pauline asked, looking up at him with her exotic eyes. Instead of seductiveness, they held a hint of fear.

"Do I?" Philip asked, trying to look amused. "I suppose you do that to me."

"That is what every woman wants to hear of her betrothed," she said approvingly.

"Did you tell your cousin?"

"Not yet. I had hoped we could announce it tonight. There will be less of a fuss if we do it publicly. Had I told him in private, he would have tied me up and dragged me back to Austria."

"I cannot think it is a good idea to behave in such a fashion. I do not want our marriage to be underhanded."

"Please, do not speak so. It gives me a headache."

He turned, the better to look at her. "Marriage is a serious business, especially our alliance. It could well create a diplomatic incident."

She frowned and walked away, through the terrace doors. He followed her as discreetly as he could.

"Pauline," he said, moving to stand behind her and putting his hands on her shoulders, "is it wrong of me to want a marriage blessed by your family?"

She pretended to consider for a moment. "I suppose it is not, but they do not care for my wishes. Do you not see this is the only way?" She turned in his arms and looked up at him pleadingly. When she touched her gloved hand to his cheek, he wanted to melt. He was powerless beneath her touch.

"I think there is more you are not telling me. Why will you not confide in me?"

She shook her head and placed her face against his chest.

"Pauline, come back inside at once," a deep voice scolded from the doorway.

She looked up with a silent plea—and returned to the ballroom with her cousin.

Philip could hardly make an announcement without speaking to her further.

He did his best to pay attention to whoever was before him, but he could not help but notice she did not seem happy. Perhaps she did just have a headache, and yet he had not known her to be burdened with the affliction before. At some point, when he had finished one of the dances, he looked around the room and could not find her anywhere. He clenched his jaw, but her cousin was dancing attendance on Maria, a sight that made him frown. Instead of seeking another partner, he slipped from the ballroom and went in search of Pauline. He expected to find her on the terrace or in the gardens, but he found only a few people seeking fresh air.

Had she gone home? He did not think she would do so without taking her leave of him, but perhaps she had been taken ill.

First, he looked in the rooms set aside for guests near the ballroom. There was a lively card game going on in the library, but Pauline was not one of the participants. He waved at their greetings but refused their entreaties to join in. Next, he surveyed the library and the drawing room, but again she was nowhere to be found. Growing worried, he was about to go in search of the archduke, but then he heard a desk drawer close in a nearby office.

"Some poor sod must be working late," he murmured, and on a whim decided to see who it was.

"What the devil?" He had opened the door to see Pauline rummaging through His Grace's desk.

She looked up when she saw him, betraying no trace of guilt

whatsoever.

"What are you doing, Pauline?"

"Why, looking for paper, of course," she answered, unabashed.

"You cannot simply rummage through Wellington's desk for paper, my dear!"

She shut the drawer with evident frustration, sat back into the chair and looked up at him. "I merely wished to leave you a note. You were quite occupied with charming that Spanish princess and I could not claim your attention to tell you I was leaving."

Did he detect a hint of jealousy in her voice? He refused to be baited when he was, in fact, angry. "I am sorry you are feeling unwell. Shall I call a carriage for you and escort you to your hôtel?"

"That will not be necessary. Friedrich has already done so. Besides, I do not wish to feel your disapproval. I already have a headache." She leaned forward, put her elbows on the desk and placed her fingers to her temples.

Now he felt like a wretch. He walked towards where she sat. Standing behind her, he caressed her shoulder for a moment before leaning over to kiss the top of her head. "Come, I will take you to your cousin. Your maid can prepare you a draught and tuck you into bed, and then all will feel better in the morning."

He had barely helped her to her feet when the door opened and the archduke entered the room. He narrowed his gaze slightly at the sight of them together, but Philip said nothing and handed her over to the man. Having watched them leave, he stood for a while, staring at the desk deep in thought, yet still able to smell her exotic scent lingering in the air.

"You must trust her," he told himself. However, something prickled the back of his neck... the thought occurring that he knew his commander and his habits quite well.

Unable to convince himself of Pauline's complete innocence, he opened the drawer where she had been searching, only to find a large stack of paper in the first one in which he saw her look.

"What the devil are you about, Pauline?" he asked out loud.

There had to be something, that was for certain, but was it a matter of international importance or one of a personal nature? He wished he could reassure himself and could only be grateful the betrothal had not yet been announced. The worst part was that he still wanted her very badly. What did that say about his own character?

He slammed his fist on the desk in frustration, knowing he would find no more answers that night. But how was he to learn the truth—and before it was too late?

CHAPTER TEN

MARIA HAD ALWAYS enjoyed the water. She had spent many an hour at her family's estate, drinking tea and staring out over the lake, never seeming to tire of it. Everything about it fascinated her, from the ever-changing color to its reflections, the way the surface would sometimes be as still as a looking-glass or as turbulent as the sea, but beneath it all there was a whole world of living creatures. Thus it was when Colonel Strickland suggested a boat ride down the Seine one day, she was only too delighted to accept. The thought was repugnant to Kate, however, which only solidified Maria's thoughts that her friend was increasing.

Maria would have preferred not to go on her own, because she suspected she would soon be receiving a proposal. That, in and of itself, was telling, but she knew she must needs come to terms with it and determined to be as pleasant as she could.

She was hardly a martyr, and if she wanted to be a wife and have children, she told herself sternly, then this was a very good prospect. By the time Colonel Strickland met her downstairs for the proposed outing, her smile was genuine.

A footman strapped a large hamper on the rumble platform of the carriage. "What is that?" Maria asked with curiosity.

"I thought we would go to Versailles and have a picnic. Is that agreeable to you? If not, we need not go so far."

"That is perfectly agreeable. I would enjoy seeing the palace."

"I suspected you might," he said, with a twinkle in his eye that softened Maria's heart towards him. He was trying to woo her and was considerate of her wishes. She should be so fortunate!

"I suspect you would also enjoy a tour of Europe. I was lucky enough to enjoy a Grand Tour before Napoleon began his tyranny."

They arrived at the river, where a small boat with a single sail was waiting for them. Once on board, they settled into two seats, the warm sun shining gloriously on the water, the wake of other boats causing them to rock a little.

"What was your favorite place of those you visited?" she asked, perfectly willing to dream of destinations to visit and live vicariously through him.

"Would you believe it if I said I have enjoyed everywhere I have been?"

She looked at him with disbelief. "Even Badajoz and Salamanca?"

"Not the battles, of course, but Spain is beautiful and has a unique culture. We spent a great deal of time there, and the fighting was but a small fraction of it."

"We only hear what is in the dispatches, of course. I am glad you found some good there, but there must be somewhere that was exceptional… somewhere you would go back to?"

He looked out over the water as they passed through Paris and into the less populated parts as they left the city behind. "I think Italy and Greece, perhaps. They are so very different from England."

"How are they so?" She had seen paintings, of course, but that was hardly the same.

"It is always warm. That may be hard to imagine being from England, but it is always summer. The water is clear and bright shades of blue. The architecture is also very different. Most of the buildings are white or golden stucco, with red-tiled roofs. There are some brightly painted houses, but they are unique. Often, they are built into sides of cliffs, as you might see in Devonshire or Cornwall."

"I should like to see that," she said dreamily, envisioning his descriptions.

"Perhaps you shall. I shall think my service worth it if we are allowed those freedoms again."

"It is a very steep price, is it not, to pay for one man's greed and ambitions?"

"Indeed," he said quietly.

They talked a little more about his travels, but very soon arrived at their destination, where they took another carriage to the palace.

The village nearby was quaint and hardly prepared Maria for the sight of one of the most beautiful palaces in Europe. She and the colonel stood before the gates, taking in the majesty of the ornate, white stone buildings, and the large stone-paved courtyard they overlooked, before strolling through the public gardens. There were a few other people enjoying the gardens, some of them young families as well as other couples. It was no wonder on such a glorious autumn day.

A servant followed with their hamper and when they found a tree on a hill overlooking the gardens, they stopped to eat.

"It is a shame we cannot go inside."

He looked up at her and smiled. "I do not think the king is in residence. Would you like me to ask?"

"No, indeed! I should have liked to have seen what it was like before. My grandmother used to dance here often… before." *Before* meaning the Revolution, where having noble blood was a crime worth the guillotine, she thought, but did not say.

"I think, perhaps, imagining from here is better."

"Probably so," she concurred quietly. They ate their cold meat, cheese and fruit with some fresh bread and glasses of wine.

"Would you care to walk through the Queen's Grove before we return to town?"

"There is a maze?"

"All proper castles have mazes," he said dryly. "But this is not a true maze. There used to be a labyrinth with thirty-nine fountains, all depicting parts of Aesop's fables."

"I do adore a good maze! 'Tis a shame, for I am very good at them," she teased. "I would have loved to have seen the labyrinth. It sounds very clever."

"Perhaps one day you shall be given your chance to show off your prowess. We can still race to the center of the grove."

While the servant packed up the hamper, the colonel helped Maria to her feet and led her beyond the formal palace gardens, where she had thought there to be nothing more than woodland. Hidden among the arboretum was a labyrinth of evergreens, far thicker and less manicured than the ones closer to the palace.

"Shall we be children again and race to the fountain?" he asked as they entered and came to a fork in the path.

She smiled widely. "I shall see you there!" she sang with glee and took to her heels. Maria was really quite good at finding her way through mazes, so this should be simple. She always had an excellent sense of direction, and they all had a pattern that, once ascertained, only had to be followed. She hurried to the end, and was rewarded with the pleasure of beating Colonel Strickland to the prize. Perhaps they could return more sedately and view each of the fountains. However, to her disquiet, she found she was not alone. Instinctively, Maria stepped back.

She saw the archduchess standing there, near the fountain, laughing as the spray caught in the wind. She looked like a portrait that someone would expend a great deal of money for, Maria thought sadly, knowing she could never compete with such artistry. Yet, besides beauty, what did Philip see in her?

A deep voice sounded, disturbing the archduchess, and Maria realized it was not Philip. The lady looked up, smiling at her companion as though he was the only man in the world, opened her arms to him. She then wrapped her arms around his neck.

"Have you discovered anything yet?" the archduke asked, as

far as Maria could make out in her limited German.

"No, very little. Merely that Wellington might soon be moving to Vienna."

"Then we must hurry. I do not know how much more of this situation I can stomach."

"As long as you know the truth," she said, and began to kiss him in a way that made Maria blush. "But you know why we must do this."

Suddenly, she was filled with anger at the woman for misleading Philip. It was clear to Maria that Philip was a pawn in whatever game they were playing, but he was obviously blind with infatuation. Why was the archduchess treating Philip in such a dreadful way? It was clear she wanted something. Whatever was Maria to do?

She heard footsteps coming up the path behind her and realized it was probably the colonel. Should she try to stop him or let him interrupt them? Better by far, she thought quickly, for he to do so than she. Being civil to the woman was unthinkable after the scene Maria had witnessed. Was the archduchess still determined to marry Philip or did she have some other purpose in mind for him?

In either case, he would be hurt.

"Oh, I beg your pardon." Maria looked up to see the couple jump apart as Colonel Strickland spoke, having arrived at a different entrance on the other side of the fountain. She saw the recognition on his face. Immediately, she turned and went back towards the exit, not wanting to speak. Would the archduchess know Maria had seen her? If she recognized the colonel, the woman must surely suspect her presence.

Hopefully, Strickland would realize Maria had seen what had occurred and come after her, for she could not stay and make polite nonsense with such a woman.

She paced back and forth at the entrance to the garden, hoping Strickland would come out soon and before the other couple. He did.

The look on her face must have told him everything he needed to know. "I take it you saw what happened?"

She nodded.

He took her arm and without speaking began to escort her away. She was grateful for the silence. He was a good man. But did he suspect her true feelings for Philip or did he think she was upset because of their friendship?

At last they entered the carriage and then the boat. The men began to row back up the river towards the city but this time she could not enjoy it.

Now what should she do? Should she tell Philip? She doubted he would thank her for it.

WELLINGTON HAD RELEASED them early to enjoy the beautiful day. Since there were no prior engagements, Philip changed from his uniform and decided he would surprise Pauline and take her for a romantic dinner at one of the cafés Paris was known for. Then, perhaps, he might take her for a stroll along the river. An evening where it was just the two of them was very much needed—in the way it had been before the others had arrived in Paris.

Philip took a cabriolet to the Austrian minister's residence, but was shocked to discover Pauline was not there.

Disappointed, he left his card and turned to leave, only to see her arriving in an open carriage with the archduke.

He clenched his jaw in frustration, trying not to allow himself to feel jealousy, let alone show it. What could he do but wait and greet them?

"Philip!" She raised her hand and waved. "What timing! Were you just leaving?"

"Indeed, we were given a free afternoon and I thought to spend it with you."

"I would be delighted. May I have a moment to change my dress? Friedrich took me to visit Versailles. Sitting around all day is such a bore, you know."

No, Philip did not know. But he inclined his head to the archduke. "It was very kind of you to alleviate your cousin's boredom, sir." He wondered if the man's English was well enough to detect the sarcasm in his tone.

"I am at her service. Would you care to join me for a glass of fine cognac while you wait for her to dress?"

"Of course." It would do no good to alienate her father's agent, and Philip wanted to better understand his role. He strongly suspected the man was far more than the pair were letting on. What man would not want Pauline?

Philip followed the archduke into a study and waited while the man poured him a glass of brandy.

He handed it to him and then gestured that he be seated. But the civility was only a temporary mask.

"What are your intentions towards my cousin?" he asked baldly.

"No mincing of words, sir?" Philip returned.

"I believe it unnecessary."

"My intentions are honorable, if that is what you are asking."

"Most of her admirers are, but I will warn you, *Captain Everleigh*, Pauline plays with men's affections. She thinks she is doing naught but flirting, but she has left a trail of broken hearts and broken engagements all over Europe."

"Indeed?" Philip murmured, trying not to show his irritation with this conversation.

"Yes, I assure you. She either jilts her lovers or her father does not approve of the match. I hear you have a similar reputation." He watched Philip over his glass as he took a sip, no doubt to judge his reaction.

Philip was not so easily flustered. "So you are here to investigate me," he stated flatly.

"A father cannot be too careful."

"She did mention her father," Philip said, in his turn attempting to pry information. Two could play this game.

"If her father does not first approve the match, then she does not receive her inheritance." He held his hands out wide. "It is a simple as that."

"She told me he has already made a choice for her."

"Of course, but she believes she can change his mind." His derisive tone of voice made it clear that such a thing would be impossible.

Pauline sailed into the room in a swath of pale green taffeta, making the room feel small and filling it with her sent of jasmine. Both of them rose to their feet at her entrance.

"Has he been nice? Or has he been telling you what an ogre my father is?"

He had no time to reply before she held out her hand.

"Say naught, I know the answer. Come, let us leave before you change your mind."

Philip bowed to the archduke, who inclined his head with a narrowed gaze, and then followed Pauline from the room. He hailed the cabriolet and saw her settled before they spoke again. Pauline broke the quietude.

"What a lovely idea! Had I known you were to return early I would not have gone to see another ostentatious palace. I swear, I have had my fill of those."

"Do you mean that? I imagine you were brought up in a grand castle and so are less easily impressed by such grandeur."

"And you were not?" She teased.

"I was," he said slowly, "although it is hardly a castle. I am not the eldest, either, so will not inherit Everleigh Park."

She made a dismissive gesture. "It is not as though we will be poor, Philip. I do not require a castle."

"That is certainly good to know," he remarked dryly. He did, in fact, have his own, very fine estate from his mother, but it was nowhere near London, which was what he liked best about it. But would Pauline be pleased to retire to the country?

They arrived at their destination, a small café in the Saint Germain District which enjoyed a lovely view of the Notre Dame.

A waiter in a white coat with a drooping moustache seated them by an open window which was open to allow the breeze to cool the warm air inside.

"Charming. I have never eaten in public like this before," Pauline remarked as the waiter filled their glasses with a white Vouvray wine.

He lifted his glass. "A toast?"

She smiled. "To our betrothal?"

"To us." They chinked their glasses together and took a drink.

"I am very pleased to know Wellington allows his men time for pleasure."

"Have I been neglecting you, Pauline?" he asked, amused.

She made a pouting face. "That is not what I said. But I am used to men…"

"Hovering?" Philip provided a word for her.

"I suppose so, but would not have chosen so crude a word."

"I will never hover. It is not in my nature."

"Do you intend to neglect me, then?"

"I intend to do my duty when I must, and I intend to make the most of our time together. You must trust me."

Something flashed in her eyes and Philip would have loved for her to rail at him so he might know what she was really thinking, but instead she smiled. "This is probably why I am drawn to you," she surprised him by saying.

"Because I do not spend every moment fawning at your feet?"

"How cruel you are!" she complained. But she laughed.

"Would you really wish for a partner in life who was such a puppy? Someone you could bend to your every whim? It would become mundane before the honeymoon was over!"

"The only thing I am concerned about, in your words, is your duty having to come first. Surely, with Napoleon captured there can be no pressing demands on the British army?"

The waiter placed two bowls of consommé before them, giving Philip a moment to compose his answer. With anyone else, he would have thought that question an attempt to withdraw information from him. Nonetheless, she had a right to know what she should expect as his wife.

"We hope that is the case, but remain vigilant nevertheless. Although Napoleon is gone, there will always be someone else willing to take his place."

She looked at him as though he had made a clever chess move. Perhaps he had. It was certainly an evasive answer. "Do you think you will remain long in Paris?"

Philip swallowed his spoonful of soup. "There is a rumor Wellington may be called to the Congress in Vienna, but we also have assembled near Brussels the remainder of our army which is not away in America."

"I see. Well, if you were to accompany Wellington to Vienna, I could show you my home."

"And introduce me to your father?" He knew he was provoking her, but it was more than a valid question – expectation – of his future bride.

"Yes, of course."

She turned her attention to the next course, a platter of Escargots à la Bourguignonne.

For some reason he could not let the matter drop. "Is there anything I need to know about your father, your family? I would like to be well-armed with knowledge of his inclinations, that I might know how to break down his differences and charm him."

"Goodness! You make it sound like a war!"

"Is it not? Your cousin certainly implied it would be."

"Oh, Friedrich." She shook her head dismissively and then took a sip of wine. "He means well. He tried to kiss me today," she said off-handedly. "But I made certain he understood we are betrothed."

Philip tried not to react. A kiss could be innocent, and she was telling him about it. "You say he is your father's pawn, but what precisely does that mean?"

She hesitated, as though deciding how much to tell him. "I have no brother, and Friedrich is my father's heir."

Now they were getting somewhere. "I see. So your father favors him?'

She lifted one shoulder in an elegant shrug. "I do not intend to marry only for bloodlines, wealth, and power."

"Then I am flattered." He raised his glass to her and took a long drink. "Do you wish for children?"

His query caused her to pause with her fork in mid-air.

"Was that not an expected question from your future spouse?"

"I had not given children much thought. Are they necessary? Neither of us are heirs, though I do have a title to pass to my children. If it is important to you, then I daresay we may have one or two."

Philip found himself surprised. He had not thought particularly of marriage, but he certainly would have expected any female to want children. Maria's face came to mind and he found himself comparing the two ladies before he then shook off the silly notion.

He and Pauline finished their dinner and walked around the square holding hands, stopping for an ice, and stealing a kiss or two. It was far easier than discussing the trivial details of marriage.

CHAPTER ELEVEN

MARIA HAD BEEN paralyzed with indecision since that day at Versailles. She was feeling wretched from lack of sleep and the worry of deciding what to tell Philip.

Colonel Strickland had said nothing more to her on the matter, and then, when she had thought to seek guidance and confide in him, he had been sent on an operation to Ghent for at least a week.

Deprived of his calm good sense, she had continued to fret. Then the answer came to her. If she were only Philip's friend, she would not hesitate to say something to him. Her indecision had been because of her deeper feelings for him, and the fear he might see through her and suspect her of jealousy.

Once she had decided what she must do, then she could not seem to find him—or, at least, not where they could be assured of any privacy. And the longer it took to confess to him what she had overheard, the more confused she was about the archduchess' motives—even if it was not her place to know.

However, she was Philip's friend and he had a right to know if his betrothed was amorously kissing another man behind his back.

And then, there were those damning words. Her German was not perfect, but she could think of no other translation.

"Have you discovered anything yet?" the archduke asked.

"No, very little. Merely that Wellington might soon be moving to Vienna."

"Then we must hurry. I do not know how much more of this situation I can stomach."

"As long as you know the truth," she had said.

Maria had to find Philip and speak with him. To that end, she spent countless hours in the garden, hoping he would find her as he had previously done, but to no avail.

Yet, when she finally did find him, it was quite unexpected and she found it hard to say the words. She had returned from a night at the theater with Kate and Jack, but not yet being tired, had stepped out into the garden for some fresh air.

Perhaps it was not the wisest course of action at such an hour, but the house was quiet and she did not feel threatened there.

When she finally grew tired, she rose from the bench to go inside and bumped straight into Philip. For all her years of knowing him, though, she had never seen him quite like this as an adult. He was in his shirt sleeves and carrying his shoes. Clearly, he had imbibed some spirits and he smelled of tobacco.

She had seen her father, and occasionally her brother, like this, but never Philip. Seeing him in such a condition made her heart hurt, especially with the knowledge that what she had to tell him would be painful for him to learn.

"Maria? What are you doing here all alone?"

"I was not tired," she confessed. "I often sit in the garden by myself."

"At night? In the dark?"

"No."

"What is wrong, Maria?"

"I have been needing to speak with you about something for some little while, although now is perhaps not the most opportune either."

"That will not fash with one of your oldest friends, pet. Come, I am the last to go up. We may speak in private."

He escorted her to a study which looked like a gentleman's purview. It had the appearance of an office, with two library tables, maps and books about. Thankfully, it was not the smoking room. The air was untainted by such odors, although she could detect a hint of lamp oil. He settled her on a sofa and went to pour a drink from a decanter on a side-table.

"Maria, you wish to have children, do you not?"

"Oh, yes. Several. That is, if my husband agrees and we are so blessed. You know this about me already, surely?"

"Yes," he said softly. "I think I should also like to have children."

"Why do you ask?"

"It is merely something that has been on my mind of late."

He returned with a tumbler containing what appeared to be brandy and placed it in her hands.

"For me? I do not need spirits, Philip."

"By the look of you, I say you do." He sat down next to her. "Now, tell me what has you looking worn to the bone. Has Strickland upset you?"

"No, no." She shook her head. "It is not about me." She lifted the glass to her lips and took a sip despite her protest. The liquid certainly did warm her from within. "It is to do with your archduchess—something I saw and overheard."

She felt him stiffen beside her, but he said, "Go on."

"At first, I did not really want to tell you. The more I thought about it, however, the more I felt it was what a friend should do."

"And you hesitated because you thought I would be angry?"

She stared into her glass but nodded her head.

"This would not perhaps be about the archduke kissing Pauline at Versailles, would it?"

She looked up abruptly. "You already know about it?" Maria asked with disbelief.

"Yes, she told me."

Maria could not have been more shocked. Had she told him how she had initiated the kiss? Maria doubted it. The woman probably knew Maria had seen and was trying to put on a bold face, yet something did not make sense. She nibbled the tip of her finger. A wisp of memory—whether seen or overheard she could not be sure—floated beyond her recognition but try as she might, she could not summon it to the present. Whatever could it be?

"Do not worry, my dear. Unfortunately, the archduke is trying to convince her to return to Austria and marry him. 'Tis what her father wants. And while it saddens me to have to say it, gentlemen find themselves very attracted to her and quite often make unwanted advances."

"Do not worry? How can you say such a thing? I have hardly slept since I witnessed that shocking scene!" Maria made a derisive sound, full of the disgust she felt.

"You are such a good friend." He answered her outburst in the calm tone one would use to pacify a child. "I will miss these talks when you marry."

"And when you marry," she said, trying to hide her distaste. Should she tell him what had really happened? Society marriages were often full of adultery, she knew, but she did not think Philip would be so open-minded about his own wife. He was being very cool about it. "Are you very sure about this?"

"Pauline is a flirt, and she apologized for kissing him. The rest of the world is not as prudish as England."

"Nonetheless, did she apologize because she knows I saw what occurred or because she was truly repentant?"

"I am not a fool, Maria. I promise I am entering into this with my eyes wide open." He took her hand and gave it an affectionate squeeze.

Maria sighed heavily. Were she giving him up to a better woman, it would not hurt so much, she was sure, but he was a grown man. What else could she do? She had warned him. "Then I shall accept there is no more to be said. I have anguished greatly over whether or not to tell you... thinking it not my place to interfere."

He smiled at her but it was tinged with sadness. "I am sure it was more innocent than you think. People kiss all the time on the Continent, and it does not mean a jot. They are cousins."

"Philip, I may never have been kissed, but this was not how cousins kiss." She blushed as she made the admission. Her mother would be proud, but secretly Maria was mortified.

"You have never been kissed?"

"This surprises you?"

"You have had several suitors and proposals if my memory serves. None of them have kissed you?"

"If you mean in the manner they were kissing, certainly not!"

He frowned. "Perhaps you should show me."

"Philip, do not be ridiculous."

She did not know if she could. She had dreamed of this for years, yet somehow, now, when they were both as good as promised to others... However, if it was the only way to convince him, so be it. "Very well. I shall try." She took a deep breath. "Mind you, I am but showing you what she did, in the interests of truth."

"Of course," Philip said, now looking amused.

Maria took another deep breath. Being so near, feeling his warmth and his familiar scent almost made her forget what the purpose was. Slowly, she raised her arms around his neck and pulled his face down towards hers. Then she planted her lips on his and began to kiss him with the same enthusiasm with which she had seen the archduchess kiss the archduke. However, she quickly lost herself in the sensation as Philip began to kiss her back, making a low growling sound in his throat as he did so.

She was carried away by the feeling of lips, his closeness, the heat spreading from her head to her toes…and she was no longer acting out someone else's kiss, but fully engrossed in her own. When she realized what was happening, she pulled back and looked down at her satin slippers. "Oh."

"Maria?" Philip asked, dismay in his voice.

She could not bear to apologize or ask for forgiveness, because she realized she could not be sorry. It had been like nothing she had previously experienced or, in all likelihood, ever would again.

She stood up without looking him in the eye. "I hope that was demonstration enough for you," she said breathlessly, before hurrying away. It was not until she was back in her chamber that she realized she had not told him the words she had overheard.

GOOD LORD, WHAT had just happened? And with Maria?

There were so many more questions rolling through his mind, his head was like a turbulent storm. If she had really witnessed Pauline kissing her cousin like that, then Pauline had much to answer for. However, the fact remained that he had just kissed Maria like that! It had quickly become far, far more than a demonstration, too. They had been kissing each other with passion and he had become carried away, even though he had known it was Maria. Neither had he stopped her.

He tossed back the remains of her glass of brandy. At least she had not kissed him whilst under the influence, he thought derisively.

He paced back and forth across the carpet. What was he to do now? He should never have suggested such a thing, but for the life of him, he had not expected more than a quick peck on the lips. The devil! He was betrothed!

He stopped at the cabinet, poured another glass of brandy and downed it in one large gulp. Unfortunately, that was not enough to allow him to erase what had just happened.

Not only had he inappropriately kissed one of his best friends and would have to deal with the consequences, he also had a betrothed who apparently had feelings for someone else. If so, why was she leading him on this merry dance? And what did he want to do about it?

"What maggot is in your head?" Jack's voice demanded from

behind him.

"And what are you doing down here at this hour?" Philip rejoined.

"I was awakened by someone crying in the room next to ours." Jack looked at him pointedly. "You would not happen to know anything about that, would you?"

Philip swore. As if he did not already feel wretched enough about Maria, now Jack was going to take up her cause against him, too.

"What do you want me to say?" Philip held out his arms.

"I don't know. Perhaps you should tell me what happened." He went over to the side-table, helped himself to a glass of brandy and then slouched lazily in the chair across from Philip.

"I wish I knew." Philip shook his head in dismay. "Everything happened so quickly – she was telling me she saw Pauline kissing her cousin and insisted it was not chaste and then I told her to show me and, by Jove, Maria and I ended up kissing." He threw his head in his hands.

"I assume it was not the simple chaste kiss you were expecting?"

"Hardly," Philip scoffed, then hiccoughed.

"Ah. Shall I call you out?"

"It would make me feel better if you were to draw my cork, perhaps, but it would not solve anything."

"You are lucky you were not caught."

"At this moment I do not feel lucky about anything," Philip snarled. "What am I supposed to do?"

"Apologize. Grovel. Beg forgiveness?" Jack suggested.

"Very helpful. I must do that, of course, but what is to be done about Pauline? Clearly there is some deeper game afoot."

"Well, we knew that—not that the ladies don't lose their heads over you." Jack took a sip and looked over at Philip. "You do not mean to tell me you have broken a spy's number one rule, did you?"

"Maybe," he answered evasively. At Jack's look of scorn he

became defensive. "What was I supposed to do? A beautiful damsel in distress needed rescuing!"

"Surely there was a better way to deal with that. You have managed to evade the matchmaking mamas of the *ton* thus far. Not only will this hurt Maria, it will create a diplomatic fuss."

"Not necessarily," Philip said, although even he did not believe his own words.

"Does Hookey know?"

"I was going to tell him about the betrothal in the morning."

"I do not envy you that conversation. Did you know he is moving some of us to Brussels? He sent Strickland to Ghent."

Philip did not want to hear that. "I need time to sort out this muddle."

"What you need is to think clearly," Jack retorted.

"What I need is to erase the past six weeks from time."

"If the archduchess is making a monkey out of you and she hears you are to remove to Brussels, then perhaps she will show her hand more quickly."

"There is also a rumor Wellington is being moved to Vienna. She could request I be sent there. If she tells him of our betrothal, then he is likely to comply."

"And what will you say if he asks you?"

"The truth—that I have been played for a fool and that I thought I could handle it."

"Rather you than me, my friend. But you had better tell him early, before this goes any further." Jack finished his glass of brandy, gave a little salute and then went back to bed. Philip did not bother. He had made a complete botch of everything and he must now do his best to make it right.

The next morning, he washed and dressed and then waited for Wellington in his office.

"Well, Everleigh? It must be serious or you would not be here waiting for me."

"Yes, sir."

"Is it about your betrothal to the archduchess?"

"You know about that?"

Wellington gave him a keen look.

"Yes, yes, you are all-knowing. Very well, am I to be repri-manded?"

"That depends," his commander said as he went to sit behind his desk. "I would like to know more about how this came to pass—beyond the obvious attractions the archduchess possesses. I, myself, am not immune to beauty, but to propose after so short an acquaintance is somewhat a surprise."

"Austria is one of our allies," Philip remarked.

"Indeed," Wellington agreed calmly, "but there is more, is there not? She is part of the royal family and her father is one of the king's advisors. We could use this to our advantage, but it could also explode in our faces."

Philip tried not to let anything show, but he felt like a guilty schoolboy. "She begged me to save her, sir. What was I to do?"

"I would have hoped you would have used your charm and fended her off."

Philip would dearly love to ask Wellington if that was how he handled the ladies, but he held back the retort. Wellington must have read his mind, however.

"Quite. But, I did a bit of digging, and she has had a long-standing betrothal."

"Yes, she informed me her father was forcing her into the marriage, but would consider other choices if they were suitable."

Wellington cocked an eyebrow at him.

Philip tried not to squirm. He was the veriest fool.

"Apparently there was a slight quarrel between the couple. Perhaps this is her way of making the archduke jealous?"

"I think there is more to it than that, unfortunately." Philip sighed heavily. "Lady Maria saw the pair kissing amorously yesterday, at Versailles."

"You have seen the archduchess since?"

"Yes, and she explained it away, and pleaded with me to put forward the announcement of the betrothal."

"Which was done last night." Wellington leaned forward and steepled his hands over his arms. "The question is, have we been checkmated?"

"In this case, who would be the prize?"

"That is what we must answer. Is it Napoleon, or simply Austria trying to gain knowledge?"

"Rather a risky chance to take, surely? What if I compromised her?"

"Mm." Wellington's features formed the expression he made when he was thinking, and Philip knew to wait. "What is in it for them? That is the question we must answer."

"What would you have me do now, sir?"

"We must somehow use this to our advantage. For now, do nothing but carry on as you have been... perhaps apply a little more of your own pressure? I assume that will not be a chore."

"No, sir." Philip bowed and left, feeling even worse than he had before. He still had to patch up the rift with his best friend.

CHAPTER TWELVE

MARIA WAS ABSOLUTELY crushed. Somehow through her tears, she made it back to her chamber and fell on the bed.

She touched her lips, and they still were warm and swollen. It had not just been a dream. The most special moment of her life—the thing she most longed for was ruined, tainted by her own passions! How could she have let herself become so carried away? And how would she ever face Philip again?

Not only that, he was betrothed to another and she expected she soon would be. As wonderful as it was, now that she had tasted the forbidden fruit, she was ruined to love another man the same way.

She could only be grateful she did not have to face Colonel Strickland right now. Surely she would not be able to hide her guilt as though she had the scarlet letter planted upon her chest.

She could return to England and pretend none of this had ever happened. But things could be worse there, and she would likely remain a spinster. What would be worse? To marry a man when you loved another? But the one you loved was unattainable? She could not be more wretched!

It was unlike her to wallow in self-pity, but for once she felt as though she deserved it. She wailed into her pillow hoping sleep would eventually consume her, though grieving the loss of losing not only her chance at true love but also a dearest friend.

"Maria? Maria?"

A soft groan escaped her lips and she turned over away from the light streaming through the window to bury her head under the pillow.

"Maria, you must wake up. It is well after noon and your things are packed!"

"Packed? Where are we going?"

"To Brussels. Jack has just received orders. We are to depart immediately. You will go with us, will you not?"

Groaning, Maria propped herself up on her elbows squinting at the light. Kate was already in a traveling dress and Bisset was packing Maria's trunks.

She could not think. Finally, it occurred to her she was in Paris and then events of the night before rushed back at her as though it were just happening. Maria fell back on her pillow and covered her eyes.

"Maria, what is the matter? Are you taking ill?" Kate reached over and felt Maria's cheek and forehead.

What could Maria say to explain what had happened? She wanted to tell her everything, yet she wanted to tell her nothing. It had been the most momentous experience of her life, yet she had to keep it to herself.

"I am well, just a headache."

Kate looked at her, head tilted with concern. "You do not look well. I can ask Jack if we can delay or perhaps you may come with Mrs. Johnson."

"No. I am sure I am well."

"If you insist. I will have a tisane sent up for you. We will be waiting for you when are ready."

Maria glanced over at Bisset who gave her a sympathetic look. "Here is your water. I will go fetch the tisane for you and then help you dress. I nearly have your things packed. You slept right through it!" Shaking her head, she left, closing the door behind her.

Maria stared at the canopy above her head. Perhaps it was for the best to leave. Would Philip be going to Brussels as well? She doubted if he did they would ride together or stay in the same lodgings. It was for the best, surely.

She forced herself to get out of bed. She splashed her face with water and even managed to fake a smile by the time Bisset returned.

She drank her remedy while the maid brushed and dressed her hair and was soon downstairs being ushered into a carriage for the trip to Brussels.

"Why the rush?" she asked as Kate settled down across from her. The men were traveling on mounts ahead of them, but Wellington had provided one of his carriages for their comfort and luggage.

"I do not know. I am no more accustomed to army ways than you. Jack acted as though it was normal."

"I suppose I should know more, but Gabriel barely speaks about his work."

"So far it has been rather like London – balls and parties. Jack assures me that is not always the case."

"I hope nothing serious has happened necessitating the move to Brussels."

"Jack says not, but neither are they sending troops back to England as if the war were entirely over," Kate reasoned.

"But Napoleon is captured. Surely he is no more threat?"

"Apparently there are still those loyal to him that could cause problems."

"And it is safer to be in Brussels than Paris?" Maria frowned.

"I felt no danger in Paris, but there are so many things we are not told."

"Very true. Being the weaker sex, we must be protected from anything we might form an opinion on," Maria retorted.

Kate laughed. "Heaven forbid!"

"How many days will we travel?" Maria asked.

"I have no idea. I believe the men will keep a fast pace since they are mounted."

"Yes, I suppose we will be the limiting factor." Maria pulled out her needlework to help occupy the time. She'd never been good at sitting still in a carriage. In fact, she'd much rather be mounted, but suspected Kate could not tolerate long days in the saddle at present.

"I hear there is a good deal of society beginning together in Brussels," Kate said cautiously.

Maria looked up from her stitching. "What do you mean?"

"I mean, that London seems to be removing to Brussels at an alarming rate. Apparently, it is the fashionable thing to do."

Maria did not know what to say.

"We will be there to support you if anyone dares to say anything," Kate said kindly.

"I suppose I have been fortunate not to encounter any vipers thus far. I could almost allow myself to pretend it had been a horrible nightmare," Maria said quietly.

"Perhaps you will be so fortunate in Brussels as well, but I did think it best to warn you."

Maria nodded. She wished she had a letter from her parents at the very least so she could know what had happened—how they were being treated. She knew nothing and though seeing Gabriel had been encouraging, he had had no such reassurances to offer her.

"Are you concerned about Strickland?" Kate asked as she studied her.

Maria had not even been thinking about the colonel, she thought with a guilty pang.

"Surely he is more constant than that? When the situation is explained, I have no doubt he will remain by your side."

"I, I," Maria's voice caught. "I assumed he already knew." She tried not to let the thought panic her. What if he did not know and put her aside once he did?

Kate reached across and took her hand. "I did not mean to distress you."

Maria was already distressed from what had happened with

Philip, though she knew she should be worried about Strickland. Yet she would not hurt him for the world. "I suppose I should have said something to him, though it felt like the world already knew. Perhaps…"

"Colonel Strickland is a gentleman through and through. "He would hardly hold against you what was not your fault."

Maria laughed harshly. "I have seen it happen over much lesser things."

"He is not one to gossip, however, and I believe he would ask for explanations first. His attentions to you have been very marked. I do not think he would be so cruel."

"No, the colonel is a very kind man, but I do not wish any scandal to taint his family."

"It will all blow over as soon as the next scandal comes, you know that," Kate tried to reassure her.

"Most scandals, yes, but being publicly accused of treason does not fade from people's minds so quickly. Especially not in a time of war. Even though it happened decades ago on another continent entirely. If only my brother would make an effort to clear our names, but he will not. Hiding only confirms people's suspicions."

"Jack and Lord Philip will stand beside you, as will Wellington, if it comes to that. Although they are not coming to Brussels immediately."

Maria felt pain welling in her breast that she wanted to keep private, yet she was stuck for hours in close quarters. At just the simple mention of Phillips's name she wanted to retch.

She had not been able to see him before they departed. She hated leaving things like this, yet she could not imagine facing him again, and seeing that the most earth shattering moment of her life had meant nothing to him—that their friendship could no longer be the same.

Would she even see him again before he married? Perhaps it was for the best. She was much more valiant in wishing for his happiness with another woman if she did not have to witness it.

HOW WAS THIS happening again?

Philip had tried to speak with Maria as soon as he had spoken to Wellington, but she was still asleep. He'd gone to some meetings, but when he'd returned to find her again she was gone.

How could this have happened twice? First, in London and now.

And of course, he was not going to Brussels with them because of his situation with Pauline. Likely, he would have to go to Vienna to see this through.

The last thing he wanted to do was leave things like they were with Maria. He could see no easy solution. He doubted Wellington would let him take a trip to Brussels for such a reason. Much though it pained him, he would have to send her a letter. He at least owed her that. If he was lucky, he might be able to send it out with one of the dispatches today.

He sat and removed paper and quill from the desk.

A little time would perhaps help them both sort things out. The kiss had been a mistake, but how to tell her that without hurting her?

His emotions had been much too high last night with knowing he'd been played for a fool by the archduchess when he had been suspicious in the first place! A few brandies into the night, he had taken liberties with his dearest friend! And he had enjoyed it! What a cad he was! Pauline and Maria could not be more opposite. How could he have toyed with Maria so?

Worse, he now had to pretend he was still enamored with Pauline when he'd rather wring her beautiful neck! Part of him still hoped Pauline was just being fickle and misguided, but Maria would hardly have made such a scene up.

What must Maria think of him?

Dearest Maria,

I was troubled to find you had left before we had a chance to speak. It is hard to put apologies into words appropriately, so I can only humbly beg you forgive my impertinence and hope we may remain friends. You may name your weapons when next we meet.

Yours affectionately,
Philip

It was a sorry attempt at reconciling with one of the most important people in his life. Maria was a very forgiving person, and the last person he would ever wish to hurt. She had been through enough and had a chance at happiness with Strickland. Philip shook his head. For some reason he had no wish to watch that courtship when he should be nothing but happy for her. Perhaps being in separate places would be easier.

He folded and sealed the letter so it would go with the next courier to Brussels, and then tried to put the kiss from his mind. He needed no distractions from what was ahead.

When work was finished for the day, Philip dressed for the evening, mulling over how best to draw Pauline out. There had to be a way for her to show her cards. What would have happened if Maria had not chanced upon the scene at Versailles? He could only be thankful his heart had not been fully engaged yet, but his pride was certainly bruised.

How far did Pauline mean to drag this on? Would she have led him to the altar, abandoned him, leaving him fully humiliated and his career blemished? Or was she simply using him to gain information? The latter made the most sense, but why was it necessary to convince him a betrothal was necessary? Mayhap it was as simple as her pre-arranged marriage was common knowledge and she needed a convincing reason to draw someone in.

"What is it you want, exactly?" he asked his reflection as he tied his neckcloth. "Tell me, Pauline. Was I the target from the start, or would any Englishman do?"

He took his sword in its scabbard along with his hat, trying to think of how best to play his part. "Perhaps a trap of some sort. Wellington is fond of those. If I only I knew what she was looking for."

As he rode to the dinner and ball, the only conclusion he could come to was that it would be necessary to pressure her. For what he had in mind, he would need his commander's blessing.

As he arrived and surveyed the ballroom, his eyes were immediately drawn to her. It was difficult to force himself to think ill of her. Perhaps it was not all false and she was being used by her father.

It would be very tempting in one who had the power to use such a tool in their favor. Poor Pauline, for her power was very great. The Fall of Troy at Helen's hands was very possible indeed.

She wore another bold gown of bright blue which shimmered green in the light. Everything she wore showed her to advantage and despite knowing she loved another, or at least did not mind playing them against each other, still did not dampen his wanting her. Lust and love were two very different things and he would do well to keep reminding himself.

"For the good of England, old chap," Wellington said into his ear as though reading his thoughts, and slapped him on the shoulder. Reluctantly, Philip moved forward towards his target not feeling completely prepared for the task.

She smiled when she saw him and took his offer of the arm. "I thought you were not coming," she said pouting her lower lip.

"Good evening," he said and pulled her free hand up to kiss it.

"The crowd is distinctly devoid of Englishmen."

"Many were sent to Brussels today," he replied as he indicated the dance floor. "Would you care for a waltz?"

"Of course."

As he led her to the floor, then pulled her close, she fit like a glove into his arms. They melted into the dance as though they were meant to be part of it, as though the music was written just for them. Philip was angry, but he would do his duty.

"Why is everyone removed to Brussels? Has something happened?" She looked up, her eyes so innocent and adoring.

How did she do that? She was a very skilled actress, he forced himself to admit. "Most of our troops are gathered in Brussels. Wellington sent those not needed here any longer to join them."

"And you shall accompany him to Vienna?"

"I have asked to do so, yes," he said, trying to remember what he was about. "I thought it was what you wanted. I am eager to meet your father." He smiled down at her, hoping he was portraying the appropriate sentiment, for even he did not know quite what that was.

"I have not yet heard back after announcing our betrothal."

"I assume your archduke would have related the information at once."

"Naturally," she answered carefully. "But there has been no reply."

"Ah. Are you afraid, my dear?"

"Of course not."

They danced the length of the floor and back before either spoke again. Philip found himself content to watch her, wondering what idea she might be hatching, for she was contemplating something. He would bet his life on it.

It was difficult to see beyond her beauty, much though Philip was ashamed to admit it, even though she was using it as a tool herself. He had done it himself in the past for information. Yet this time he'd been caught in the spider's web. She had counted on it. But he did not intend to let her feast on him.

"It is warm in here," he remarked. "I am going to stroll through the gardens."

"May I join you?"

"Of course. If your watchdog will allow it."

"We are betrothed. I am permitted a few more liberties now."

Philip no more believed that than he did she was allowed to

marry whoever, but he said nothing and escorted her outside. He did not want to compromise her and yet he had to find a way to discover what she was after. The longer this went on the harder it would be to avoid uncomfortable consequences.

They walked among some rose gardens in silence, save the sound of their dancing slippers crunching on the pebbled path and the stringed instruments escaping the ballroom.

"What is the matter, dearest?" he asked.

She laughed harshly. "You will think I am playing games with you."

"Perhaps," he admitted. "But you had best tell me."

"I do not wish to return to Vienna."

That was not what Philip expected to hear. He raised his brows and waited for her to elaborate.

"Can we not go to Brussels? Or remain here? It is so much more pleasant here." She looked off in the distance and he saw her chin began to tremble.

He had to harden his heart against this brilliant piece of acting. "I will not force you to do anything against your wishes," he replied. "But if my commander orders me to go, then I must."

"You must?" She turned and looked at him with surprise.

"Indeed. You have to realize I am merely a soldier, Pauline. Unless you fear for my safety, I have no objections to make that would be valid." He turned away trying to consider his next move.

"Am I not reason enough?"

"To me, yes of course, but to the Field Marshall of the Army? No." He turned back and she thrust herself in his arms and began to sob. Crying females were certainly not his forte. He wrapped his arms around her and held her to his chest. The one thing he had discovered was nothing he could say would make it stop any quicker. One thing was for sure, the tears were real, but what were they for? Certainly not for him.

CHAPTER THIRTEEN

B RUSSELS WAS CHARMING, and while built on a much smaller scale than Paris, Maria adored it. The town lay nestled inside a brick wall, with lush green countryside and surrounded by a mixture of tall forests and rolling hills of farmland, the latter dotted with quaint brick cottages and barns. The city square was an exquisite four-sided market-place, surrounded by seven guild houses built for seven dukes, the Town Hall, which boasted a Gothic tower, and a bread house which had humble origins, but was a four-storied marvel of balconies covered with tiered arches. The rest of the city was simpler yet equally charming, filled with slate-roofed, reddish-brown brick houses, as well as parks bursting with beautiful trees and bright flowers.

The only thing that was less than ideal were their accommodations. Captain Owens was looking for a larger lodging, but they had only been able to find a small set of rooms above another family in a terraced house that was small to begin with. Kate and Jack were all that was kind, but it was quite apparent she was *de trop*. It was a far cry from Wellington's hôtel in Paris.

Maria did her best to stay out of the newly wedded couple's way, but she prayed Captain Owens would be able to find something larger soon.

Kate had not been exaggerating when she had said London Society was flocking to Brussels. Apparently, with the Peninsular

War and the one against America currently splitting her forces, the costs in England were high and one could live far more economically in Brussels. Then there were those who did not want to miss any social occasion or excursion of pleasure. Since the largest portion of marriageable young men were quartered in the town with the army, it was a natural migration… much to Maria's chagrin, for it threatened her wish for anonymity.

Thus far, Maria had not attended any Society events. Once everyone was settled, she knew their small circle of officers' wives would at least visit one another. She did not know if there would be anything official, as in London or Paris, but for now she was content to walk in the park. Her thoughts and feelings were still in a state of torment. She expected she would have to face Colonel Strickland soon, and determined to speak with him about her family before he would be faced with the embarrassment of having to withdraw from an engagement.

As they walked through the park, the lovely scent of fresh baking filled the air and she sent Bisset across the street to purchase some fresh rolls. They had no luxury of Wellington's pastry chef here—only a very basic cook, as far as Maria could surmise.

"I will wait for you here," Maria said, gazing at the fountain. She was in no mood for conversation and was content to call her humor reflection, although those who knew her might call it melancholy.

The water trickled through the fountain, the sound soothing her as it always did. Since the season was growing colder, she did not permit herself the luxury of removing her glove and running her fingers through the spray. In all likelihood the fountain would soon be closed off for the winter, she thought sadly.

"Maria? Is that you?"

Maria turned to the familiar voice. It was Philip's mother, an elegant lady of near fifty years who still bore the signs of having been a rare beauty. "Lady Marsden," she said with pleasure. "What are you doing in Brussels?"

"Why, we came along with the rest of town, it seems. but I thought you were in Paris with Philip? He mentioned you in his last letters."

"We arrived just two days ago. I came with Captain Owens and his wife, but I believe Philip is to go to Vienna with Wellington."

"Oh dear, I was so hoping he would come here. Marsden told me Wellington would soon be sent to Vienna, but I persuaded him to bring me to Brussels anyway."

"I am happy to see a familiar face, ma'am."

"The three of you must come for dinner tonight and Captain Owens may tell Marsden the latest news."

"I am sure we would be delighted. I would invite you back for a cup of tea, but I am afraid our accommodations do not boast such luxuries." They could make tea, but they had no real servants.

The lady frowned. "Where are you staying, Maria? Is it horrid?"

"Oh no, ma'am, I did not mean to imply such a thing. It is merely small and we have the upper floor of a family's home."

Lady Marsden made a face of distaste.

"I am told this is quite common whilst the army is traveling. We did stay at Wellington's new hôtel in Paris and it was very beautiful. I enjoyed it very much." She hoped her cheeks did not betray just how much as she recalled the kiss with Philip.

"We have plenty of room. The three of you shall remove to our lodgings at once!" the marchioness proclaimed.

"Oh, my lady, that is quite unnecessary! Captain Owens is looking for a larger apartment." No sooner had the words left her mouth than Maria wished she might unsay them. Now what had she done?

Bisset returned then with Maria's purchases. Stopping when she saw who was speaking with her mistress, she dropped into a deep curtsy.

"I am glad to see you have not forgotten all the proprieties,

Maria. Now, take me back to your lodging so I might see for myself what indigencies you are suffering."

"Yes, my lady." There was no gainsaying Lady Marsden when she was decided on a course. Her mother would have been just the same.

She made a slight gesture of her head at Bisset, who understood the need to go ahead and warn Kate immediately. The maid quietly slipped away while Maria strolled in a more leisurely fashion with the marchioness.

"What were you doing here in the park alone, my lady?"

She sniffed at the question as though she did not wish to answer it. "I was merely taking a constitutional myself. We are staying in a house on the other side of the square."

Maria did not mention that their lodgings were not on the square, but the lady would see for herself in a few more minutes.

As they reached the house, Lady Marsden narrowed her gaze when Maria opened the door herself and led her up two flights of stairs to their humble rooms.

"Kate, look who I happened upon in the park."

"Your ladyship," Kate said as she curtsied. Thankfully, she appeared well this morning. "I am pleased to see you, again. Shall I make you some tea?"

Lady Marsden's look of dismay was comical. "No, I thank you. In fact, I have come to beg the three of you to stay with Marsden and myself. We have a large house, far larger than is needful for the two of us. You would be doing me a good turn. I would appreciate the company."

Kate looked at Maria, clearly a little shocked, but then she smiled.

"Maria said Captain Owens was looking for a larger establishment, and if I may not have Philip, then I consider Jack the next best thing. And of course, my dear Maria."

"I will need to ask Jack, of course. You are most generous, my lady," Kate answered.

She waved her hand as though it were a mere formality. "I

will send my carriage to collect your luggage," the Marchioness said, making to leave. "Maria, will you walk with me to my hôtel?"

"Of course, my lady." She smiled at Kate, along with a look of chagrin, behind Lady Marsden's back.

Once they were again in the street, Lady Marsden took Maria's arm. "Now, my dear, tell me about this woman who thinks to entrap my son?"

"The Archduchess Klementine?" Maria asked carefully.

"Indeed."

"She is very beautiful."

"As all his flirts have been," she said acidly. "But none have ever made him wax into ridiculousness as this *innamorata*."

Maria agreed, and she could hardly say what she really thought about the woman, could she?

"Tell me the truth about her. I trust your judgment completely, Maria."

"It is hard for me to say, ma'am. Philip is very dear to me and it is hard to consider anyone good enough."

"So she is a trollop! I knew it!"

"That is not what I said," Maria objected. "She is very elegant and refined."

"You do not need to defend her, my dear. A mother knows these things." She patted her arm. "But how to go about extricating him?" She pursed her lips and Maria tried not to groan. An interfering mama was not at all what Philip needed.

"Perhaps Marsden can persuade Wellington to send Philip here. That would be just the ticket."

Maria knew better than to argue, so she changed the subject. "Had you any word from Mama before you left? None of my letters have been answered."

"No, my dear, but Marsden called before we left. We went to check all was in order on the estate before leaving, you know."

"And?"

"And he was turned away."

"Gabriel says he would have heard if something were amiss."

"He is correct. They just need time to lick their wounds in private, as my sons would say."

Time. That was something the luxury of which Maria did not have.

PHILIP WAS NOT looking forward to asking Wellington to send him to Brussels. Even though Wellington knew it was necessary to go where Pauline went, he would not be pleased. He liked having his belongings ordered just so. He found the duke breakfasting alone.

"Good morning, sir." Entering the room, he filled a plate from the sideboard and took the seat to the right side of his commander.

"Well, Everleigh? Any new information?" A footman filled a cup of coffee for Philip.

"No, I am still trying to determine how to draw her out. However, she was adamantly opposed to returning to Vienna when last we spoke."

Wellington took a sip of his coffee, contemplating the information. "Does that mean she is acting on behalf of her father or behind his back?"

"It is curious," Philip agreed. "The news must surely have reached him by now."

"If it were intended to reach him," Wellington pointed out. "What do you think? I am fairly certain I will be required at the Congress. The Austrian minister is leaving by the week's end to preside over the Congress."

"I fear I do not follow, sir."

"He is the one who is hosting Pauline," Wellington reminded him.

"Perhaps she was unaware of the connection?"

"In which case, is it in our best interests to keep her away from Vienna?" Wellington asked.

"Maybe for now, while keeping the possibility open, but who would introduce her in Brussels?" Wellington was a brilliant strategist and while Philip would prefer to end the matter quickly, for his own personal reasons, there was much more at stake here.

"Good question. If you think it best to go on to Brussels for the sake of the operation, I will have Strickland return here. Had I known earlier, I would have kept Owens here in your stead."

"Thank you, sir. I will report this evening."

He stood to leave, then Wellington stopped him. "Oh, by the by…" He wiped his mouth with his napkin, put it on the table and then stood up. "I received a letter from your father with this morning's dispatches. It might be your answer."

Philip followed him into the office, where the Duke handed him the letter. Thanking Wellington, he at once read the first lines.

By the time you receive this we will, in all likelihood, have arrived in Brussels.

Philip cursed. "What possessed him to do such a thing?"

"Keep reading." Wellington was now sitting behind his desk and perusing other correspondence.

Philip hastily read through his father's familiar script.

…I assume you are aware of this betrothal, my lord duke? Does it meet with the court's approval? I confess, I am quite shocked. As to his mother, I have at least for the moment prevented her imminent arrival in Paris…

Philip looked heavenward with a muttered oath.

"Keep reading," Wellington ordered without looking up.

"It gets better?"

"Just so."

Since it seems London is leaving en masse to enjoy instead the entertainments provided by the soldiers garrisoned there, my Marchioness wishes to join them.

"Poor Maria!"

"Lady Maria?"

"Oh, indeed."

"Have I just sent her to the wolves?" Wellington asked.

"If what Father says is true, I fear it might be so."

"Then it should be a good thing your mother is there. Perhaps she may introduce your betrothed as well."

That much was true. His mother would protect Maria as much as she was able. Philip scanned the rest of the note, but the remaining lines were concerned with more administrative business from the War Office. He returned the paper to Wellington's desk and took his leave again, wondering why his parents had not written to him, and why they could not be pleased he had decided to marry. Never mind the fact the betrothal was a farce—they could have no notion of that!

He left the hôtel to visit Pauline and determine the next move, trying to swallow the bile seeping into him. If forced to go to Brussels, he would have to lie to his parents. Perhaps by now Pauline knew her uncle would be returning to Vienna, and would spare him that drama.

He would vastly prefer not to have her living under his parents' roof.

"Captain Everleigh for the Archduchess Klementine," Philip said as he entered the Austrian minister's residence and handed the butler his card. It was clear by the hive of activity within the house that it was no longer a secret von Metternich was leaving Paris.

He was shown to the same parlor where he had been interrogated by the archduke. Now he was allowed to sit alone, thankfully, but he could not keep from wondering what Pauline's plan would be, for he had little doubt that if she wished to avoid Vienna she would have a plan to do so.

He did not have to wonder for long.

"Philip!" She sailed into the room in her usual fashion, leaving him feeling as though he had been caught in a storm of muslin and perfume. He bowed and kissed her offered hand.

"We are leaving for Brussels in the morning!" she said with delight.

He tried to adopt an expression suitable for one who should be surprised. "I cannot say I am delighted. I thought your uncle was to lead the Congress?"

She waved a gloved hand in the air. "He is, but my aunt is not. She has heard Brussels is quite gay with society and wishes to go. Everyone seems to be leaving Paris."

"Everyone but me," he said, looking stern.

"I thought you intended to speak to Wellington and convince him to send you there?"

"I have told you before, I am not my own man. Unless I have an excellent reason to plead my case with him, I cannot do so. He believed himself to be doing me a good turn in thinking I would prefer to go to Vienna with you should that come to pass. He has already sent a staff to Brussels, and has himself not yet been deployed to the Congress."

Pauline pursed her lips in a pout. Perhaps this ploy would prevail and she would reveal something. Even a morsel of intelligence would be welcome at this point.

"We must think of something."

"I thought you would be pleased," Philip grumbled.

"But I told you I did not wish to return home just yet. Father will make me marry."

"Yes. Marry me—or did you not mean what you said?" He could not keep some of the anger from his voice.

"Of course I meant it! You do not understand."

"Then help me to. I thought, by meeting him and being in his presence, he would be more readily convinced. I cannot but think becoming betrothed without his permission is unlikely to win me any favor with him."

She remained quiet, studying the floral and paisley print on her gown. He waited for her to answer, now thinking of her as someone to interrogate, to draw information from. Silence was often the best tool. The seconds ticked by, yet he waited.

Finally, she gave a heavy sigh. She looked up and her eyes were pooled with tears. "My father does not know."

Philip kept any emotion from his face. He was a skilled card player because of this particular talent.

"Will you say something?" She slapped her hands down on her thighs.

"What do you wish me to say?" he demanded. "You have been toying with my affections and using me as a pawn in your games, but to what end?"

She shook her head and let the tears fall. "You misjudge me."

He turned away and walked to the window, his hands behind his back.

"Philip, please!"

"You will have to direct me on my next move, madam, since I am evidently your puppet to do with as you wish."

"That is not fair." He heard her rise and come up behind him. She put her hands on his arm and tilted her face to his. "You must trust me. I know I will be able to convince my father, but I need more time."

"Then why the need for the public display here in Paris? Are your aunt and uncle a party to this charade?" And Friedrich… was she also playing him in this manner or was he a party to the game? Or was she baiting them against each other for a scheme of her own? But what was that scheme?

She looked down. "I asked them not to say anything as yet. It was a select group at dinner that night if you recall. No one else would be communicating with my father."

"I see."

"Do you?" She looked up at him again, with the expression designed to bring men to their knees. Even while knowing what he did, he was not immune to it. How he wanted to believe her!

She cradled his cheek with her hand and brought her lips to his. "Will you speak to Wellington?"

"I can make no guarantees," he warned, "but I will promise to say nothing to your father should we meet in Vienna. For now."

CHAPTER FOURTEEN

I T HELPED TO be away from Colonel Strickland and Philip for a few days, Maria reflected, even though she was now living with his parents.

She had been given her own lovely chambers again, appointed with pastel shades and a view of the park, while Jack and Kate had rooms on the other side of the house.

Apparently, the residents of Brussels were only too happy to lease their homes to British aristocracy while they themselves spent the winter on the Mediterranean.

That sounded quite lovely to Maria—as opposed to attending an at-home Lady Marsden had planned for that afternoon. It would be her first real encounter with members of Society since her family had retired to the country after the scandal.

While it was likely no one would say anything to her face in Lady Marsden's presence, she had been in Society long enough to know those present would say plenty behind whispered hands and behind her back.

She dressed with less daring than she would have done in Paris, knowing she would be judged for every action. Selecting a jonquil muslin with Alençon lace, cut in one of the latest Parisian designs, she felt about as demure as she could be. Bisset wound a matching ribbon through her short curls and then she went downstairs to join Lady Marsden and Kate, who were both already in the drawing room.

Kate looked up and saw her face. "Do not worry, Maria. We will not allow anyone to say anything against you."

"I know, dearest, but you cannot stop their thoughts."

"No, that is true," Lady Marsden agreed. "But we can influence them." She looked Maria up and down, clearly viewing her toilette with approval. "You will do nicely."

"Thank you."

"Now, if anyone dares to bring it up, we will remind them that your brother was cleared of any wrongdoing. As far as I am concerned, your father did what most gentlemen would have done, even now."

"It does not make it right," Maria said quietly.

"Perhaps not, but you should not be judged for it."

Should and would were two very different things, but Maria refrained from saying so.

"The Duchess of Richmond will be here, and I know she and Lady Georgiana will also stand by you. If anyone dares to say aught against you they will find themselves without many invitations whilst in Brussels."

Despite Lady Marsden's assertion, the duchess was known to be quite volatile with her moods and whom she chose to bestow favor upon. Maria would not count on it, but having her Grace's approval would be welcome.

"Lady Capel and Lady Greville have also accepted the invitation and Mrs. Robinson, who is bringing out her eldest daughter this year."

Mrs. Robinson's family was one of the wealthiest in England. Certainly, they were not there to economize, unless either she or her husband had fallen prey to the epidemic of gambling.

The very select circle of ladies soon arrived and if they were surprised to see Kate and Maria there, they were tactful enough not to show it. Maria stayed between Kate and Lady Marsden while tea was poured and then served with some tiny cakes filled with melted lumps of pearl sugar, as well as chocolate confections molded into heart shapes and swirls.

"These are exquisite," Lady Greville said, biting into a cake. "What are these?"

"Gaufre de Liège, the chef calls them."

"We may always rely on Lady Marsden to steal a march on all of us," the duchess said. She was known to be one of the most competitive hostesses.

"Thankfully, the owners have left their chef and he informed me these are local specialties. When in Rome?" Lady Marsden held up one hand and smiled sweetly.

"You are newly arrived in Brussels, I take it?" the duchess asked abruptly, turning in the direction of Maria and Kate.

"Yes, we have come from Paris, Your Grace."

"Is that where your gown is from? You cannot buy anything like that in London," Lady Georgiana said in a mournful tone.

"I imagine there are some excellent modistes here, but I would be delighted to show you some of the designs," Maria said.

"How happy it is to know we might once again be able to attain such things," Lady Capel said.

"How did you find the society there?" Mrs. Robinson asked.

"Very grand," Kate answered. "It felt as though there were more balls than in London during the Season, if you can imagine. There were many diplomats present, from all over Europe."

"Will they come to Brussels soon as well?" Lady Georgiana asked hopefully.

"Perhaps some of them will, but many of them were removing to Vienna," Maria answered, trying to will the lump in her throat to go away.

"And how are your parents, Lady Maria? I am surprised to see you here, I confess," Lady Capel interposed.

"Lady Maria is here as my guest," Lady Marsden said in a pointed voice. "She is like a daughter to me. Her parents were well when we called before our departure."

"What is there to amuse oneself with here in Brussels?" Kate changed the subject, earning Maria's undying gratitude.

"Oh, there is so much to do!" Lady Georgiana answered, her face blooming with the excitement of being in the know. "There are as many balls and dinners as at the height of the Season at home, picnics on most afternoons, the men are off racing and hunting, and even the Prince of Orange attends us as if we were his own subjects!" She giggled.

"Lord Lyndoch gave a fête for the Prince in the Forêt de Soigny. 'Twas really delightful!" Georgy gushed. "The party was very large and agreeable, the day quite lovely and, you must know, the scenery was beautiful." She looked around the circle of ladies and smiled with satisfaction that she had their full attention. "Tents were pitched and the Band of the 52nd played during breakfast, and horn music was placed at a distance which vibrated through the Forest," she added with relish. "I never saw a more animated scene or a more Motley Group, consisting of Ladies, brilliant Uniforms of various Colors, Hussars attendant upon the General officers, Peasants and 'Sprigs of gentility' from the Village of Soigny."

"I am sorry to have missed such a spectacle!" Lady Marsden said, appropriately impressed.

"How long do you intend to stay in Brussels, my lady?" Maria asked Lady Marsden. She did not feel quite comfortable initiating conversation with anyone else, even though she had known them for quite some time and all those present had been friends with her family socially. At least, they had before…

Lady Marsden waved a flippant hand. "I suppose for as long as it amazes me to be here. Marsden had some business here in any case, so it seemed a good idea to visit. Perhaps we shall see Philip as well."

"Do you think the army will remain here once the treaties are signed?" Lady Capel asked.

"March does not seem to think they will not make an immediate return. With so many of our regiments away in America, they will not want to give anyone the upper hand here," the duchess answered.

"I like it here very much. It is warmer and does not rain quite so much," Miss Robinson remarked shyly.

"If only they could have been so agreeable as to garrison themselves further south," Lady Capel added sardonically.

"It would have been considerably less convenient to travel so far!" the duchess retorted.

"Not everyone travels with three dozen servants!" Lady Capel quipped bravely.

"And a dozen children to boot!" the duchess added in rare good humor.

Maria believed the number was thirteen, the last she had heard, but supposed the Earl of March could hardly be considered a child.

"Did I hear a rumor that Wellington would be leaving Paris for Vienna?" Lady Greville asked.

"That is where they are to hold the Congress to sign the peace agreements. Castlereagh is there for now."

The butler entered the room, walked over to Lady Marsden and spoke in a quiet voice only she and Maria could hear. "A Colonel Strickland has called for my Lady Maria," he said.

For an instant, Lady Marsden looked at Maria with surprise in her eyes, then hid it well almost at once.

Maria gave a slight nod. They had not yet discussed the situation, but word would soon spread that he had called, and she was ready now to face the reckoning, after agonizing over it for days.

She stood up. "Will you please excuse me, ladies? A friend has called and perhaps has news of my brother." She wanted to offer him an excuse should he wish to escape.

They murmured their consent, not masking their curiosity. Maria hurried away from the wolves, but not before she heard Lady Greville say, "Strickland? He must be unaware. Someone had better warn him away."

PHILIP RODE ON to Brussels the next morning, carrying dispatches as an excuse to ride on his own. He needed two hundred miles to clear his head and to plot out the various possibilities which might happen.

He also wished to speak to his parents alone. He did not imagine the conversation would be pleasant and he needed to decide how much information to give them. Part of him still strongly desired for this to be a misunderstanding – that somehow he could still have Pauline—yet he knew in his heart that the odds were not in his favor.

After two hard days of riding, he was pleased to pass through the Soigny forest and then on through the Namur gate into the city.

He had been to Brussels once before, on a scouting trip with Wellington. He enjoyed the simplicity and forthrightness of the Bruxellois, who he feared, from the reports he had read, were a little shocked by the English. If Society had truly removed itself to the city for the nonce, then he could only imagine what it would be like. There had been reports of gambling, races and hunts—on top of the more harmless balls, parties and picnics.

All of which was only to be expected when the entire British army was garrisoned there and drink was cheap. Part of what Wellington had commissioned him with was to report back on whether training was still being accomplished despite the immoderate pastimes. Wellington understood the need for gaiety, but he also understood tired soldiers were less ill-behaved soldiers.

He returned in his mind to the problem of Pauline; he had decided to dig into her father's connections and business dealings. There had to be something more under the surface that would explain her need to do something as a rash as betrothing herself to a foreigner without her father's permission.

Philip suspected that perhaps there was treason involved. There usually was. But was her father simply conducting business for greater gain or to garner favor with Napoleon, or were there revolutionist loyalties to the cause? That seemed unlikely, her father being royalty himself, but stranger things had happened in history.

Philip's own father would be one of the best people to help him, but were he to tell his sire, he would have to confide his suspicions. Why was it hardest to confess one's shortcomings to those one respected most? Wellington had been bad enough, but Philip's father would be even harder. He supposed he deserved that.

Maria would tell him he was being ridiculous. He smiled despite the heaviness in his heart at the thought of her. She should have received his letter. Would she have forgiven him by now?

Dear Maria. She would never think of betraying him like Pauline. Her heart was as pure as fresh snow.

He slowed to a trot as he considered her. Never would he have guessed she could cause a physical reaction in him. She had always been like a sister…yet she was not.

When he stopped at the British headquarters to deliver his dispatches, a friendly face greeted him.

"Oh, Captain Jack. I knew we could not stay apart long." He leaned against the doorframe as he spoke.

Jack looked up with a grin. "Fancy seeing you here. I thought you were headed to Vienna. This is not exactly on the way, you know."

"Matters have changed. Pauline wished to come to Brussels."

Jack raised his brows, but Philip gave a slight shake of his head. There were too many ears to hear and he would explain later.

"I should have known you would turn up. Kate calls you my army husband. What am I supposed to think of that?"

Philip laughed. "I think it means we like each other and we spend too much time together."

"As to the former, I suppose so. As to the latter, most assuredly."

Philip dropped the parcel of dispatches on Jack's desk. "I hear my parents are in town."

"They are, along with half of London," Jack retorted.

"Where are their lodgings? I should pay my respects."

Jack began to laugh.

"Kindly apprise me of the joke," Philip said disapprovingly.

"Kate, Maria and I are all billeted with your parents! There are no decent lodgings left in the entire city. Why, according to your mother, even Richmond had to take a place on the undesirable side of town."

Philip would have been shocked, but he knew his mother too well. "Managing females," he muttered.

"Just so, but I was not going to be the one to say nay to your mama."

"Therein lies the problem. No one will! Even Wellington is afraid of her."

Jack answered with one of his comical expressions which involved a single raised eyebrow.

Philip slumped into a chair, not in quite the hurry he had been before. "How is Maria?" he asked quietly. He needed to know if she had said anything.

"Lady Marsden has taken her under her wing, as would be expected in such circumstances. She used it as part of her reasoning to inveigle us under her roof. Not that our accommodations were quite acceptable for a married couple and a companion, but they were luxurious when compared to many of our accommodations in the past."

"Understood."

"Not that Kate or Maria complained, mind you."

No, Philip could not see either of them doing such a thing.

"The house your parents have let has a much finer prospect over the park and a walled garden. Maria likes to spend a great deal of time outdoors. 'Tis number twenty—on the street opposite."

"That she does," Philip agreed.

"As far as Maria is concerned, I do not believe she has faced any difficulty as yet, although your mother was receiving some Society ladies this afternoon."

Philip looked at his pocket watch. He ought to go and show his support, he thought, placing his hands on his knees to rise. "Is there any news on the diplomatic front?"

"Is that a sly way of asking if there has been some revelation regarding a certain archduke?" Jack whispered loudly.

Philip looked at the ceiling with exasperation. "It was not sly and you have never needed an explanation before."

"Well, I do know that Strickland was to arrive from Ghent today. He is, most likely, the man you need to speak with."

"Strickland is coming here?" Why did the name taste like dirt in his mouth? It was nonsense, of course, for him to be jealous, but he knew that the colonel had never kissed Maria and he had. What did that mean? "If you see him before I do, then please let him know I wish to speak with him. Wellington wanted him to replace me."

"Aye, aye, Captain." Jack saluted him in his mocking way.

With a shake of his head, Philip departed. He left his horse to rest in the stables, under the care of the army grooms, but retrieved his saddle-bags and walked across the park. He regretted the fact he would arrive in his mother's drawing room in all his dirt, but it could not be helped.

Maria would once again be staying under the same roof as he. It could be a blessing or a curse. He would not want his presence to cause her discomfort in any way.

His parents had found a large brick house overlooking the park, just opposite the army headquarters. He hated to think how his parents had come by such a place, but at least they were one family not in need of economizing and Brussels was far less expensive than England at the moment.

He was greeted by their butler, Percy, whom he was not surprised in the least to find in Brussels. His mother had doubtless brought a good part of her household from home, the better to entertain with.

"Lord Philip." Percy bowed. "May I say I am delighted to see you, my lord? Was her ladyship expecting you?"

"No, it was a very last minute change in my plans. Is she holding some sort of party?"

"Indeed, sir. She is entertaining several ladies at this very moment."

Now that he was here, Philip hesitated and debated whether or not to interrupt. He had just decided to see if Maria needed rescuing, when he overheard her voice across the hall.

"Is that Lady Maria?" he asked Percy.

"Yes, my lord. A Colonel Strickland has called for her." He held out a hand, indicating where they were.

"Thank you. I will announce myself."

Percy bowed and left him alone. He stood in front of the wooden door leading to the parlor where Maria was greeting Strickland. It was ajar, as was proper, but Philip did not know what to do. He had no wish to enter a drawing room full of ladies when the purpose for so doing was not in that room.

He closed his eyes and stood there with indecision. Was Strickland proposing? He had no business interrupting, yet he needed to speak with the man. He would simply have to wait.

He sat in the fauteuil chair in the marbled entrance hall, and could not help but listen. Eavesdropping was part of his profession and it was hard to block out the words.

"I was not expecting to have the pleasure of seeing you here," Strickland said. "I was delighted when Captain Owens gave me the news this morning."

"I trust your visit to Ghent was all that you hoped?" Maria asked.

"It was useful, yes. I must spend the afternoon writing reports, unfortunately. However, I did wish to speak with you. I have had a great deal of time to think this week."

Philip sat up at his tone. It certainly was not amorous.

"You have heard about the scandal, then."

Strickland did not say any words – he must have made a gesture.

"I do not blame you if you wish to distance yourself from me, sir. It had not occurred to me that you had not heard of it, but then you could not have heard. Forgive me if you feel misled."

"I believe this will pass, Lady Maria."

"Good day to you sir," Maria said hastily.

Philip stood quickly, fearing she would catch him loitering. Maria ran from the room and almost straight into him. He caught her and looked down into her eyes; they were trying to hold back tears.

"Philip? I must go," she said hurriedly and at once ran away.

Philip let her leave; he would speak with her later. But first, he must speak with Strickland and in a professional manner when, unfortunately, he wanted to plant him a facer instead.

CHAPTER FIFTEEN

PHILIP WAS HERE? Maria stopped and moved out of sight behind a corner beyond the stairs. She could not go back into the drawing room, yet he would see her if she went towards the stairs. How much had he heard? Based on the look of pity he gave her, it had clearly been enough.

Strickland had acted in the manner she had expected. How silly of her to think her family's disgrace had not mattered to him! Perhaps he had written of his intentions to his family and they had forbidden it. In the polite world, alliances were made or broken by such considerations. She had always thought the maxim "being punished for the sins of the fathers" to be ridiculous. Now she was living it.

The worst part was that she felt her pride to be damaged more than her feelings. It was one of the most lowering moments she had ever experienced. Perhaps he would have followed through, but she had given Strickland an opportunity and he had taken it. No doubt it was for the best. Maybe it would be better to be a spinster than to settle for something simply adequate.

Having left the little parlor in which her humiliation had taken place, she stopped and took slow, deep breaths to calm herself. That was when she heard Philip speaking with Strickland. It would have been too much to hope Philip would not speak with the gentleman. Would he defend her?

"You are the very man I was hoping to see, sir," Philip was saying.

"Would this be about Lady Maria?"

"Actually, it is a matter of business, but now that you mention it, may I enquire…if you have withdrawn your suit?"

The Colonel hesitated with a long pause. "Not precisely. I have a great admiration for Lady Maria and had I been able to discover Lloyd's whereabouts before my trip to Ghent, I would have sought his permission. However, I was not aware of what had occurred with Mottram, and thus Lady Maria and I have agreed to wait a while longer for the scandal to settle."

Was that what they had done? That was not what Maria had heard or felt or agreed upon.

"I see." Philip's voice indicated he did no such thing. He cleared his throat. "I care very deeply for Lady Maria and want what is best for her."

Maria's heart gave a squeeze on hearing those words. If only she had the beauty to hold his attention, she thought sadly.

"As do I," Strickland said.

There was another uncomfortable pause.

"I have left a dispatch for you from Wellington. He requests you to replace me in Paris. Perhaps that is for the best now, especially since you were rather pointed in your attentions to her there."

"I cannot deny it. My wish is not to hurt her."

"Indeed. I hope it will not." Now it sounded as though Philip was pacing up and down. Footfalls sounded with a lighter tread than Maria associated with the Colonel. "I also wanted to ask something of a more discreet nature."

Maria's ears perked up. She knew she should not be listening, but she could hardly betray herself now and expose the fact that she had overheard the entire conversation.

"With regards to Austria, have you any suspicions in that

quarter? Anything at all?"

One of the gentlemen's boots cut across the floor as if they were doing so methodically with their thoughts.

"Nothing obvious, of course, or it would have been remarked upon before."

"Something has given us a reason to cause suspicion, but we have no possible connection or evidence as yet. His Grace has asked me to make discreet inquiries. Who from their contingent was present in Ghent?"

"Baron von Wessenberg, and he was returning directly to the opening of the Congress. Do you suspect a plot?"

"Thus far there are but some inconsistencies and untruths."

Maria smothered a gasp of surprise. What had happened?

"You may not have heard that the archduchess and I have become betrothed. You can see why it is a matter of great importance that I investigate this matter fully before any official arrangements go ahead…especially if it could involve treason."

"I understand perfectly. Is there anyone in particular you wish for knowledge of?"

"Anything to do with the House of Klementine or its direct associates."

Maria heard a few more of the clicking steps across the parquet floor.

"Does something touch a chord?" Philip asked.

"Nothing I would take an oath on, but I do seem to recall a royal nephew or some such being a revolutionist."

"Hmm. That could take many forms. I wonder if this is the cousin who is heir to Pauline's father. It would explain some things, but not what the current plot is."

"I will consider it as I ride to Paris and send word if I remember anything else. There are others in a position to know whom I will ask. They may remember more than I," Strickland said.

"I am grateful to you, sir," Philip said and it sounded as though they might be shaking hands. "Godspeed on your journey."

A few more clicks of some boots sounded, as though Strickland was heading to the door. Instinctively, Maria held herself closer to the wall, but there was no reason for him to come in this direction, away from the front door.

"Oh, and Everleigh? I know you will take care of Lady Maria, but please know I care for her deeply. If anyone should talk…"

"I will do my best," came the terse reply. Then she heard the entrance door close as Colonel Strickland departed.

A fist slammed down hard on something, coupled with an oath at Strickland. Maria jumped with surprise.

Without thinking, she turned and walked back into the parlor where Philip now stood. He was leaning on the back of a chair with his head down.

"Philip?" He turned and looked at her over his shoulder. Then, with an expression of raw pain in his eyes, he turned and held his arms open. Without thinking any more about it, she stepped into the embrace. His arms came about her and she instantly relished being surrounded by his warmth once more—something she had not thought possible to feel again.

"Am I forgiven, pet?"

"Yes, but not because of your horrid excuse for apology."

He chuckled, and she felt a deep rumbling in his chest against her cheek.

"Not that I accept an apology where none was needed, mind you."

"I was not sure if you had received it yet."

"Yes, Jack made certain of that. I had not thought to see you again so soon."

"Circumstances changed rather suddenly."

"Has something happened with the archduchess?"

"You have been listening around corners again? You are the most complete baggage."

She nodded against his chest, ignoring the second part of his remark. "I had not meant to eavesdrop, but I was caught in the hall and was not sufficiently composed to return to the drawing room."

He gave a murmur of understanding. "I still wish you had not heard all of that."

Reluctantly, she stepped back from his embrace. It would be difficult not to make a fool of herself again while he was holding her.

"If you are regarding the parting of Colonel Strickland and I, then that is for the best."

"Your heart is not injured?" The look of concern he studied her with near undid the fragile composure she had achieved.

"'Twas more my pride that was injured, I fear, but you know as well as I that Society can be cruel and unjust."

"I do think he will come about, but it may take longer than you wish."

"I do not wish, Philip. I hardly want a man who has to 'come about,' as you say, in order to have me."

"I did not mean it that way. I meant that he still wants you… which is more than I can say for my own situation." He ran his hands through his hair, causing him to look more handsome in his dishevelment.

"What has happened?"

"I wish I knew. After learning how she had kissed another man, I confronted her."

Maria did not point out that they had also kissed in such a manner, but at the memory her body reacted with a flush to her cheeks.

"I did not mention the kiss, but she was hesitant to return to Vienna, so I used it as an excuse to ask her if she was toying with me."

His face told her many of the words he was not saying. He was hurt.

"Did she admit as much?" Maria had misjudged the strength of his feelings, if that were the case.

"Of course not. She had a reason – an excuse – for every-thing."

"You still have hope of her?" When next she saw the woman, Maria would find it difficult not to choke her for leading Philip around by the collar.

"I have spoken at length with Wellington. We both believe there is something amiss, but must tread cautiously."

"And you are a man of honor and are therefore obligated."

He inclined his head and she could tell he was debating whether or not to say more. She knew he still wanted the archduchess, and that what was the bitterest pill of all to swallow.

Maria vowed to do something to help him see the archduchess for what she really was. Perhaps he already did, but if she could find a way for them to separate without Philip compromising his honor, that would at least keep him out of a ruinous marriage—one where he would be toyed with. Indeed, on one sentiment she agreed entirely with Lady Marsden; Philip needed to be extricated.

Hopefully, Maria reflected with sadness, his heart would heal in time.

⇶⇶⟫⟨⇷⇷

THE RELIEF PHILIP had felt while holding Maria in his arms had been a balm to his battered soul. Her familiar scent of orange blossom soap wafted through his senses in a peaceful and comfortable way, a notion he did not attribute in any way to Pauline.

Why had he not told Maria the whole truth? Would he tell his father the truth?

Certainly, it would be easier for people to participate in the charade if they believed in the betrothal. Yet for some reason he wanted to tell Maria everything.

He needed to return to Headquarters, but first he needed to wash and remove his road dirt and then greet his parents. Perhaps his mother's callers would be gone by then.

He returned downstairs about an hour later, when Percy informed him that his father had returned and was in the study. Headquarters would have to wait, he thought dourly.

"Philip!" his father boomed, smiling and rising from his leather armchair to greet him. "Percy told me you had arrived. I must say I didn't expect to see you immediately."

"Wellington and I thought it would be the best move, considering the current state of affairs."

His father understood instantly. He walked over to a cabinet, poured himself a drink and held up a second glass to ask if Philip would like one. At Philip's nod, he brought them across to two chairs flanking the fire and joined him as Philip sat down.

Without troubling to spare his own indignity, Philip wasted no time in explaining the facts to his parent, who listened without interrupting.

The only part Philip omitted was kissing Maria. He still did not understand that part and did not wish to taint Maria's name in any way, especially with his parents. Secretly, he thought they had always wished for a match in that quarter. Who would not want Maria for a daughter?

"First, I shall give you my professional thoughts. The House of Klementine was under suspicion during the beginning of the Peninsular Wars. Your betrothed's father cleared his name, however, supposedly by ferreting out the source within his own family. I do not recall exactly who it was but a brother or cousin, I believe."

"Strickland also believed there was something in the past but could not remember anything specific. Is this all from memory or did you take it upon yourself to investigate when you received my letter?"

"I investigated as a matter of course."

"And is the Klementine family now in his Majesty's good graces?"

"Reports did not indicate if that is now the case or not."

"I wonder if knowing who the person was would matter

now. Somehow I think it will."

"I will try to discover more. But do you believe you were specifically targeted or a means of opportunity? What are the pair trying to accomplish, do you suppose?"

"I wish I could answer that. When I look back, it seems as though it was chance. Pauline could not have known I would be there that night."

"Perhaps she was simply waiting for the right opportunity." He set down his glass. "Let us consider what we do know." He held up one finger. "She forced an Englishman into a betrothal." Another finger went up. "She is betrothed to an Austrian cousin of hers, of whom her father approves and she seems enamored."

"We assume."

"Yes. We assume." A third finger joined the others. "She is avoiding Vienna and wants the betrothal to remain secret from her father." Finger number four. "There is a possible history of disfavor in her family." He looked directly at Philip. "If you were looking at this objectively, what would you tell one of your colleagues?"

"One could surmise she needs information to prove something, mayhap, or to continue what was begun before."

"Vindication?" Lord Marsden asked. "Or revenge?"

"Why me?" Philip slammed his glass on the side table.

"I would suppose, if she wanted to pry information out of a close source to Wellington, you would be the most believable choice for the rumored greatest beauty of her time to favor with her attention."

"Thank you, sir—I think," Philip answered dryly. That was some small comfort. "What do you advise I do?"

"Continue with her game for now, but be very, very wary. We will continue to dig for more specific answers and perhaps even dangle some bait to see what entices her to bite."

"I was afraid you would say that." Philip leaned his head back and stared at the smoke-blackened wooden cross beams in the low ceiling.

"As a father, however, my answer would be to run in the opposite direction as fast as you can. Her history is akin to that of a poisonous spider. She traps men like insects and drinks the lifeblood from them."

Philip tried not to wince outwardly at the severe analogy.

"Now begun, I am afraid you must see it through. Perhaps even a betrothal ball may answer the purpose if it is to be announced publicly. Anyone who knows your mother would find it odd were she not to host one."

"That could force the lady in question's hand—especially if she thought to contain such a falsehood within Paris. Brussels substantially widens the circle of our acquaintance… which brings me to my next question. Why did you come? It is only happenstance that I was able to come to Brussels."

His father scratched his forehead. "Your mother read your letter and was less than pleased."

"She who has been after me to marry this past decade," he murmured under his breath.

"Mothers wish for their sons to be married happily. Even she has heard of the infamy of this woman."

Philip swore. He hoped Pauline would arrive and prove them all wrong. "I do not think she is poisonous, as you believe, but having Mother already against her will not help in the quest to discover her purpose."

"We cannot have it both ways, but I will beg her not to make her distaste a matter of public concern. She will be offended that I say anything of the sort, of course; then will claim a lady knows better than to display her true feelings in public and that she most certainly *does not* make scenes."

Philip smiled. It was just what his mama would say.

"When does the Austrian contingent arrive?"

"I left before they did, so I surmise we have another day at the least, two at the most."

His father nodded and took a sip of his drink.

"Can you tell me how Lord Mottram does? Maria mentioned

she had had no reply to her letters."

His father's face took on a grave look. "Your mother and I called when we went to visit Marsden Park. They would not see us."

"You are sure they were at home?" Philip found it hard to believe they would refuse their oldest friends.

"The butler did not even attempt to play games with us. In fact, he seemed concerned and relieved that we had called."

"And are rumors still rife in town?" Philip asked.

"At first they were what you would expect. Some of the Whigs wanted blood, but most of the Tories stood by him, agreeing it had not been his place to interfere. But you know how public humiliation is. It is hard to recover from such a blow."

Philip did know. "Was anything further said about Major Lloyd?"

"Not much. It is unfortunate Newsom made those accusations in such a public manner, but we have been able to dismiss them as the ravings of a lunatic trying to place the blame on an innocent party."

"False accusations could happen to anyone."

"Nevertheless, his silence does not help his career or his sister. Have you seen much of Maria?"

"Indeed I have. There were several gentlemen interested in courting her. Strickland has been paying her marked attention and all of us were waiting in daily expectation of an offer."

"You speak in the past tense, I notice. What happened?"

"He received a warning from his parents in response to his letter announcing his intent. He had thought they would be pleased. Fortunately, nothing formal had been announced."

"Did he not know about the scandal before?"

"As fantastic as it sounds, apparently he did not. He told her he was still very interested, but he needed time for the situation to quieten."

"Poor Maria. She deserves none of this."

"And now that half of Town is in Brussels, I fear it will not improve," Philip growled.

"We will do everything we can to support her."

"I know. That will help."

"The Duchess of Richmond has also agreed to foster Maria's cause. She was here earlier and pledged her support."

"Was she, now? Lady Georgiana will also stand friend to Maria. Thankfully, Strickland was leaving for Paris to replace me. Having him here would have made matters worse."

"And see you pay attention to the gal. That always seems to help. Not that Maria is unattractive, mind you. I have no idea why she accepted none of the offers she had before."

"She needed no help attracting gentlemen in Paris." *Including me*, Philip thought, but did not say. "She chose to reinvent herself a little, being out from under her mother's thumb."

"I have not yet had the pleasure of witnessing the transformation," her father remarked.

The dinner bell sounded. "It looks as though you will now have the chance, sir."

CHAPTER SIXTEEN

MARIA NO LONGER knew what she believed anymore. So much of what she had always felt most strongly about seemed no longer in black and white. Apparently there were many shades between the two, and decidedly she did not like gray. It was disconcerting to say the least.

Had she shared this level of intimacy with Philip at any time before, she would have allowed herself false hope. She had done so for years, had she not? But now that Colonel Strickland had rejected her and Philip was betrothed, it was though her heart were slowly dying. There was no hope, and she knew it.

Fortunately, they had no engagements this evening, so she wore one of her Parisian gowns which she would not dare to wear around the disapproving matrons of Society.

It might be a while before she had the chance to dress like this again – if ever. Even though Colonel Strickland had said he might still have her, she did not believe he was anything but thankful for his lucky escape. Now she was hardly in a position to turn down any respectable offer.

Maria laughed to herself when she thought of the vicar from *Pride and Prejudice*. She did not think herself quite ready to fall on the sword for a Mr. Collins... most definitely she preferred spinsterhood to one such as he.

Even though she teased Kate for the amount of reading she

did – she had, in fact, forced Maria to take turns with her in reading aloud on the journey to France—Maria somehow felt that the authoress understood her. Certainly, she was not the most dashing of females, nor the biggest catch on the marriage mart, thanks to her family's scandal, but somehow she still held on to that little shred of hope that she was worthy of someone who cared for her.

A knock on her door caused her to jump and realize she had been staring out of the window, lost in thought.

"One moment!" she called, rushing to the door to find Philip standing there.

"Have I kept everyone waiting? I do apologize."

She stepped out into the hall and took the arm he offered.

"You are not late. I was walking past your chamber and thought to see if you were ready."

"I am always early. I was wool-gathering while I waited," she admitted, giving him a sheepish smile.

Philip looked her over from head to toe. Maria felt herself blush. No one had ever looked at her like that. She now questioned whether the clinging crushed velvet without a fichu was a wise choice.

"You look very well, Maria. That color becomes you."

"Thank you. I imagine I will be relegated to my mother's choice of gowns again shortly. I thought to have one last night of freedom."

"Do you believe you must dress like a demure maiden to gain their approval?" he asked, clearly not pleased with the notion.

"Of course I must. Surely you must understand I am hardly in a position to be daring?"

"The stuffy matrons who decide what should be worn should be drawn and quartered. If they are trying to attract husbands, they are mistaken. Such fripperies and furbelows do the very opposite."

Maria could not but laugh. "You are quite abominable."

"I am truthful," he corrected. "Young girls are already at a disadvantage by being taught to be silly, and then they are dressed like a doll with flounces and lace which makes most men of my acquaintance run as fast as they may in the other direction."

"How is a lady to make a match, then?"

"You must prove your worth through some other means, unless you have a large enough dowry that your suitor will overlook flaws of character."

"I have always suspected as much, but such are the rules."

"I should very much like to rewrite these rules you speak of."

"So would I," she said with a heavy sigh. "The thought of wearing one of the ruffled pastel gowns my mother selected makes me grow pale."

"Then do not do it."

They had reached the drawing room. Philip stopped and turned to look at her. "Maria, please do not hide yourself. If anyone takes offense because of your beauty or the color of your gown, then they do not deserve you."

Oh, dear, dear Philip. "How I wish it were the case."

"There is nothing you could do that would be truly scandalous. Even in the cut of your gown that you think fast, you do not appear half as daring as Pauline, in the toilettes she wears!" There was anger in his voice. She could hug him for coming to her defense.

"Philip, you must know that no one would condemn her, because she has the title and beauty to carry it off. Instead, they look at me and think I am trying too hard." She laughed with self-deprecation and looked down at her beautiful gown. "And now I sound like a self-pitying fool."

He lifted her chin and bent down towards her. She could feel his breath on her cheek. "You have as much beauty as she. Do not let anyone ever make you feel otherwise."

Maria could feel emotion boiling within, her throat already tightening in the effort to hold it back.

"Philip? Is that you?" Lady Marsden peered around the door. Philip stepped back. "Yes, Mother. Maria and I were discussing something."

She raised a querying brow. "Something important, I gather. Come, join us."

Maria took a steadying breath. Now, what would Lady Marsden think of her?

Philip took her arm and leaned down to whisper in her ear. "Smile, pet. 'Tis only friends and family tonight."

"Thank God," Maria muttered as they entered the room.

"Is that my little lady?" Lord Marsden asked, a bit too loudly, from across the drawing room. "Why, Philip was right! You do look fetching! He said you were attracting all the gentlemen in Paris."

Philip had said that about her? To his father?

"You have been hiding your light under a bushel, eh?" he continued, and Maria could feel her cheeks burning like fire.

"Stop embarrassing her, Father," Philip scolded as he handed her a glass of sherry.

"Maria is like a daughter to me. I think she knows I mean no harm."

"Of course, sir." She managed a shy smile at him.

"Maria had a caller today," Lady Marsden announced. "Colonel Strickland."

"Ingram's eldest? That would be an excellent match."

"He is not my suitor, I am afraid." Maria decided she had best address any false hopes before they became out of hand. She had not yet had the opportunity to explain what had occurred to her ladyship.

Kate and Jack walked into the room at that very moment and overheard.

"What is this about Strickland?" Captain Owens asked. "I thought he intended to ask for your hand?"

Maria could only be grateful the company was confined to friends and family that night. Nevertheless, it did not lessen her humiliation.

"He heard about the scandal and has decided now would not

be the time to declare an engagement," Maria said, in barely more than a whisper.

"Oh, dear. That was not well done of him, then, to court you so openly in Paris." Kate frowned.

"Do not blame him. It is my fault. I thought he knew."

"You are too generous, Maria," Kate muttered her disgust.

"Thank goodness he has already left for Paris. I do not think I could be civil if I met him in public," Jack added.

The support her friends were showing her almost made the situation harder, but she loved them for it nonetheless. "I do not think things will be easier here, and I certainly do not wish to put a damper on anyone else's enjoyment. Perhaps it would be for the best if I returned home."

"Nonsense!" Lady Marsden interjected. "You know the best way to deal with scandal is to face it head-on."

Not hide away in the country as her parents had? It seemed an attractive option at the moment, as opposed to being discussed under her nose like an infectious boil that needed treatment.

"It will still not solve the issue—not if the rumor spreads that I have been jilted. It will only make things worse."

"There was never a betrothal, was there? You were wise to say earlier the colonel was bringing news of your brother. And you did not behave like a goose by mooning over him in front of the ladies today."

"There were too many people in Paris. Word will soon spread." Maria was a realist. It took very little fact to set tongues to wagging.

"We can make certain none of the officers will say anything," Jack offered.

It was all too much. She shook her head and was grateful when they went into the dining room. Not that she had much of an appetite, but she hoped that the conversation would steer away from her and her problems. Her wish appeared to be granted, until they began to speak about the one thing which pained her even more.

"When is this archduchess arriving?" Lady Marsden asked, not masking her distaste.

"Tomorrow, I expect, Mother."

"So soon?" she asked with an unladylike scowl.

"She is my betrothed. You could try to be a little more pleased," Philip remarked dryly.

"Mayhap you could throw a ball for them. You are always looking for reasons to host something or other," Lord Marsden said as he cut into his fillet of beef.

"It would be nice to host a ball here in Brussels, but must it be a betrothal ball? I have not even met her."

Maria watched the interchange, feeling very much in sympathy with the marchioness and wondering how she could endure much more.

PHILIP WAS IN no mood for pretense that morning, yet he had just received word that Pauline and the Austrian entourage had arrived in Brussels. She had summoned him to ride with her that afternoon, in a surprise note handed to him by Percy. There was to be a review of troops and she wanted to watch. It was a popular pastime amongst the civilians in the town to watch the troops train, so he supposed it was harmless enough.

Methodically, he dressed in his uniform, thinking through all the past meetings and conversations, wondering what he had missed. What did she want? Quite likely, the key was something to do with the previous plots on her family's name, but what could that have to do with him? The only two possibilities he could ferret out were that she wanted to pass information on to a traitor or she somehow thought to clear her family name and restore favor to someone. But whom? And how would it help to betroth herself to him?

There were no possible secrets he could know to help her. In fact, with the current peace and pending treaties, there was a decided lack of information being passed anywhere.

Could it be something to do with those treaties? It was certainly a possibility to consider, but again, how did she think he could help her?

Having gathered his hat and sword, he went downstairs. His father and Jack were in the breakfast room.

"The very gentlemen I wanted to see," he said, by way of greeting.

"Not something I hear every day," Jack quipped.

A footman poured him some coffee, then his father signaled for the servants to depart.

"What is it, son?"

"Is there something of hidden import taking place at the Congress?"

The marquess wiped his whiskered mouth with his napkin and set it down. "Besides the redefining of boundaries, do you mean?"

"Will that affect Austria?" Philip asked. "I am aware it will create the Kingdom of the Netherlands, returning France's recent gains."

"They stand to gain a great deal of territory, as do Prussia and Russia."

Philip threw up his hands. "I have racked my brains but I cannot think of what she is after. She cannot think I have any influence over Austrian boundaries!"

"Perhaps it has less to do with Austria than something more personal," Jack suggested.

"Go on." Philip looked up.

Jack shrugged one shoulder. "Perhaps I am wrong and she is a highly trained spy, but I suspect this has more to do with her affections than her political views."

"You think the traitor was the archduke? That this was all a ruse for him?"

"I find that more likely," Jack confessed. "I cannot puzzle out how your involvement helps, but it is a feeling."

"Your notions are usually correct," Philip drawled.

"Much though you hate to admit it," Jack teased.

"I am inclined to agree with Owens. I do not think there is political treason involved this time. It makes no sense."

"I agree, if she used me as a lure, but then why continue the charade now?" Philip felt as if he was running mad. Could he be missing something which was right under his nose? "There has to be some other component to it, I would think," Marsden said thoughtfully.

"Maybe we are thinking too deeply about it. Perhaps she simply meant to lure the archduke here with rumors of other men."

"But again, why continue the game?"

"To buy herself more time? She did not want to go to Vienna," Jack said.

"That much is quite true," Philip said reflectively. "Perhaps once I have given her the invitation to Mother's ball, she will show her hand."

"Do you mean the one announcing your betrothal to all of Society on the Continent?" Jack asked rhetorically.

"The very one."

"Please say I may accompany you," Jack said, like a greedy child wanting sweets.

"For once, I would welcome a second pair of eyes to witness her reaction. Are you attending the review, Father?" Philip asked as he finished his coffee and readied himself to leave.

"No, I have dispatches to prepare for London. I will await your news with bated breath."

Jack laughed. Philip shook his head.

They walked to Headquarters, where their horses were stabled, saddled them, and having mounted, rode on to the address Pauline had provided in her letter summoning him to her side. 'Twas it only a month since he would have gladly answered such a call? To that very same call he now rode with dread, fearing his ability to act.

The house was a beautiful red-brick mansion, overlooking the river and near the city's central square.

"A palace fit for a princess," Jack remarked as they dismounted. The drive was lined with a multiplicity of carriages. "It looks as though they have just arrived. The place is at sixes and sevens."

What Jack had said was true. The door was wide open. Servants were carrying trunks to and fro, and no one paid them any mind as they stepped over the threshold.

He and Jack stood there for a few minutes, thinking someone would eventually take notice of them, but they did have to be in position at the review, after all. He finally stopped a servant to enquire after Pauline.

"Is the archduchess at home? Captain Everleigh has called to escort her to the military review." He asked in German, hoping that was the correct choice.

The servant looked taken aback. "I am not certain, sir. I have just arrived with His Grace."

Philip exchanged glances with Jack.

"Would you please find someone who might inquire? I have come at her request."

The servant bowed and left, even though it was clear he would rather do anything but.

"Do you think it is someone important?" Jack asked.

"I believe it is her father," Philip said. "If so, it will certainly make things more interesting."

They were kept waiting more than a quarter of an hour, standing impatiently on the marble floor while servants continued to move about them as if they were not there. Finally, Philip spotted Pauline at the top of the grand, curved staircase. She looked anything but pleased to see him. It gave him a small measure of satisfaction to know she was rattled by her own doing.

"Hoisted by her own petard?" Jack leaned over and asked as she hurried down the stairs. This was no ladylike, grand entrance as she was used to making.

"Perhaps," Philip considered as he and Jack bowed to her.

"You cannot be here!" she said in a loud whisper. "Everything has changed and I can no longer go this afternoon. I apologize. I was unable to send word."

"Has something happened?" Philip asked, even though he knew very well.

He saw her hesitate. "We have had some unexpected guests arrive."

"I will not keep you, then. We must not be late."

"We are duty bound," Jack added with a bow.

The relief on her face would have been comical if it had not been so pointedly directed at his departure.

A moment of deviltry stopped Philip just as he was about to walk through the door. "Oh, my dear, I almost forgot to mention… my mother has decided to throw a betrothal ball. The invitations should be arriving shortly."

Pauline appeared speechless…and panic-stricken. "But we agreed not to announce it yet."

"Word has spread, I am afraid. I had already written to my parents before you apprised me of the fact it was a secret." And after she had pushed him to announce it in Paris.

"The marchioness throws very grand parties," Jack muttered mischievously. "No one ever refuses one of her invitations."

"But my father," she whispered.

"Is he here?" Philip smiled brightly. "I would be delighted to make his acquaintance at last."

Pauline was disconcerted and Philip was more amused than he should be.

Jack pulled out his pocket watch. "We must be off," he said.

"Yes, we must. Auf Wiedersehen, *my dear*." He kissed her hand with deliberate slowness while at the same time looking into her eyes. If only he knew what game she was playing.

CHAPTER SEVENTEEN

MARIA'S HAND ACHED from writing the many invitations needed for the forthcoming ball. The last thing she wanted to do was celebrate Philip's betrothal to a woman she could not like, but it did give her something to do other than attend events with people who seemed to wish only to gossip about her. Reprehensible though it was, Maria had to admit she was enjoying the fact that Lady Marsden had chosen to omit mentioning on the invitations the dance was a betrothal ball...except on the one sent to the archduchess. She had written it on that one. How curious, Maria thought. Did the lady still hope to end the betrothal before the ball? That being the case, she had less than a week in which to do so. Maria prayed that something would happen to save Philip, but even as the wish crossed her mind, she knew his marriage to another was inevitable. Of a certainty there would be someone else, yet was it too much to hope that Maria might like the lady?

She finished the last card and placed it on the stack with the others. It had only provided a few hours' reprieve from thinking of her own dreadful situation. Much though she did not want to return home to Lloydstone, she also did not wish to be the object of pity, gossip, or censure. She had enough self-pity.

Regardless, there was no question of returning home before the ball. Lady Marsden had made it clear she quite depended on

Maria and Kate to help her. Sighing, Maria stood up and collected together her most recent stack of invitations, to place on the table in the hall for the footman to deliver, before then going to find Lady Marsden to ask what other tasks she needed help with.

As she stepped away from the table, Maria looked across at Kate, who had fallen asleep on the sofa in the little parlor. She shook her head. Someone ought to tell her—and soon.

"There you are!" Lady Marsden said, coming into the room in a hurry. "I have secured an appointment with a florist and they will be here shortly! This must be the finest ball Brussels has ever seen, Maria. I must raise the flag so high Charlotte must see it and be green with envy." Charlotte, Maria knew, was the Duchess of Richmond. Lady Marsden laughed, rubbing her hands together with anticipation. As she did so, she glanced across the room and saw Kate sleeping. "When do you think she will realize she is increasing?"

"I was asking myself the same question."

A sleepy Kate then opened her eyes, looking confused. "Did I fall asleep again? I do not know why I am so tired of late."

"My dear girl, you are with child," the marchioness said without preamble.

Kate looked dumbfounded, but Lady Marsden did not appear to notice.

"It is quite obvious to the rest of us. It is best that you should know. Now, shall we remove to the ballroom? I believe I know just how I want things to be arranged, but I have never thrown a ball in a strange house before!"

She hurried out of the room, leaving Kate still looking confused. Maria went over and gave her a hug before helping her friend to her feet. "It will be wonderful, Kate."

"Do you think Jack knows?" Kate asked.

"Gentlemen never notice these things," Maria said, patting Kate's arm as they walked slowly through the house.

"Why did I not realize?" she asked, as though in a daze.

Maria laughed. "There have been many significant changes in

your life. I do not suppose you have a lot of experience with these things."

"No, none," she agreed, "but I do think I would like to be a mother."

"That is certainly a good thing," Maria said, more sardonically than she had intended.

When they reached the large apartments which were to be used for dancing, Lady Marsden had already gathered her army of servants to rearrange the ballroom.

"I think we are superfluous," Maria remarked, but received no response. Kate was still coming to terms with the news. Smiling at her friend, Maria thought it would be the most wonderful news she could imagine, but then she had been brought up to a life of ease, where she had dreamed of little else. Kate had not.

"If you truly do not think I am needed, I would like to go to my chambers," Kate whispered.

Maria frowned. "Should I accompany you? Do you wish for me to send for a soothing draught, or perhaps some tea?"

"No, no. I merely need a few moments to think."

"Yes, of course." Maria watched Kate leave and debated whether or not she should send for Jack, finally deciding that would be too much interference. Kate would tell him in her own time. Instead, she turned back to the task at hand.

"Maria! Do you think we should place the musicians at this end or that?" Lady Marsden demanded, as she indicated both ends of the long room with either arm. It was devoid of furniture and carpets, and the wooden floors had been polished to a high shine.

Maria thought it would not matter one whit, but she pointed to an alcove at the far end, trying to imagine her own betrothal ball and where she would place decorations and the orchestra. While such an event was unlikely to happen for her now, she nevertheless wanted the very best for Philip. Fleetingly, she wondered whether or not the archduchess should be participating in the plans, and then remembered Lady Marsden's distaste for the betrothal in the first place. No, perhaps it was best to keep that notion to herself.

Although Maria did little in the way of actual help, she humored the marchioness as she ordered ornate floral arrangements and the placement of seemingly thousands of candles. Her ladyship even arranged for a cascade along one wall of the room. The only addition Maria suggested was hanging crystals from the ceiling.

By the time Lady Marsden was satisfied, Maria needed a walk. She excused herself and escaped to the park, barely remembering to take a maid with her. It was not as though her reputation could afford such a lapse. It was not as though it would help it either, she thought bitterly.

Bisset followed behind her mistress in the proper manner. She always knew when Maria needed to be alone. At a time like this it was difficult not to feel an impending sense of doom. Besides her own, crushed expectations with Colonel Strickland, she felt as though Philip's downfall was inevitable. Maria had been certain his association with the archduchess would come to an end after she had witnessed the woman kiss the archduke – and after she herself had kissed Philip.

Just then, Maria's mind took an uncharacteristically devious turn of thought. Was it possible to stop the betrothal? Philip would never end it of his own volition—he was far too honorable.

The archduchess and the archduke were residing under the same roof, so it was not as though arranging clandestine meetings were a possible avenue to pursue.

There had to be some way to expose them! Dejectedly, she sat on a bench. It was as though she were watching a tragedy unfold before her eyes while helpless to stop it.

She did not know how long she remained seated there. Nor did she realize she was shivering with cold, or that the light was fading into darkness, until a familiar voice disturbed her.

"Maria?"

She looked up suddenly, to see Philip and Jack standing before her, dressed in their uniforms.

"What the devil are you doing out here at such an hour? You will freeze to death!" Philip scolded, his beautiful face frowning with concern.

Glancing about her, she saw Bisset a few feet away, huddled inside her cloak.

"Come. We will return to the house at once and warm you both," Jack said, motioning to the maid. "There will be time enough later for explanations."

Philip helped her to her feet and put his arm around her. Jack and Bisset were already walking ahead of them.

"What is wrong, Maria? How long have you been out here?" he asked, ignoring Jack's advice.

"I fear I lost track of the time."

"That is most unlike you."

It was also unlike her to forget her maid, yet she frequently spent hours out-of-doors on her own. She found it easiest to think when in the fresh air… and while she had resolved to do what she must, she was far from certain Philip would thank her for it.

Nonetheless, she was already ruined and if he would not free himself, then she would do it for him. It would be her last gift to him. Then she would return to England alone. Strangely, while she should be terrified at what she planned to do, she felt at peace for the first time in weeks. With luck, something would happen to save him before she was forced to take action, but she was prepared to do anything to release him from that harpy. Hopefully, one day, he would understand why.

She remained quiet except for the chattering of her teeth as he guided her across the street and into the house. He ushered her before a fire which was blazing in the small parlor and placed a glass of brandy in her hand, wrapping her frozen fingers about it and lifting it to her lips.

She took a sip and felt the liquid fire burn all the way down, as he had doubtless intended.

He knelt before her. "Maria, will you not tell me what has upset you so?"

"I am not upset," she replied. It was the truth; she was not upset any longer.

"Liar."

She turned to look into his dark blue eyes and smiled. He was so very dear.

"Maria?" He looked at her with concern, as though he feared she might be a little mad. Perhaps she was.

"Truly, Philip." She finished her brandy, then rose and went to her rooms.

⇒⟫⟪⟸

SOMETHING WAS AMISS with Maria, but she clearly did not wish to tell him. She had excused herself to her bedchamber and did not come down for dinner.

"Has Maria been unwell?" Philip asked his mother after they were seated at the table with an onion soup before them.

"She seemed perfectly hale this afternoon, although perhaps I asked too much of her." She pursed her lips, wrinkling her brow in concentration.

"No, I am sure that helping you to prepare for the ball would not have upset her."

"Perhaps she is more affected by Colonel Strickland's abandonment than she would have us believe," she suggested.

Philip did not like the thought of that at all. A strange emotion suddenly consumed him. Good God, was he jealous? She had assured him her heart was not wounded. Had she lied to him just to keep him from worrying? *She thinks you are in love with Pauline,* he thought guiltily. He barely tasted his soup.

"How did the preparations go for the ball?" Kate asked his mother. "Forgive me for leaving you. I needed to rest."

His mother waved her hand as though it were nothing. "I had

Maria to support me. You need your rest."

"She does? Is something wrong, Kate?" Jack's brow was furrowed with concern.

Philip looked first at Kate and then at his mother, whose lips formed a moue of guilt as she paused in her eating, a forkful of sole a few inches above her plate.

"I have noticed you have oft been tired of late. Should we send for the doctor?" Jack asked.

"I am quite well, I assure you," Kate said, a hint of pink forming on her cheeks. That was when Philip realized Kate was with child, and for the second time that night he experienced the unwelcome emotion of jealousy.

In the midst of the second course being laid, a short while later, after his father had neatly drawn the conversation into less troubled waters, Philip thought he heard a knock at the front door. It was a strange hour for such a thing in his parents' home, though messages came and went at all hours at Headquarters. It was but a moment before Percy entered and whispered in his father's ear.

"As soon as we have concluded the meal," his father replied and with a bow, Percy quietly withdrew.

Philip raised his brows in question and his father gave a slight nod.

It was difficult to sit through the meal after that, and he gave silent thanks it was not one of his mother's grand dinners. As they were *en famille*, it was a simple five-course affair.

As soon as the covers were removed, Jack and Kate excused themselves, as did his mother, who claimed fatigue from all the preparations for the ball. She was quite used to her husband dealing with political matters at all hours.

Philip followed his father into the study, where a packet sat atop the desk. He wanted to rent it open and read the contents for himself but he refrained. Percy had left a carafe of port, with three glasses, filled for them. He had assumed Jack would be joining them. Ah, well, Jack was about to be shocked by some more pleasant news. Philip smiled and toasted his glass upstairs to where he hoped Kate and Jack were celebrating.

He then set a glass next to his father, who was already sitting at the desk, sifting through the reports.

Sitting in one of the arm chairs near the fire, Philip crossed one leg over the other, trying to relax as he hoped for news that would set him free.

"You are being remarkably patient," his father remarked, looking at him over the spectacles he had donned to peruse his correspondence.

"I am doing my best to appear so. You never did approve of anyone hovering."

"I shall reward your good behavior." He chuckled as he handed a letter to Philip, who did his best not to snatch the sheaf of paper.

"'Tis almost ten years old," his father said. "I had forgotten most of the details, and while not proof of the current predicament, it is insightful. I had quite forgotten I was present for part of it before returning to England to assume the title."

His father moved to light his pipe, filling the room with the aroma of floral and spice, while Philip began to read.

It was a file on the House of Klementine, one of the branches of the royal house of Hanover, though not the direct line.

Inside, it held the precise details of how Karl Klementine had sided with one young Napoleon Bonaparte, and even gone so far as secretly pledging troops and funds.

Philip murmured and whispered lines as he read to himself, while his father sat silently beside him. There was certainly enough evidence to damn the man, but he had already been dealt with.

"What has happened to Karl now? Was he executed?" Philip asked, looking up from the middle of the lengthy report.

"I believe he is imprisoned on house arrest, very likely condemned as mad. The shame of it, however, would be enough to taint his descendants."

"And now the descendant happens to be the heir." Philip sat back and looked into the flickering flames of the fire. "One his daughter wishes for herself."

"He is also the one her father formally betrothed her to as a child," his father added, pointing the end of his pipe towards the fire.

"Then why not rescind the betrothal?"

"Perhaps he has, and this elaborate ruse has been designed to prove something to her father."

Philip shook his head. "At least now we may assume we know why she selected me… but what, do you suppose, does she intend for me?"

"I should think I would be the more likely target of revenge." He did not mask his sardonic tone.

"Yet what can they hope to accomplish? It is not as though they can clear his name by exacting revenge. Besides, you did nothing more than provide evidence. She has not attached herself to any of the others listed here." He tapped the back of his hand against the reports in his lap.

"To prove Friedrich's loyalty?" his father suggested.

"We shall soon find out. The Archduke of Klementine arrived today."

"And I believe your mother sent the betrothal ball an-nouncement this afternoon." His father took a draw on his pipe.

Philip felt sick at the mention of the betrothal. Never before had he allowed himself to be so entrapped during any of his duties—or intrigues, for that matter. "Do you think he will stop it?"

"He will certainly not put a stop to the ball, but the betrothal? Who can predict the whims of such a one?"

"I fear this may be putting you in danger, Father. With her father, the archduke, arrived, it will force their hands. His arrival was clearly unexpected. I was there. Pauline was flustered and wanted me gone immediately."

"She needed time to spin her tale, and to tell him what she

wanted him to hear."

"Undoubtedly," Philip agreed, "but we must be prepared for desperation, which means your life could be in danger."

"That seems rather a drastic way to exact revenge, and creating a diplomatic incident with England would hardly endear them to the king."

"What else is there?"

"I cannot tell how they would even make the connection that I was involved."

"Perhaps it is a coincidence, but nevertheless we cannot be too careful," Philip said.

"If the father hears of the betrothal, I expect he will want an audience with you before the ball."

"I am hoping Pauline will come to me before then. Mayhap she will call the entire thing off."

"We can only pray that will happen," his father muttered.

"What, sir, you as well?" Philip turned a little to face his father.

"Parents only hope for their children's happiness, my boy. I cannot think how she would make your life happier."

No. Even Philip had to agree, although he still wanted her.

"I think you have laid the trap nicely, but what if she fails to show her hand before the ball? What will you say to the father?"

"I may be well and truly trapped, but I do not think she will allow it to come to that—and I suppose I will lie to him as I am doing to everyone else." *Tell Maria the truth,* his conscience said. Why was he thinking of her at a time like this?

"Be very, very careful, son."

"I intend to. Nevertheless, I must stay one step ahead of her." That meant knowing what she intended to do before she did it.

CHAPTER EIGHTEEN

MARIA WAS NERVOUS as she donned carefully chosen dark clothing and set off alone into the night. She knew the address of the Austrians from the invitations she had written earlier—a fortuitous thing, she supposed.

She had no real plan, other than to make a hunt for information that would free Philip even if he did not wish for it. The risks were high. Her already clouded reputation would not recover if she were caught. Strangely, she cared little for that. It mattered more that he was free.

It was a cold night, made more so by a wind coming off the river which tugged at her cloak as she walked along to the house. The city was mostly quiet, since the Bruxellois retired earlier than Londoners. When she reached the gates to the estate, she stopped to rest and watch for signs of activity. It did not appear as though they were entertaining, which she supposed was a good thing, although it would have been easier to enter had there been a lot of people. After ascertaining that no one was likely to open the gate for her, she moved through the large park which surrounded the house, moving steadily towards the servants' entrance. They were usually open and she walked straight inside through the narrow iron gate in the stone wall.

A few lanterns showed from near the house, but there was nothing to guide her within the back garden, which was thick with trees and the scent of pine. It was a place she would not mind being lost in for hours, were it another time and place.

Slowly, she crept forward, her senses heightened by the clandestine nature of her presence. Every step she took sounded like a roar to her ears as branches snapped, pebbles crunched and even the frosting grass rustled beneath her boots.

Her breath, steaming in the cold air, was enough to give her away if anyone chanced to be looking. She huddled closer inside her warm cloak and pulled her woolen scarf over her mouth and nose in order to conceal herself further.

It was silly of her to imagine she might happen upon the archduke and archduchess outside in such weather, let alone in conversation, but for Philip's sake she had to try. She skirted a small formal garden and, as she drew closer, saw it had a shadow cast upon it from the lanterns on the house.

She stopped to allow her eyes to adjust to the lamplight, looking for an escape route should she be discovered. She noticed there were small gates on either side of the park, but where did they lead? She hoped she did not have to find out.

Tentatively, with legs trembling, she moved towards a room with long windows through which light was streaming out—presumably a drawing room where people might be gathered. She leaned backwards against the brick façade, trying to become one with it, and crept sideways to the edge of the first window. By angling her head sideways, she managed to observe one side of the room. Immediately, she spotted her quarry—both quarries in actual fact, for in the far corner, the archduchess was sitting on a stool in front of a grand pianoforte, with the archduke standing behind her. They were speaking to one another as they looked at sheets of music, perhaps deciding which piece she should play next.

Maria looked around her, feeling as though she had a bright target painted on her front and back, but she had to get closer. She pulled her hat as low as she could to conceal any hint of light on her face. Taking a deep breath for courage, she then fell to her knees and crawled beneath six full-length windows, hoping the foot of clearance under the sill was enough to hide her.

She reached the end and stopped beneath the far corner of the last window, feeling her blood pound through her ears like a drummer boy calling the troops to war.

With extreme care, she lifted herself to a crouched position and placed her ear as close to the window as she dared. A Haydn sonata began, which she knew well and had played many times. As unsurprising as the lady's choice of music, Maria recognized at once that she was an accomplished pianist...but unfortunately also a distracted one. Maria knew she had to act swiftly. Heart in mouth, she looked up, to see the archduke leaning over to turn the pages while at the same time handing the archduchess a note.

The sonata seemed to go on forever, but Maria did not turn her eyes away from the pair. When the last chord had been played, the Archduchess unfolded the note and placed it before her as though it were more music.

Maria squinted and strained to see the words. The bold, slanting script was too difficult to decipher, especially in a foreign language. There had to be a way to discover its contents.

A moment later, however, the archduchess folded the note and tucked it into her skirts, most likely into a hidden pocket well beyond Maria's reach. She felt as though the wind had gone from her sails. There was something on that note that would help, she was certain. If only she had been able to read it!

As dejected as one of her father's hounds when there were no scraps to be had from the cook, Maria wanted to weep. It was silly when she'd had no expectations of finding anything when she had started out, yet now that it seemed there would be deliverance, it was just out of reach. If only she could put her hand through the glass and snatch the note away unseen.

Laughter close by startled her and she realized the recital had ended. The archduke was assisting the archduchess to her feet and Maria's best chance for reading the note had gone.

Turning over, she leaned her back against the wall, knees up and her head back with despair. "I shall have to think of something else." She whispered the encouragement to herself. Was she to scale the wall or wait until the servants were abed in order to enter through the kitchens? "You do not make a very good spy," she chided, both herself and the fear she felt in attempting such a thing. It had been all well and good to want to do such a thing, but the reality of it was terrifying.

She turned back to peek through the window again. It appeared as though the intimate gathering was ending, and Maria was so very cold. Nevertheless, she continued to watch as the inhabitants exited the drawing room, wondering what they might do next. At her own home, they might play cards or converse over tea. It did not appear anyone was inclined to linger, she observed, trying to decide who was whom.

A handsome older gentleman, with an impressive set of whiskers, put his hand on the archduchess's arm. Her father? The similarities were striking.

The archduke cast a look of longing at the archduchess and Maria felt more disgust and anger at the woman's betrayal of Philip. She did not deserve him. If it was within Maria's power, then the Austrian would not have him either.

The gentleman she presumed to be the father spoke to the Duchess von Metternich, who must be his sister. Another look passed between the archduke and archduchess and Maria knew they were planning something—a clandestine meeting, perhaps? Would it be tonight? If she waited, would she be rewarded?

The four left the room and Maria sighed heavily with defeat. She brought herself back to her feet, using the sill of the window to stand when she caught sight of a flash of white from the corner of her eye.

The archduchess had dropped the note.

Maria had to reach that paper before the servants did. Wondering how long she might have, she began a desperate search of the window sashes, hoping at least one of them had been cracked open. It was unlikely, with the night so cold, but she had to try.

The one closest would have been the most convenient, but it did not budge and neither did the next three. When she reached the fifth window, the sash was loose, and she was able to lift it open. With one last glance to ensure the room was still empty, she climbed in before she lost her nerve. She crawled across the room, quickly retrieved the note and hurried back from whence she came. By the time she had climbed back through the window, she thought she might die from nervousness, if such a thing were possible. Certainly, her breath was stertorous and the blood was pounding at a fierce pace through her body.

Barely had she finished closing the window behind her and begun to unfold the note with her trembling hands, than a deep voice spoke in her ear. "What the devil are you doing here?"

"PHILIP?" SHE ASKED in a loud whisper, her voice trembling.

Philip had never been more angry or frightened in his life as when he realized Maria had broken into the Austrian house. When at first he saw the intruder, he immediately tried to decide who else would be spying on the house, yet also prepared himself to attack.

"You are fortunate I did not hurt you," he said in her ear as he wrapped his arms around her from behind and pulled her into the shadows of the house. "Would you care to explain why you are here?"

She tipped her pert little chin up in the air defiantly, her eyes flashing briefly with guilt in the dim light. The mists of their breath mingled, he was holding her so close. He would wait for her answer. "If you must know, I am here to help you."

"Help me?" Was he hearing her correctly?

She nodded. He could see the indecision on her face. She must have thought better of what she was going to say, since she then clamped her jaw shut.

"What is it, Maria?" He had never before felt such frustration with her. He did not wish to start now, but there was something she was not telling him. Had she overheard him speaking with his father? "Why would you take such a risk to *help* me?"

"I was hoping to discover what she is about."

"All because of the kiss you witnessed? Why would you take such extreme risks?"

"Because of what I overheard."

"You failed to mention that part. Would you care to enlighten me?" If Maria had the information he needed all along… he wanted to be furious, but it would change nothing. Maria was not vindictive; Pauline was. He needed to remember that.

"The archduke asked her if she had discovered anything, and she said no—only that Wellington might be moving to Vienna soon. Then she reminded him why they must do this and kissed him. She does not deserve you, Philip."

"You thought to fight my battles for me?" He ought to be flattered. It was touching, really, but somehow it stung that everyone he cared about seemed to disapprove of Pauline. He had been blinded by infatuation, that much was true, but this information still did not clarify what Pauline sought.

"What are you doing here yourself, lurking in the garden? Or were you inside and saw me?" Fear crossed her face, very likely along with the realization of how close she had been to discovery.

He really ought to let her believe that, though he could not bring himself to lie to her when she was risking her reputation – possibly her life – for him. He ought to tell her he had no intention of marrying the woman, but knew it would be for the best to continue the charade for now, never mind how good Maria felt in his arms. That was something he could not dwell on now. "I was trying to discover information myself… which leads me into my next question…" he began when he saw her open her mouth to interrogate him further. "What did you go inside to find?"

He could see the indecision on her face and the moment she

decided to confide in him at last. Did she not realize he was not an enemy?

With resignation, she held up a note. "I have not yet read it. My fingers were trembling too much with nerves and cold."

It served her right. "Good. What was your plan if you had been caught?"

"To run," she answered simply.

"I will address your complete loss of sanity later." For now, he needed to see what was in that note.

He realized he was still holding her close, and had to release her. "Stay here." He unfolded the note, then moved enough to gain the faint light from a lantern.

"What does it say?" Maria whispered in his ear.

"I thought I told you to stay where you were?"

Maria ignored him and pressed close behind to peer over his arm. It was hard not to become distracted.

We must act soon.

Meet in half an hour in the garden.

Behind him, Maria sucked in her breath. "We must hide!"

"We?" Philip asked in a voice that clearly indicated *we* would do no such thing—except he would not allow her to travel across the city alone at night, so unless he wished to miss the assignation, she would be with him.

"You surely do not think to be rid of me now?" Maria had the gall to scold.

He thought that very thing. God save him from infuriating females. "I would not have thought you capable of something like this!"

"You can be cross with me later. There is no time now."

"The devil," he muttered. She was right. He took her hand and they followed in the shadows back into the woods where they could better observe the house.

"Will they not hear us, if we move?" Maria asked.

"They will not hear me. You might have to remain here." Thankfully, she did not argue, but remained glued to his side, shivering in the cold air. Hopefully, it would not be much longer, and he would learn the truth, for Philip was in no mood for this—not anymore.

A flicker of a shadow indicated someone was near the house. The archduke had clearly followed much the same path they had, but then continued on, farther into the woods where a summer house stood. He had not seen it before, but it would allow them to move closer unseen. Drawing Maria with him, he fell back into the shadows until, not ten minutes later, Pauline arrived—huddled in a dark coloured, hooded cloak—and went inside. Philip edged as close as he dared in order to listen.

"This must end now, Pauline. It has gone too far. The risks are too great."

"Why did Father have to arrive now? He has ruined everything!" Pauline turned back on him. "You should know I had not counted on your arrival so soon in Paris, either."

"Can you blame me for disliking your plan? Kissing other men? There has to be another way, mein liebster. I also do not believe this will prosper. In making the formal betrothal announcement, the affair is very public. He might force you to marry the man."

"Nein, nein, nein. He loathes the English, and Marsden, for what they did to your father."

"Not enough to reinstate my inheritance," he said dryly, "and by forcing his hand, I think you will only make him angrier."

"Even if we shame my betrothed and avenge your father's name?"

"It is a very big risk to take, Pauline. I would rather take my chances with marrying you now in the hope he will accept the marriage and reinstate me as his heir in all good time. I have been making progress with him, I believe."

"I want both." Her voice was filled with petulance.

"We cannot keep the ball a secret forever. It is only a few

days away. What will happen when he finds out what you have done without his permission?"

"We could return to Vienna and not attend the ball. That would humiliate them, no?"

"But it would achieve nothing else. What would be the point? Please, I wish you will put a stop to this now."

"How would we live, Friedrich? We are dependent on his whims!"

"Do you think he would cast us out? I think his pride would prevent that."

"I cannot give up. Can you not see that?" she argued.

"Someone is bound to be harmed by this, Pauline. Is it worth that?"

"Do you care naught for what happened to your father?"

"He defied his king. Even by shaming the house of Marsden, you will not change that."

"I think you are wrong. I think my father would approve."

"Let us not argue anymore. We must return to the house."

PHILIP AND MARIA watched them leave the summer house, having to endure, in silence, a passionate embrace between the two before they returned to the house. Philip believed it would have been preferable to have his nails pulled out one by one in a torture chamber.

Maria took his hand and squeezed it in a comforting way. When he was certain they were alone again, he moved, pulling Maria along with him, returning through the park and out of the gates before either spoke again.

"It sounded as though Pauline had instigated this entire situation in order to gain favor for her beau. Whatever did your father do to them?" Maria asked.

"Very little, according to him. He did play a part in discovering the Austrian duke's treason."

"What, do you think, she intends to do at the ball?"

If only he knew. "Either deny the betrothal or make some

false accusation, I expect."

"As happened with Gabriel," Maria said quietly.

"You know well the effect of such accusations, even if untrue. Keep your hat low," he murmured as he led her around a group of late-night revelers who were probably British.

"At least, being a gentleman, you have options besides spinsterhood."

He looked sideways at her then and drew her into a hug. He had not fully understood the depths of her plight. *It is difficult unless one is faced with them*, he reminded himself. If only he had found her before returning to Paris, they might have been wed. Maria—his wife. It seemed a much better prospect than the one he was facing now.

"Perhaps it might be time to mention your mother did not announce the betrothal on the invitation. Only on the one addressed to the Austrian contingent."

Philip looked up in shock. It had to be too good to be true, and he had to prevent himself from smiling.

CHAPTER NINETEEN

Rain was pouring against the window pane, but Maria scarcely saw the blur of green as she stared out of the window from the bench seat in her chamber overlooking the back garden. It had been three days since Philip had caught Maria spying, and she had scarcely seen or spoken a word to Philip unless they were around other people. He had made her swear not to leave the house again on her own, nor interfere in his business with the archduchess.

She had no notion of how to help other than confronting the woman, but in the end, it was Philip's decision. But how could she just stand by and let her ruin his life? Had she not given him the information he needed to free himself?

Maria wondered if the archduchess would attend the ball or not. The last laugh would be on her, since no one else knew of the betrothal. It would certainly be the simplest solution, would it not?

However, there was so much anger and vengeance in her tone the other night that Maria did not think she would give up so easily. The woman intended to humiliate Lord Marsden and his family, but how would she accomplish that without making herself also look a fool?

"I will have to confront her before any kind of announcement is made," Maria remarked. But how could she do it without causing a scene?

She could not understand why Philip didn't simply stop the charade from continuing, unless he still wanted her regardless of her own true feelings. Maria knew how it felt to love someone even if they did not return your affection. Would he be able to love enough for both of them? Somehow the hate in the archduchess's heart made Maria think nothing but misery would come of it. Philip deserved better. Maria knew she could make him happy even though he would never share a grand passion with her.

Someone knocked on her door and she groaned to herself. She would much rather sit on the bench and mope all day, but there was much to be done for the ball. The fateful ball.

"Enter."

"There you are," Kate said, as she opened the door and stepped inside. Her cheeks were flushed in a bloom like a fresh rose.

Maria felt a pang of guilt. She had not been the best of friends to Kate of late, so consumed was she with her own plight. "How are you feeling?" Maria asked.

Subconsciously, Kate's hands rested on her abdomen. "Mornings are a bit treacherous," she confessed. "But other than needing frequent naps, I feel quite well. I am still becoming accustomed to the idea of being a mother."

"You will be wonderful," Maria assured her.

Kate sat in the chair at the dressing table and looked a bit pensive. "How are things with Philip?"

"What do you mean?"

"His betrothal is to be announced tomorrow evening… I know this must be hard on you."

"It was bound to happen sometime." Maria was caught off guard. She did not feel up to discussing it. "If only she were worthy of him, I could be happy."

"You should tell him how you feel, Maria. Before it is too late."

"What good would it do? He wants her—even if she doesn't want him." Maria did not know how much to say.

"Then shall we try to divert you? I could use some gloves for my gown."

"I must look desperate, indeed, if you are willing to shop. Bisset could purchase them for you. But yes, let us shop. I will see if Lady Marsden needs anything as well."

"What gown will you wear?" Maria asked.

"One of my Parisian ones, of course. Perhaps the peach. Hopefully with the higher waistline I will be able to wear them for some time."

It was hard not to be envious.

"And you? I think you should wear the deep gold one that matches your eyes."

"If only I could. I must be on my best behavior, you know that."

"Do you think by dressing plain and blending into the wallpaper that it will make the matrons be less critical?"

"Of course." Kate had not spent as much time in society. Any boldness on Maria's part would label her negatively in one way or another.

Kate shook her head. "Do not do it, Maria. Be yourself. Let them see you the real you. Let Philip see."

The sad part was, Maria had been showing Philip her true self. It was not enough. It would never be enough.

Kate stood and went to the wardrobe and pulled out the golden gown, tempting Maria. For once she wanted to be herself, Society could rot. Was she not about to risk her reputation anyway?

Maria felt herself drawn to the gown, and went over to finger the delicate silk, letting it flow over her skin.

"Perhaps I shall have one more night," Maria whispered to herself.

"What do you mean?" Kate asked.

"I believe I will return to England after the ball. After what happened with Colonel Strickland, I do not think anyone else will want me."

"But I love having you here. At least you will have some adventure. But am I being selfish? Is it so very hard to be here? Some people are horrid."

"I assumed once you had the child, you would return to England," Maria said.

"Perhaps I will feel differently then," Kate admitted, "but there are many who bring their children along. I think until Jack decides to resign his commission, we will stay with him. As long as it is safe."

"I would want to do the same," Maria remarked.

"Why not wait to make a decision? I know it seems hopeless now, but perhaps the dust will settle. We have only just arrived in Brussels."

"Perhaps. I will think about it," Maria said as she hung the gown back up and gathered her cloak and bonnet.

Once they were inside the carriage on the way to the shops, Maria could not stop thinking about the ball and what the archduchess might say or do. How she longed to confide in Kate and seek her advice, but she had promised not to interfere.

Maria had considered many options from confronting the woman to tying her up. No options allowed a graceful return to Society afterwards if she were caught. She would be utterly ruined. Unlike now where she was not completely ruined, but not good *ton*.

Yet, she had to say something to the woman. She could not simply stand by and do nothing. Perhaps drawing her into the garden during the ball was her best chance, before any announcements were made. She did not think the Archduchess would ignore a summons from her lover. It was trickery, yes, but that was nothing new to Her Grace. Hopefully Maria's courage would not fail.

"What has you so distracted?" Kate asked as they alighted from the carriage, ducking under the umbrellas the footmen were holding to usher them into the milliner's shop. "I just asked you if the sun set in the east."

"Forgive me, I cannot stop thinking about the ball tomorrow."

Kate held up a ribbon that matched her evening gown and quickly selected a pair of long gloves to go with them. She paid and then led Maria towards the door, where a footman went to hail their carriage. "I can see shopping was not the best of choices."

"At least we are not sitting at home."

"At home, we would be warm and drinking chocolate by the fire." Kate shook her head.

Thankfully, the carriage arrived quickly, and they were back inside, though shivering from the damp cold. "Please tell me how I can help."

Maria debated for a moment, and knew Kate to be trustworthy, but it wasn't entirely her secret to tell. Yet...having an ally at the ball might become necessary. "Very well, but you must promise to keep it to yourself."

"Of course you can trust me!" Kate looked offended.

"I know that, but this involves Philip, and I am afraid you will be tempted to say something to Jack at the very least."

That pacified Kate a little. "As long as you or he are not in harm's way, then I promise it remains between us."

That was as much as Maria could expect, so she unburdened herself to Kate, sparing no details. "Will you help me?"

"Philip kissed you!"

"That is all you have to say? I should have left that detail out."

"Of course you should not have! It changes everything!" Kate admonished.

Maria shook her head. It had upended her world, but had not been enough to change Philip's heart. "Sadly, not, but you understand why I must save him now."

Kate reached over and squeezed Maria's hand. "I will do everything I can to help."

❯❯❯❯✕❮❮❮❮

PHILIP HAD BEEN trying to call on Pauline's father for the past three days. But every time, she would circumvent the attempt as if she had been watching the door for his arrival.

Philip was determined. He took up watch and waited until she left the house. Now that he knew there was no treason involved – simply a personal vendetta – he was perfectly willing to let the father know. Hopefully, that would put an end to it, because there was very little likelihood that he would allow the betrothal or the marriage.

It was a cold, soggy day, which did not improve his disposition. Philip made his way down the drive to the front door, which was opened by a very cool, disapproving butler. He was tall and thin, with ice-white hair and pale blue eyes to match his demeanor.

He handed the man his card, the formal card with his courtesy title.

"I will enquire if His Highness is receiving." The butler turned to go, not bothering to show Philip the courtesy of a reception room this time.

"Please mention I am Lord Marsden's son," Philip mentioned as an afterthought, quite sure he would be refused admittance otherwise.

The butler's only acknowledgment was a slight pause in his steps.

It was not long until the butler returned with a smug look on his face. "His Highness sends his regards, but he is not now, and will not ever, be receiving, and has also extended that edict to that of his daughter."

Exactly what Philip had expected. He reached into the pocket of his coat and pulled out an invitation to the betrothal ball. Extending it, he remarked, "Then perhaps you would be so good as to give him this." Then Philip turned on his heel and exited the house.

"Let Pauline deal with that when she returns home."

And that was that. It was an unsatisfying ending to one of his less fortunate pursuits. He would not even be present to see her reaction. She had been bested, and Philip would have enjoyed seeing that.

He returned to the stables, where he saddled and mounted his horse and took himself off. He needed a long, hard ride and knew just the place. Once he negotiated traffic to the Namur gate, he headed south to the Soigny Forest, trying to rid himself of Pauline Klementine once and for all.

He hoped her father packed her up and took her straight back to Austria. He no longer cared what happened to her. He could only be thankful there had been no more serious consequences and that he had found her out before. Not that Pauline would have gone through with marriage to him, but she certainly planned to try to humiliate his family. That should at least be prevented, and he had Maria to thank for that.

What would happen to Maria now?

You should marry her, his conscience spoke loudly.

He should, but the thought of marriage was a bitter taste in his mouth at the moment. Although he been prepared to marry her before, things were changed between them and it was no longer a marriage of convenience he had in mind. He shook his head. It was too soon and his feelings were too conflicted. But he did care for Maria. He even desired her, but he owed it to her to court her properly.

The irony of the cold hard rain was fitting for washing away the ice princess. Two hours later, he found himself in the charming village of Waterloo. He continued riding south until he reached a valley of farmland, now fallow from the impending winter.

He dismounted near a farm called La Haye Saint and the rain began to lighten. He walked Midnight for a while looking out over the valley until he saw a large château upon the hill.

Hougoumont, he believed it was from some maps they had drawn of the area. They'd done extensive scouting when Napoleon had made no secret Brussels was one of his intended targets. It was always better to be prepared than sorry, and he hoped Boney was rotting on his Mediterranean island.

He had little doubt there were those even now working to free him. It was hard to believe his interactions with Pauline had been based on revenge. Or were the reasons so benign? Would he have found himself labeled a traitor had he not realized in time? It was hard to completely dismiss this mistake as over and done with – but his bruised pride and reputation could not seem to fathom there was nothing else to it. Could she and her love be plotting to free Bonaparte, or sending troop information to his sympathizers?

He looked out over this quiet, peaceful valley and hoped it remained that way. Wellington had at once thought a battle might have to be waged in this area. He walked past the château, whose charming stone wall surrounded a cottage with a chapel and barns. He could see the remnants of an orchard, now gone dormant. It was a picturesque farm in a setting of lush green fields. It was something he would not mind owning one day…settling down.

His feet carried him on northward to the village, and he stopped at a public house, to give Midnight a rest before returning to Brussels. By the time Philip had left the horse with a groom to see to him, the sky had darkened and he scarcely made it in the door of the pub before the Heavens opened up with a torrential downpour.

'Twas the bad thing about staying with your parents—they were more likely to notice when you did not return home. Hopefully, with the preparations for the ball, no one would notice he was not there for dinner. He could hardly send a chap out into weather he wasn't willing to ride in, could he? He would leave as soon as the rain let up, but he might as well have a pint of ale and a warm meal.

There was not another soul in the dark, musty taproom save the innkeeper. No one else was dumb enough to go out in the weather like this, he thought ruefully as he looked at the window with water streaming down against the dark sky. It was a small inn for a small village, and with its dark walls and low beamed ceilings, it looked as though it had been there for centuries already. As a warm meat pie and some fresh bread were set before him, the door creaked open with a rush of cold wind and rain.

The innkeeper made a grunt-like noise at the sight of another sodden traveler whose great coat and hat were dripping on his floor.

"Evening," he said. "There is a hook by the fire if you want to hang your things to dry."

Philip paid the man little mind as he sat to his food. He had not eaten since quite early that morning, too engrossed by his need to get away from Brussels to have thought of food.

He was several bites into his meal before he noticed the stranger standing near. He stopped and looked up.

"Lloyd?"

His old colleague gave a nod. "May I join you?"

Philip stood and extended his hand. "Of course. You are the last person I expected to see at this moment."

"Of that I have little doubt, but I consider it a lucky coincidence as I was headed to Brussels in search of you."

Philip indicated for Lloyd to sit and signaled the innkeeper to bring another meal for his friend.

"It must be serious to bring you so far."

Lloyd waited until the innkeeper had brought him a meal and a pint and walked away before he spoke again. "Indeed. Strickland arrived and told me about Maria."

Philip waited. Gabriel Lloyd was a secretive man of few words and when he spoke, one listened.

"I wanted to call him out," Lloyd confessed.

"It was all I could do to restrain myself from it," Philip admitted.

"She shouldn't have to suffer for my sins. How is she?"

"Maria is well, though not as free as she was in Paris. There is a great deal of London Society here."

Gabriel grunted, his thoughts of that institution apparent. "Thank you for looking out for her."

"You know I would do anything for her," Philip answered, not willing to commit any further than that, but he met Lloyd's gaze—his questioning gaze, but he nodded his satisfaction.

"That was not the only reason I came."

Philip had been assured of that from the moment he first recognized him. Lloyd would never blow his cover or risk it without good reason.

"Strickland mentioned you were looking for evidence against the House of Klementine."

Philip leaned forward. "Do you have something? The only thing my father discovered was old."

"I have been watching them for some time."

Philip waited while Lloyd took a drink.

"Like father, like son," he said cryptically in that way he had.

"So the son is a Napoleon sympathizer?"

Lloyd nodded. "Staunch revolutionist. That is why the father opposes the Archduchess's marriage to Archduke Friedrich and has disinherited him."

So there was more than he expected. Had they realized they were being listened to before? "So why the ploy with me?"

"She was looking for information. Knowledge is power. Anything to further Napoleon's cause."

"What evidence do we have?"

"Letters upon letters." He reached into his jacket and pulled one out. "This is the latest."

Philip took the letter and then unfolded it. It was written in Pauline's slanted, feminine script.

I will go through with the marriage if that is your wish. I trust your word to make everything right in the end, once you have regained power.

Your devoted servant,
PK

Philip set down the letter and looked up. "She is doomed for disappointment."

CHAPTER TWENTY

MARIA HAD HAD difficulty falling asleep due to anxiety of what tomorrow would bring and fear for its irreversibility. Philip had not been home for dinner, and though unlike him not to send word, both Jack and Lord Marsden seemed to think little of it. Maria could not but worry with so much at stake. He still had not come home by the time she had at last been overtaken by sleep, and then she had spent the day helping the marchioness with last minute details—rearranging last minute place cards at the dining table, showing the florist where to put arrangements, and soothing the chef's temper when one of the undercooks accidentally burned a souffle.

Now it was time to prepare for the ball, and still no sign of Philip.

She rang for Bisset, who curled her waves into beautiful works of art with a string of crystal spangles woven through. Then she helped her into her most daring Parisian gown which was empire waisted, yet the bodice was crossed to allow a veed neckline, in which the gold faded up into translucency as swaths of fabric hinted at a capped sleeve. The skirt was covered in spangles like those in her hair, which were designed to sparkle like stars in the candlelight.

She hardly spoke as her long-time maid helped her dress. Her usually calm disposition was on tenterhooks and she felt as though she might explode at any moment.

Her hands shook as she slid on her gloves and waited for them to be buttoned. To finish, Bisset placed a simple teardrop diamond necklace and clasped it around her neck. Maria fingered it with sadness, the tear was fitting as her heart ached for what was to come.

"You look beautiful, my lady."

"Thank you, Bisset." Maria surveyed her reflection in the looking glass and hardly recognized the person staring back at her. She did look fine, but it mattered not anymore, she thought with sadness. More importantly, though, she felt like a warrior ready to do battle.

She made her way downstairs, taking a path by the ballroom where the servants were lighting the thousands of candles for the evening's festivities. She smiled as the lit candles caught the hanging crystals that sparkled across the floor like dancing fairies. It was as magical as she'd envisioned.

Looking down at her gown, her spangles caught the light, protruding their own sparkle. She had dreamt of this moment for years—she had watched Philip longingly across ballrooms and drawing rooms, then when he left for the army, she had read every single dispatch for news of him and Gabriel from the war. It would have been magical, she thought, if it had been her own betrothal ball. Instead, it felt like a life sentencing affair, one that would condemn multiple people to a life of misery if it went wrong. She could not fail.

SHE TRIED TO envision the perfect opportunity to pull the archduchess aside before any announcements or harm could be done. As early as possible was the key.

When she arrived in the drawing room, it was crowded with guests, but not Philip. No archduchess. She muttered an unladylike oath.

"Maria? What is the matter?" Kate asked, coming up beside her. "You look upset."

She tried to relax. "I just want everything to end well."

"I know," Kate said, squeezing her arm.

"Have you seen Philip?" she asked as she looked out over the crowded room.

"I have not. Jack might know something."

"I'm sure he will be here. After all, the ball is in his honor." Maria looked at Lady Marsden who also seemed to be looking around for someone. As if timing his arrival perfectly, Philip appeared in the doorway, looking more handsome than ever.

Percy had been waiting on his arrival and announced dinner almost on Philip's heels. There was a ball to follow dinner and there was time to keep, after all.

Maria desperately wanted to go to him, but it was neither the time nor the place. He greeted a few of the guests as he made his way towards his mother. He whispered something in her ear, and the lady smiled as though she had been given the best news of her life.

"Curious," Kate whispered in her ear as though she had noticed the same thing. "We should find our partners."

Everyone was pairing off to walk into the dining room but Maria did not see the man to whom she'd been assigned, and the room was quickly emptying. She began walking towards the door, trying not to look at Philip. He would see she was up to something and try to stop her.

"Here is my partner, the most ravishing lady in the room."

She knew it was him before she turned to see his face right next to hers. His fresh scent of soap and bergamot were strong and his hair was still damp from his bath. "Philip. While flattery is appreciated, falsehoods are not."

"I speak only the truth." He held out his arm.

"How come you to be escorting me to dinner? I was certain it was to be a Captain Willems."

"We adjusted the seating arrangements last minute."

"Oh?"

"Indeed. I think you will be pleased." He drew her into the

hallway and down the corridor to the dining room.

"What is going on?"

"You will see." He took her to a chair which was not at all where she had originally been placed. After all, she had put the place cards there. She had put herself far away from him and from the archduchess, not wanting to witness them together.

But nothing was going as planned. She had already hoped to have spoken with the woman, but she was not here. She was not there. Where was she?

She did not have to finish the sentence. "Pauline is not here, nor will she be. May I have the pleasure of sitting next to you?" Philip asked.

"Of course, but how?"

"Does it matter? It is over," he whispered in her ear as he helped her into her chair.

Maria sat in stunned silence as Philip greeted Lady Georgiana on his other side, and thankfully Jack was to her right. She smiled at him, not yet capable of words, but he grinned and filled them in for her.

"Good news, eh?"

The footman filled their glasses with claret and she raised her glass to mimic Jack's. Good news was an understatement. Her heart leapt for joy. She was so happy she scarcely tasted her food and then she thought it would burst from her chest when it was her turn to talk to him.

Philip smiled at her as though he truly saw her. "Lady Maria, may I beg the honor of the first dance?"

"It is very presumptuous of you to think I have any dances left," she teased.

"Who is it?" he practically growled.

Maria laughed with a lightheartedness she had not felt in years. "Lord Marsden," she confessed.

"I will deal with my father, the rogue."

"Are you going to tell me what happened?"

He took his wine glass and swirled it in his hand. "There is little to tell. I informed her father."

"That is all it took?" She could not believe it.

He inclined his head. "She is not here, is she? I have not heard from her, though I would have paid a fortune to see her face when she arrived home to meet his wrath."

Maria could not hold back a laugh. "As would I have."

He smiled at her then, but shared a secret smile like they would have shared as children. It was good to see him free again. Life and reality would get in the way again, but for tonight she would enjoy the celebration of a narrow escape.

As if her reading her thoughts, he toasted his glass to her. "To narrow escapes."

"And friendships."

They both took a sip of their drinks.

"What did I miss?" Jack leaned over and asked.

Philip looked over at his best friend, annoyed. "Shall we go over manners once again, Captain? You are to speak to your other dinner partner while I speak to mine."

"Mine is half-deaf and does not care for English," he said unapologetically. "And I know your conversation is vastly more entertaining. Did you tell her how your almost betrothed was using you?"

"How she wanted to use me," Philip corrected. "I was on to her from very early on and gave nothing useful away."

Jack scoffed.

"Is that true?" Maria was not sure how she felt about that. Part of her was glad he had seen through the ruse, but the other part of her was a little hurt that he had not told her. She was not certain even when they had kissed, he fully believed her.

"Maria?" Philip asked as though she'd been wool-gathering. She supposed she had.

"Oh, look at the time. Now Maria is mine," Jack said unapologetically. "Do not ignore Lady Georgie," he said shooing his fingers away.

"You are terrible."

"I am," Jack agreed. "Someone has to keep Everleigh in line."

"And now poor Kate has to do it for you."

"Miracle of miracles, I don't think she minds," he said as his gaze went across the table to his wife who was deep in conversation with the Duke of Richmond.

Maria wanted to be looked at like that. She swallowed hard trying to tamp down her jealousy. She would not allow such a base emotion at a time like this, which was cause for joy. She would take this victory as a gift from above.

PHILIP HAD ALMOST been late. After spending the night in the Waterloo village, he and Lloyd had stopped to help a family whose cart had been swept away and stranded by a washed out bridge. Then, when he had arrived home, it occurred to him that he had not informed his mother that the betrothal was off and there would be place settings to be removed. She would have his head for making her look anything but prepared and perfect. With Percy's help, they removed and rearranged everything to look as intended. He never could have managed that on his own, and everyone else was busy with last minute details. But Percy did not complain, understanding the necessity of making it right without bothering Lady Marsden. He'd rushed to bathe and make himself presentable and barely had time to inform his mother there would be no betrothal announcement.

Then there was Maria. How had he ever thought her plain? She looked like sunshine and fire and pure temptation in the gown she wore. But most importantly, that package wrapped up everything that mattered and everything that was good to him.

He thought she cared for him, even loved him, but could she forgive him? Lord knew he did not deserve it or her. It would be difficult to be patient and court her properly for he wanted to shout to the room how he felt about her.

The pure pleasure on her face when he told her that Pauline was gone from his life and the evening was enough to bolster his confidence in the end prize.

He released Maria to stand beside his parents and greet guests arriving for the ball.

"Well, boy, you met with success?" his father asked.

"I was unable to speak with her personally, but I made sure the duke knew this was her betrothal ball. Thank God mother had the foresight to only mention that on their invitation."

His mother did not hide her smug smile.

"By the by," he remarked. "I am stealing your dance with Maria."

"I am happy to relinquish her to you. I suppose I may scandalize everyone and dance with my wife," he chuckled.

His mother made a face of mock horror before bussing Lord Marsden's cheek in a tender moment no one else was privy to.

That is what I wish for, Philip thought with conviction. His eyes sought out Maria, wishing she was there by his side. She was chatting with Jack and Kate, and his attention was taken with new arrivals.

When it was at last time to open the ball, Philip found Maria and bowed before her. He extended his arm. "My lady?" Never before had he meant *my* lady so much. "May I have this dance?"

Her eyes twinkled and she took his arm and he was certain his answering smile made him look like an idiot, but he was happy.

The strings of a waltz played, and Maria looked up at him in confusion.

"I told the orchestra to change the dance when I saw you in that gown, pet."

"You rogue," she chastised without heat.

"If you say so, it must be true. You know me better than anyone."

"I suppose I do." She smiled, but there was some sadness there. He thought he knew the cause and would remedy it when the time was right. He took her hand in his and put his other on her waist, still surprised by the reaction he felt.

Dancing was something one did as part of one's duty as a gentleman, as one of Wellington's officers, as part of society. With Pauline, he'd felt attraction, nay infatuation, but with Maria in his arms it was something else entirely. And it scared him a little. He tried not to shy away from it, because Maria needed none of that. But it did make him hesitate from telling her more.

Yet, it did not prevent the release he felt at his freedom, or the enjoyment of having the partner he wanted.

"How do you feel?" she asked.

"Like I have been released from a trip to the gallows."

She studied his face for a moment as if to see how genuine his words were, those familiar wide, amber eyes searching. "That is a relief to hear, because I for one feel very, very pleased that you are out from under the clutches of that woman."

Philip laughed. "How do you really feel about her, Maria?"

A look of guilt crossed her face. "I have a confession."

He raised his brows. "Pray tell."

"I had intended to stop it tonight. Someway, somehow. Even by drastic measures if necessary."

She looked like a warrior queen, all fierce and ready to do battle. He could not believe how much he wanted her in that moment.

"I am almost sorry to have deprived you of your moment of glory. I should have liked to have seen it."

She laughed and the sound was musical. He looked down at her and it seemed like a fairytale. She was smiling up at him with bloom in her cheeks and the candlelight looked as though it was spreading fairy dust upon her.

"I scarcely notice ball decorations anymore, but I like these very much." He waved his hands up at the crystals.

"I will take credit for those," she said proudly. "I rather like them myself."

"I am impressed my mother allowed anyone else to give ideas

or opinions, even though she asks for them."

"Perhaps they were not good enough before."

He liked this new, unleashed Maria who flirted with him. He allowed himself to get lost in the rhythm of the dance, feeling enjoyment and lightness of heart. He allowed himself to consider her for a different role beyond that of a friend. How many times had he danced with her before? But this time was different. Did she feel it, too?

Suddenly, he was eager for what came beyond the ball and Pauline. To see if his feelings remained the same once Pauline was gone for good. He wasn't sure what Wellington's plans for him would be, but he thought he might be allowed some more time there in Brussels.

As the dance ended, Maria looked over his shoulder and halted a moment before speeding up their progress from the floor, pulling at his arm. They had barely stopped at the edge of the dancing before she bobbed a quick curtsy and excused herself. She began to disappear through the crowd and he made to follow, wondering if he had said something to upset her. But then he saw what she was after. Pauline Klementine had arrived.

Philip sped up, realizing Maria was about to do something drastic, after all. And he did not want to watch her pitted up against the ruthless evil of the archduchess that no longer had anything to lose.

CHAPTER TWENTY-ONE

"THE GALL OF the woman!" Maria could not keep from scowling as she went towards the archduchess. She would not allow Pauline Klementine to ruin this ball, or Philip's life.

How dare she make an appearance at the Marsden ball? Since Philip had broken the betrothal and asked her not to come, why had she been allowed in? Whatever was Percy about? It was too late to think about that though, Maria realized abruptly; the archduchess had already arrived. Maria would make sure she left again with considerable haste.

She had been itching to give the woman a cutting set-down and now that she knew Philip did not want her, Maria moved through the crowd with more determination, more confidence. In her zeal she jostled and brushed by people but did not stop to apologize. The woman would not escape her. For if she knew the betrothal was over and yet still had come, then there was nothing but trouble to follow. It was one last thing Maria could do for the one she loved.

The archduchess appeared to be standing alone, looking around the ballroom, when Maria reached her. She was dressed in dark blue: a simple frock with a high waist, her hair drawn up in a simple knot, and none of her usual ostentation. Quickly, Maria looked about to see who had accompanied her, but no one was by her side. She was evidently seeking someone—very likely Philip. Then her gaze met Maria's. Instantly Maria's heart raced with fear, for the woman's eyes looked wild, full of her desire for vengeance. Her gaze narrowed.

Maria stepped forward, lifting her chin and drawing herself upright. Even though she was shaking with fear, she would not let the archduchess see it. "I know who you are looking for. Come with me." That was a hum if ever she had told one, but nevertheless the woman followed. Maria led her out of the ballroom and far away from the curious, often malicious, tongues of those members of the *ton* who were present.

Maria was not so naïve as to think Philip would not have noticed, nor that he would not follow, but she hoped to have her say before he arrived.

She pushed through the doors that had been closed off to the guests and onwards to the private drawing room. A small lamp had been left burning, but otherwise it was dark and quiet.

"Where are we going?" the archduchess demanded.

"Somewhere private."

She scoffed and stopped. "And if I do not wish to be private with you? Nein. I will find Philip and speak with him in the ballroom."

Maria locked the door behind her and dropped the key into her bodice. "You shall not have a choice until you have listened to me."

That was decidedly not the answer the woman wanted. Narrowing her gaze again until she resembled a cornered cat, she came at Maria. *Let her.* Suddenly Maria felt very calm.

"What do you think you are doing?"

Maria stepped sideways and put a chair between herself and the other woman. "I intend to keep you away from Philip and his family. I know he has made it clear he wants neither you nor your betrothal."

The Archduchess scowled in a manner which removed all pretense of civility and folded her arms over her chest. "How very sweet you are—and pathetic. Do you really believe he will have you if I do not marry him?"

Maria shook her head. "I am not doing this for myself."

"At least you realize you could never have him…but you are wrong, you know. He did not call a halt to the betrothal. I want him and I intend to have him. Now, give me that key and let him decide for himself." She held out her hand as though demanding something from an insolent servant.

"Every word you utter is a falsehood. I saw you with the archduke at Versailles. You are here for no other reason than your pride." Annoyingly, Maria could not accuse her rival of desiring vengeance or it would reveal her own less than honorable spying activities.

The archduchess paced across the floor, her jaw working as though she were thinking hard. "It is my belief you know not of what you speak. You have no experience with gentlemen or with how to use them to get what you want. Kisses mean nothing."

Maria tried not to let the barbs pierce, but they did.

"Now release me. You cannot keep me locked in here against my will."

"Do you agree to leave this house and not return?" Maria asked in one last desperate attempt to end this respectably.

"You have no authority in this house or in Brussels," the archduchess snapped. "I received an invitation to the ball—one which bore my name and the intelligence my betrothal was to be announced."

"Yours was the only invitation inscribed thus."

A brief flicker of doubt crossed her face. "How would you know that?

"I wrote them myself," Maria said defiantly.

"Does Philip know of this trickery? Are you the one who has arranged this whole affair?" The woman stepped closer and closer, slowly stalking her prey.

"I wrote them in the manner I was asked to do so by Lady Marsden." Maria stood her ground, despite the fact that she had not expected the lady to turn aggressor. Perhaps she had helped to sway Philip against the archduchess, but she did not regret it. "Philip and I have no secrets."

"Now who tells the falsehood? Have you told him how you pine for him?" she mocked. In a swift movement, she reached for Maria's bodice.

Maria thrust her back. "Keep away from me!"

"Not until you release me!" the Archduchess shouted. She rushed towards Maria again. "How dare you meddle in something which is beyond your comprehension? How dare you imagine that to him you are anything more than a mousy little childhood friend?" She struck Maria hard, knocking her backwards and causing her to stumble into a table.

The door rattled in its jamb, and there were shouts in the corridor beyond which Maria could not quite understand. Her head was reeling, her ears ringing from the blow.

Once more on the attack, the archduchess had a vase in her hand. Maria grabbed a book from the table. It was the closest thing to hand.

"You are out of your senses!"

"You are the one who has trapped me in here. You have but yourself to blame!"

"I did not do so with the intent of killing you!" Maria cried, using the book to deflect the vase hurled at her head, the resulting crash of the porcelain echoing in the room. The archduchess darted at Maria, ripping her bodice and tearing at her shift in a maniacal desperation to find the key. Maria fought and scratched to hold off the assault. The Austrian woman was as one possessed, and forced Maria up against the wall.

"Where is it?" the woman demanded, continuing to rip and rake at Maria's body and clothing with her nails as she searched for the key.

"Tell me why you are doing this to him!" Maria demanded, battling for her very life. She struck hard at the woman's arms with the heavy book. The archduchess bit her lip. *Good,* thought

Maria, *you deserve the pain.*

"You could not understand, you little fool! I do this not for my own sake! This is about freedom! This is not nor has ever been your concern!" Her voice rose with each successive statement until she screeched the last. She was losing control.

Maria was very much afraid, yet could not draw back now that she was so close to the truth.

"Freedom for whom?" she spat. "These are the ramblings of a traitor!"

The archduchess jerked her head backwards as though struck, her eyes starting from their sockets. Her mouth opened on a terrifying scream and her fingers curved into the claws of an enraged tigress. Maria had now gone beyond fear; the woman was truly insane. One hand lifted to the simple auburn knot…and in one, swift movement produced a wicked-looking silver pin. Hand raised, she drove it towards Maria…

In the same instant the door crashed in and all hell broke loose. Maria heard shouts in German and then the firing of a pistol. Flame from the powder flashed in the dim light, the loud bang which followed deafening in the small room.

The woman's weight flung them both against the wall. Half-dazed, Maria barely registered her assailant before sliding to the floor. The duke, the archduchess' father, ran to his daughter, taking her in his arms, weeping and crying her name as he did so.

"Why, my daughter? Why did you force me to do this?"

Philip's face swam before Maria for a moment as a feeling of warmth spread across her abdomen, and then she, too, slumped down the wall.

"No! Maria!"

Why was he shouting? Vaguely she pondered the oddity as she felt his arms come around her. She would have known it was him by the feel of him.

"Send someone for the surgeon!" he shouted again. "Stay with me, Maria!" he commanded in a stern voice he had never before used with her. It was probably something he had learned as part of his soldiering, she thought distantly. She was growing tired. "Look at me!" he pleaded. While she very much wished to, she could barely keep her eyes open; she was so very tired. Sleep beckoned, despite his entreaties, and she thought it was not so terrible to rest in his arms.

IT HAD HAPPENED so fast, yet in slow motion. How could he have been so stupid to imagine Pauline would not fight back? The truth was, he had thought her father would control her. But Maria had seen Pauline before he had and had at once set off after her. As he had struggled to follow Maria, the crush of the crowd closing in to bar his way, he had known a deep sense of foreboding.

He had then caught sight of Pauline standing on the steps looking out over the gathering. It was as though she had peeled her mask away, for she looked wild and ready to do harm…

…And Maria was cutting straight towards her, prepared to fight his battles.

He ignored as many people as he could, but was unable to follow completely unimpeded. By the time he had discovered the two ladies' whereabouts, he could hear shouting, and then something crashed behind the door. He rattled the wooden panel and shouted, but the occupants took no notice.

He looked desperately about for assistance but all the servants were in the other wing, helping with the ball.

Cursing doors and locks, he debated going for Percy when he heard a scream. This was no mere slaying with words; someone was going to be hurt. Someone could already be hurt. He hammered on the door with his fists.

As he considered whether he could kick in the solid oak, footsteps sounded along the hall, and he prayed it was Percy come to help.

"Where is she?" An older man, presumably the duke, shouted frantically as he ran towards him.

Philip inclined his head and once more debated attempting to kick down the door.

His cheeks red with exertion, the duke immediately began to bellow at his daughter, commanding her to open the door. However, bare seconds later, one voice rose in progressive screeches, easily loud enough to permeate the heavy wood.

"You could not understand, you little fool! I do this not for my own sake! This is about freedom! This is not nor has ever been your concern!"

Philip could wait no longer. Fear and anger lending strength to his body, he stepped back and kicked down the door. In hindsight, had he known the duke was going to shoot his own daughter, he might have done things differently, but he had been too worried about Maria to think properly.

With a swift glance to see if the duke had any more weapons to hand, Philip ran inside to see if Pauline still lived… if she could possibly have survived.

Her father's aim had been all too true and it was evident the life had drained from her. Already at Pauline's side, the duke caught her as she fell to the floor, weeping and asking why. "Why did you force me to do this? I had no choice. How could you leave me no choice?"

Philip shook his head, understanding more than he wished and knowing the duke had been forced into the untenable choice by his daughter's treason.

He looked away, his gaze finding Maria against the wall, probably frightened beyond belief. No matter what she had intended, Philip would wager anything it had not been this scene.

Then he made the wretched discovery. Maria was not merely frightened, she had been hit. The bullet must have gone through Pauline and into Maria. A red pool was already spreading from her abdomen in an ever-expanding circle, and Philip shouted her name as she began to slide down the wall. Running forward, he took her in his arms, screaming for help. This could not be happening, not when he had just seen the light. He had been caught in the archduchess' web of darkness and had lost what mattered most.

More in desperation than any real hope, he leaned forward and put his ear close to her face. A feeble breath brushed his cheek.

His heart leaped. Maria was not yet gone—and he refused to let her go.

He tore off his neckcloth and held it to the wound to stop the life seeping out of her. Her heartbeat was growing weak and something needed to be done quickly. He had lost too many men on the battlefield not to recognize the pallor and shallow breathing of the afterlife overtaking a body.

Realizing help was not coming, he dashed to the fireplace and violently jerked the bell-rope. Returning to Maria's side, he picked her up and carried her towards the stairs. In answer to the summons, a manservant came running from the nether regions of the house and Philip at once directed him to fetch a surgeon and send another footman to aid the duke with Pauline. The man ran off again while Philip struggled to carry Maria's limp body to her chambers, whispering words of encouragement and love in her ear every step of the way.

As soon as he had laid her on the bed, he stripped away the ruined gown as fast as he could and tore strips of linen from the bedding, pressing them into the tiny hole which hardly seemed as though it could have caused so much damage. He tied the bandage tightly around her and then waited. Clasping Maria's small, white hand in his large, blood-stained one, he sank on to the bed and took up a vigil at her side.

It felt as if hours had passed by the time help arrived, so that when a tap at last came on the door, the bandage seemed to have slowed the bleeding. Philip knew that removing the bullet and stopping the bleeding were not the worst foes they faced, although if Maria lived to fight the inevitable infection, he would be grateful.

"Och! What is this?"

Philip turned to see an old friend and army surgeon, Dr. Wheeler, enter the room, his own parents hot on the man's heels.

"A very long story, Wheeler, that I will not trouble you with at this point, which ends with this fair lady having a bullet in her abdomen."

The marchioness gasped. "Maria!"

"Right. I will need my instruments from my gig, some spirits and a good deal of hot water," the older Scotsman said through his white whiskers, beginning to remove his coat and waistcoat and roll up his sleeves.

"Father, would you be so good as to deal with the scene in the drawing room? The bullet went through the archduchess first."

Lord Marsden's eyes widened a little at the news, but he nodded and left the bedchamber, pulling Lady Marsden with him. "Come, wife, it seems we have work to do."

Philip was grateful beyond words that his parents could be relied upon to deal with the situation downstairs that at the moment he had no capacity for. He could not think beyond Maria.

"Help me lift her, lad," Dr. Wheeler commanded as he unwound the bandage to survey the damage done. "It appears there is indeed a bullet to extract."

A servant entered quietly with everything the doctor had requested. He set out his instruments on a clean cloth in readiness for his procedure, while Philip held linens against the blood which still oozed from the small hole, and silently willed Maria to fight. She had smiled wistfully up at him before losing consciousness, and that worried him. Did she no longer have the strength, or will, to fight?

"You have to fight, my love. For me. For us," he whispered in her ear.

"Hold the lass tight now. She willna like this," Dr. Wheeler warned as he prepared to rinse the wound.

Philip had seen this time and again. He held Maria's arms against her sides while the footmen held her legs. She flinched a little as the doctor worked, first cleaning away the clotting blood, then using his instruments to probe for the ball.

Once found, he held it up for inspection. "'Tis wondrous how such a little thing can cause so much damage."

He set it down, and in its place picked up the bottle of spirits. "Hold her again, lads." He then poured some very fine brandy into the wound, a strange trick the Scot swore by. Philip did not question it, because the surgeon's reputation preceded him.

Maria did flinch and stiffen a little, but was still too weak for Philip's liking.

Dr. Wheeler packed some lint into the area and covered it with linen strips, after which Philip helped to lift his love while the surgeon wound the bandage tightly around her.

"I will send her maid in to clean her up," the doctor said as he began to wash and pack his instruments away.

"What are her chances?" Philip asked, knowing what he would say.

The doctor hesitated and wiped his brow. "If we are stating simple facts, I would say she is fortunate that the bullet went through someone else first, which reduced the force. However, she bled a great deal when the ball lodged itself in her spleen. She is safe enough for now, but I canna say how she will tolerate the fever."

The fever. The inevitable infection. With all the advances in medicine, there was still nothing to combat that.

"The rest is in God's hands." Dr. Wheeler repeated the words he always said, and Philip wished they gave him more peace. He needed to do something. As Bisset came in to change and wash Maria, Philip moved to stand at the window, looking out into nothingness, willing life back into the ghost who lay on the bed behind him—willing God to let her live—willing Maria to want to fight to stay with him.

CHAPTER TWENTY-TWO

MARIA KNEW PHILIP was there, beside the bed. He had been there for a long time—or had it been in her dreams? She felt as though she had been asleep for weeks, but now, although her mind was awake, she could not open her eyes. It was most odd. And she was hot... uncomfortably so. Her brother Gabriel had been there as well, had he not? But how could that be?

She tried to shift position to make herself more comfortable, but the movement was accompanied by a dreadful stinging and slicing pain. *I am not dead, then. Why can I not wake up?*

She tossed and turned, her limbs tangling in the sheets. Her skin was damp with sweat and she longed for a bath...to be clean, but she did not have the energy to say so, much less ring for one.

"Hush. Settle yourself, now. I am here. I will always be here," Philip whispered in her ear. She felt a cold compress on her forehead.

"She is uncomfortable. Give her some laudanum." Kate's voice came from the other side of the bed.

"Perhaps a little more will not hurt. I was hoping she would wake without it, but she is clearly still in pain."

"Maybe she cannot wake up. Maybe she will not..." She choked and began to weep.

"Now stop that. She will awaken to find you sobbing like Halcyon." Jack's voice sounded. That was not the right thing to say to Kate. Why was she sobbing? Maria knew there was a reason, but she could not think. Perhaps she should sleep a little more.

"How long can a person stay like this? It has already been days!" Kate sounded nearly hysterical. Maria had never known her friend to be so upset. She tried to comfort her, but her body would not cooperate.

"I do not think it will be much longer," Philip said softly.

"I should stay with her. She would not leave me," Kate protested. "Maria, you must wake now," she said to her, the tears throbbing through her words.

"Come. You need to rest. Everleigh has her in hand and will let you know if anything changes. Getting upset is not good for the baby, Kate." Jack tried to pacify her.

Of course, Kate was increasing. But why was she so upset? Maria tried to think, but was so devilishly warm her mind would not follow her bidding.

"Philip has been with her the whole time. Should he not rest?"

"Everleigh will not leave her, beg him though I may. Let us know if her fever breaks," Jack seemed to say as the sound of footsteps faded from the room.

"I will," Philip said.

Fever. Who had a fever?

That was when she remembered. Maria had taken the archduchess away to speak in private, then the woman had refused to leave—had refused to give Philip up. Then she had run mad and begun to attack Maria—and confess her motives. But someone had shot the Archduchess. Had Maria also been shot? She must have been.

She tried to remember. It was as if it was happening to someone else, far away.

"What happened to her?" she tried to ask.

"Maria? Did you speak?" She heard Philip rush to her side and felt him take her hand.

She struggled to say something, but her throat was too dry.

"Here, my love." He held a glass of cool barley water to her lips and she drank. "Thank God," Philip said as he kissed her brow.

Maria thought she smiled, but she was too tired to care.

"Maria? Can you open your eyes?"

She tried, she truly did, but it was too exhausting.

"Sleep, then, dearest. I will be here when you are ready to awaken."

Maria relaxed, knowing Philip was there, the cold drink and laudanum taking effect on her senses. She was aware of him holding her hand, giving her drinks, and wiping her brow. Yet why was Philip there?

He had been there the whole time, they had said; for days, they had said. Philip had been in her dreams with his tender words, soft touch, and familiar scent. Not only that, he had also changed bandages, applied salve and kept cool cloths on her brow. Many times she had felt on the precipice of awakening, but the fear of reality without him had kept her just shy of it, along with the pain consciousness seemed to bring.

"How is she today?" Maria heard Lord Marsden's voice ask. He sounded distant, as though she were in a tunnel.

"About the same, I believe, although she has drunk some barley water on her own."

"That is hopeful."

"Aye," Philip responded, but he sounded tired. "Has there been any more word of the Austrians?"

"No. They have completely disappeared, along with the archduchess's body."

"I still cannot believe they were gone by the time you reached the drawing room," Philip said with a sigh.

"Not only that, there was hardly any sign of the incident at all. Just the cracked vase and a missing carpet. He must have had an army of servants waiting. He knew what he was going to do."

"It is for the best."

"Whitehall seems to think so, but I cannot imagine having to shoot my own child to protect my country." He took Maria's hand. It was plumper than Philip's and gave a firmer squeeze. "While I am glad it is over with, I pray Maria will recover. I have delayed in writing to her parents, hoping there will be nothing to tell."

"There won't be," Philip said gruffly, as though he were fighting back emotion.

"People are asking after her already. Her absence—all of our absences this past week—is being remarked upon."

Philip growled.

"I know, my son. Your mother has put it about that we are afflicted with the ague, but we will not be able to keep it a secret forever."

"I know," Philip whispered. A moment later, he was stroking her cheek with the back of his hand. She wanted to lean into it and stay there forever. "I need her to wake up, Father. I have things I never had the chance to tell her."

"You know we love her as though she were our own, but…"

"Do not say it, Father," Philip warned.

"How the devil did that bullet go all the way through the archduchess and into her?" he asked as though he had not asked it a hundred times.

"I do not know, but it did, and I will never forgive them for it. Maria did not deserve any of this. To think she was tainted by *her* bullet, when she was trying to defend me, is incomprehensible."

The marquess sighed heavily. "'Tis very like Maria to be so selfless. None of us could have anticipated this."

"No," Philip whispered.

"You need to rest, son. One of us can wake you the moment she comes to herself."

"I will not leave her. I will rest on my cot. It is no hardship to be with her; in fact, it would be harder to leave her."

"As you will." Lord Marsden seemed resigned and Maria heard him leave again.

A moment later, she felt pressure on the bed next to her.

"Maria. What am I to do? Why will you not wake up?" She felt him lay beside her and put his arms about her. This was a dream she most definitely did not want to end. "I have words I need to say to you," he whispered in her ear.

Say the words now, she willed him, hoping he would somehow understand.

"Maria." His voice cracked and he sniffed, as though trying not to cry. Philip in tears was not supposed to be in a dream. "Please don't let me be too late." He stroked her face with one hand while the other clung to her.

Too late? For what could he be too late?

"You cannot die, not now. Not when I have finally realized how much I love you—how desperately I need you." He kissed her brow, and warm drops fell on her face. "Please, my love."

She had longed to hear those words for as long as she could remember. If only this were not a dream...

PHILIP WOKE TO a knocking on the door. It took a moment for him to realize where he was and get his bearings. He was lying on the bed, holding Maria in his arms. She was unnaturally still and limp...but cool.

He crawled out from beneath her, settling her on the mattress as gently as he could.

"Enter," he called as he tried to straighten himself. He looked dreadful after scarcely leaving her side for days and nights on end.

"You need a bath, Everleigh," Dr. Wheeler remarked in his usual gruff tones, sniffing in pantomime fashion.

"Amongst other things," Philip agreed.

"Has the lass wakened at all?"

"I thought perhaps earlier she might, because she drank some water easily. I thought she tried to speak."

"'Tis a good sign. She needs more than water to fight the fever and blood loss. Maybe she will wake when I change her bandage this time."

Philip made to help as he had been doing every day. "Has her fever perhaps broken? She was much warmer earlier."

Dr. Wheeler stopped rummaging through his case and put his hands on Maria's hands, then her forehead, then her neck. "I believe she has."

"Thank God."

"Aye. I didna think she had the strength to fight, poor lass. Usually I can tell, but I am delighted to have been proved wrong on this occasion." He pulled back the sheets and cut away the bandages. "It looks mostly healed from the outside. There is little else I can do. Keep it clean."

Philip helped the doctor dress the wound with fresh linen and then wrap more about her limp body. Having rung for the maids to come in and change the bedding, he placed her gently on the chaise-longue.

"What comes next, Doctor?"

Dr. Wheeler shrugged as he packed his medicaments back into his case. "Now we wait for her to wake—if she is going to, that is. It shouldna be long, now."

Philip watched the man leave on those less than encouraging words. He had to do something. If she had survived the blood loss and fever, then it was for Maria to decide she had something to live for.

He took the opportunity to wash himself while the maids stripped off the old linens and replaced them with clean ones. While he changed, Philip decided he had to try something drastic.

Leaving his beloved for the first time in days, he went in search of Percy, to put forward his strange request, while Bisset and two other maids dressed Maria. Then, once he was told everything was ready, he returned to Maria's side and carefully lifted her into his arms. Carrying her down the stairs, he took her out into the gardens, to the makeshift swing which had been hastily prepared. Carefully, he lowered himself into position with Maria in his arms and began to rock gently back and forth.

"I have brought you to your favorite place," he said in her ear, hoping she was listening, "or as near as I could manage. I know how much you love the garden and how you escape out of doors every chance you get… So I thought, perhaps, bringing you out here might be good for you, despite how cold it is, but I will keep you warm." He nestled his face into her neck while he spoke.

"It is a little dreary out here, I will confess. It is not an ideal vista to lift one's spirits, though somehow I know you would still find beauty in it."

His control was threatening to lose itself. He could feel his throat tightening with emotion and his chin beginning to tremble. "Maria. I need you to wake up. You have fought so hard, so long. Now it is time for you to wake up. Please do not let a mere lead ball destroy you. Not when I have just discovered how much I need you, how essential you are to my happiness."

He laughed harshly. "That sounded selfish, but I also vow to spend the rest of my days ensuring your happiness. We will make each other happy, I know it—along with parcels of little Philips and Marias running around to add to our happiness."

"Now you sound ridiculous."

"Maria?" He looked up to see the prettiest amber eyes he had ever beheld. It was something he had for days been fearing he would never see again.

She smiled at him. "We are outside," she said as she squinted up at the sky. "It is very bright."

"It would be to one who has had their eyes closed for days. I have been unable to get you to wake up for days. I will admit it is a desperate measure."

"Are we swinging?" she asked sleepily.

"Another desperate measure," he said, feeling slightly sheepish all of a sudden.

"Thank you," she said, simply nestling into his chest.

He rocked them back and forth for a few minutes in relieved contentment, feeling more grateful than he had known possible.

"How do you feel?"

"Sore. Tired. I have been dreaming a great deal," she said softly.

"I am glad to hear someone has been dreaming, because you have put me through the worst nightmare imaginable."

"I would never do that on purpose," she protested.

"Mm. Do you even remember what happened?" he asked skeptically.

She closed her eyes. "I remember we danced. And the archduchess arrived, intent on causing trouble. We argued, then she came at me, and then there was a shot. Did she…?"

"Yes, she died by her father's own hand. The bullet went through her and into you."

"That is unthinkable. Her father shot her?"

"And you, unintentionally."

"I remember someone saying I had a fever."

"At first, I thought you would bleed to death. Thankfully, the bullet was not lodged deep, but Dr. Wheeler said it hit your spleen. Then it became infected."

"How many days?" she asked, wonderment in her voice.

"I have lost count. Six? Seven?"

"That is a long time to dream."

"And what did you dream about?"

"Mostly you," she answered without pretense.

"Oh?"

"You said a lot of things to me."

"I am not sure that was you dreaming. I did say a lot of things to you."

She opened her eyes again and looked at him, searching.

"Do you wish for me to say them again?" he asked tenderly. "I have been waiting, hoping, praying to say them again."

"Philip…" She hesitated and swallowed, as if she were parched, shifting slightly in his arms. "I think, perhaps, they were said out of guilt and maybe obligation."

"Then cease to think! I assure you, the things I said to you were nothing of the kind. I realized how much I wanted—needed—you before the ball. I was merely waiting for a chance to court you properly before confessing all."

She closed her eyes again, as if in pain. "I do not know if I could bear it, Philip."

"My love is too much to bear?" Was he hearing her correctly? Of all the responses he could have fathomed, that would not have even entered his head.

"How could you love one such as me? I am dowdy to your dashing, plain to your sophistication, and simple to your elegance."

Philip tilted her chin up. He knew she needed to look at him to believe him.

"You are anything but plain! And if dashing is what I have just experienced, I want no part of it. Maria, what we have is so much more than those considerations could ever be."

She still looked doubtful.

"Do you love me?"

"I have always loved you, Philip."

"Then allow me the chance to prove myself to you." He was begging.

She shook her head, and his heart sank.

Then she closed her eyes again. Whatever she was going to say would not be welcome, of that he was convinced.

"Look at me when you say it, Maria."

"Philip, I believe you love me, but do you desire me?" Maria asked, not quite meeting his gaze, her face awash in bashfulness.

"How can you doubt me?"

She sniffed and then winced from the pain. "Please do not make me list my inadequacies!"

"Perhaps, then, you will allow me to list your attributes." A tear rolled down her cheek and he kissed it away. "None of that," he commanded, and she smiled faintly. "Better, my dear. I believe

I will start with my favorite. Your eyes are what I have missed most of your physical qualities. Besides the beauty of their color, which is like one of the most precious jewels, they do not hide your thoughts or your mischievous wit. They are positively enchanting."

A pink flush was slowly rising to her cheeks. Encouraged by her response, he continued, "Although I miss your long hair, I love these short curls as well. I do believe they make your personality shine. Though I have always known of your inner beauty, you have finally allowed others to perceive it too."

Maria firmly shook her head.

"Your skin is like the finest porcelain, yet softer than a kitten's fur." He stroked his hand down the side of her face to prove it. "But as for desire, when you kissed me, it opened a treasure and allowed me to fully see. I am surprised you can doubt my feelings after that."

"I have heard over and over again that kisses mean nothing. I have heard the archduchess say it more than once," she answered harshly. "Even you said as much when you asked me to show you."

"I cannot call that a mistake, for without it, my eyes might never have been opened."

Although she said nothing, she remained snuggled in his arms. He had just laid his heart wide-open to her and, of all things he might have expected, she remained quiet? His insides twisted with dread.

"Say something, Maria. You have never been one to mince words with me."

"I think I may be dreaming again. How am I to know the difference?"

"Perhaps I could show you?"

Her eyes shot back to his in disbelief.

He laughed.

"If you think you are about to kiss me when I have been on the sick bed for a week, you have feathers in your cock-loft," she declared roundly. "If you could taste what I do, you would not suggest such a thing." She wrinkled her face adorably.

"'I will love thee ne'er the less, my girl!'" he said approvingly, "but if you think such a minor detail is going to stop me, *you* have feathers in your cock-loft! Such language on a lady's lips… I see I shall have to take you in hand."

As she opened her mouth to protest, he took instant advantage, allowing his lips to descend upon hers. He proceeded as best he could to prove his love to her through a deep and meaningful kiss, although she was rather defiant and resisted his charms.

"For one who has been on a sick bed for a week, you show remarkable strength in resisting my affections," he teased.

"For one who has waited so long for those affections, I want them to be perfect," she snapped.

"Then I will cease for now, if you will promise to give me the rest of our lives in which to prove them."

"You are certain I am not dreaming?"

"Shall I pinch you instead?"

"I do not think that will be necessary," she said primly.

"Maria, please make me the happiest of men and marry me," he pleaded.

She held his gaze for a long moment. "Very well. But only because you went to so much trouble for me." Then she laughed.

"Minx," he scolded.

"No longer pet?"

"You have advanced."

"Very well, my lord knight."

"This is how it is going to be, is it?"

"I might point out that you were the one who began the name-calling." Her accompanying smile was enough to make him forgive everything.

"As long as I am your lord knight, I will tolerate it."

EPILOGUE

DUE TO THE delicate nature of the situation, the banns were not called. Maria was still weak and they did not wish word to spread of what had happened. Maria also wanted her brother to give her away, and he could not stay for long.

Although Maria's strength was not what she would have hoped for wedding Philip, she found enough.

In nothing short of a miracle of arrangement, Lady Marsden had managed to have made a beautiful gown of pearl white, with sleeves of the finest silk and the bodice covered in tiny clusters of seed pearls which then descended out like a waterfall over the skirt. Bisset had placed a circlet of pearls over Maria's short curls and Lady Marsden's string of abalone pearls about her neck. Maria felt like a princess.

"You look beautiful, sister," Gabriel said when he came to help her down the stairs and out to their carriage. His dress was very subdued and he had his hat pulled low on his head, over his eyes. It was a cold December morning, quiet and rainy, and so he did not appear in any way untoward.

"Thank you, Gabriel. I feel very fortunate."

"As do I. None of this should have happened."

"Do not blame yourself. Everything happens for a reason. There is no point in dwelling on it. It has turned out very well."

"As long as you are happy, I am pleased your wish has come

true."

The carriage pulled forward from the drive, out onto the cobblestone road, the horses setting a slow, rhythmic pace.

"Certainly, I could not have predicted this outcome," she said wryly. "When will I see you again? I do not like feeling as if this is the last chance I will have to speak with you or, at the very least, it will be a long time before I may once more set eyes upon you."

"I cannot say what may be ahead, but at least I know you will be well taken care of by Everleigh."

"Gabriel, what is next for you?" she asked, adding, with a little half-smile, "I assume you will escape into the night as soon as the ceremony has ended."

"I do not know what is next for me. I suspect I will continue to live in the shadows until it is time for me to take up my duties as earl."

Maria huffed her displeasure. "I, too, am still angry with Father, but he is our father."

"You forgive him if you wish, but do not ask it of me."

Maria watched Gabriel's face. It was filled with suppressed emotion. He was in a dark place, his soul disturbed. "What Father did – what he put that family through..." Breaking off, he shook his head and looked away. "I am grateful he did not commit treason, but what he did was dishonorable. It goes against everything I stand for... everything I fight for."

Maria took his hand in hers and squeezed it.

"But this is your blessed day, sister. We shall not dwell on what cannot be changed. I do hope that your future together is easier than your story has been thus far."

"As long as I may engage to stay out of the path of bullets, it cannot be less than an improvement," she remarked.

"But that should not have happened. I let down my watch, because not once did I suspect he would commit filicide."

"Would you not have done the same, had Father been guilty of treason?" she argued. It was a difficult question, but Maria knew the answer even if Gabriel did not respond.

"I would have tried to ensure no one else was hurt." He was looking out of the window, refusing to meet her gaze.

"I was an unfortunate casualty, but I do not think he dreamed it would hurt me. Nevertheless, I am here, and I believe I am the luckiest woman alive."

Gabriel turned and smiled at her, but did not say any more.

"I hope it will not be so long before I see you again. Do try to find some measure of happiness, Gabe."

"Happiness is not for everyone, dear sister."

"At least promise me you will be willing to accept it if it comes to you."

He did not answer. They had arrived at the chapel and there was no more time for speech. A brown stone building, the chapel was lined with narrow, stained-glass windows. Above their heads as they entered, the ceiling arched up towards a beautiful steeple with a belltower at the top, ringing the hour.

Inside, Lord and Lady Marsden were waiting, accompanied by Jack, Kate and a few of the servants, including Bisset and Percy.

Maria's gaze slipped past them all, for standing near the altar was her heart. Philip was waiting for her, glorious in his full-dress regimentals, which enhanced rather than detracted from the beauty of the man himself. Maria was still in awe that she was actually marrying him, but she would not question her good fortune. As she walked down the aisle towards him, she resolved to do her best to ensure neither one of them regretted the marriage, for he had chosen her, and who was she to question it? Only heartache would lay in that direction, so she would close the door on her insecurities and relish his love.

From the looks he gave her, she sometimes wondered if some spell had been cast on him, but if so, she was as equally enchanted.

Therefore, on that quiet, rainy, December day, one of the army Anglican chaplains married them in a small Brussels chapel near the parc.

It was a small but beautiful wedding, Maria's only regret being that her parents could not be there, as they would have been had her father's past indiscretions never happened. Unfortunately, they had, and not for a king's ransom would she wish to delay wedding Philip. At least she had Gabriel to support her, and she had a suspicion he would need her more in the future.

When the ceremony was over, they returned to the house to partake of an intimate breakfast the servants had laid out in celebration. Lord and Lady Marsden seemed truly pleased.

"We have always considered you our daughter, now you are so in truth," Lord Marsden said as he kissed her cheek.

"Of course, I would have wished for a grand Society wedding, but we will hold a celebration ball when you are strong enough, Maria," Lady Marsden added.

Philip groaned, causing Maria to laugh. It still hurt to laugh.

"Do not exert yourself, my love," Philip said when he saw her wince, at once concerned.

"Do not make me laugh, then, husband." She tried to look stern, but knew she had failed when his eyes twinkled at her with amusement.

"I intend to devote the rest of my life to making you laugh—when it no longer hurts, that is," he added softly, gazing down at her with the deep affection she had given up hope of receiving.

She turned in her chair, which stood next to his, and placed her head on his shoulder. "And I intend to make you happy."

"I am already happy," he said, dropping a tender kiss on her head.

A throat cleared loudly across the table. They both looked up. Jack was standing beside Philip, looking down upon them and clearly entertained by their absorption in one another.

"If I might have just a moment to make a toast?"

"If you must," Philip retorted as Percy placed glasses of champagne in front of them.

"Of course I must." He cleared his throat again, as if Philip had interrupted a thought of great import. "As you know, Philip and I began our careers together as wee lieutenants."

"Wee?" Philip interrupted in mock offense. "I was never *wee*."

Jack looked at the ceiling as if seeking patience. "We have been through years of service together, fighting battles, amongst other unmentionable things, and forging a bond as brothers—a bond I never thought could be improved upon. Now," he continued as if Philip had not spoken, "we are wizened old captains who have taken wives—wives who neither of us deserve, I might add…"

"Hear, hear!" Kate interjected, drawing laughter.

He winked at her, but continued as if finishing his sentence, "…but nevertheless make us both better men. I wish you as much joy and happiness together as Kate and I have found. And selfishly, I look forward to many more years together, our bond a little larger." He charged his glass. "To Philip and Maria."

Everyone toasted and sipped from their glasses, and then Philip looked at Jack. "That was almost eloquent."

"I thought so." Jack grinned.

About the Author

Like many writers, Elizabeth Johns was first an avid reader, though she was a reluctant convert. It was Jane Austen's clever wit and unique turn of phrase that hooked Johns when she was "forced" to read Pride and Prejudice for a school assignment. She began writing when she ran out of her favorite author's books and decided to try her hand at crafting a Regency romance novel. Her journey into publishing began with the release of Surrender the Past, book one of the Loring-Abbott Series. Johns makes no pretensions to Austen's wit but hopes readers will perhaps laugh and find some enjoyment in her writing.

Johns attributes much of her inspiration to her mother, a former English teacher. During their last summer together, Johns would sit on the porch swing and read her stories to her mother, who encouraged her to continue writing. Busy with multiple careers, including a professional job in the medical field, author and mother of two children, Johns squeezes in time for reading whenever possible.

www.ingramcontent.com/pod-product-compliance
Lightning Source LLC
Chambersburg PA
CBHW061243210726
48293CB00003B/872